W9-BVI-902

PRINCESS
in
Practice

Also by Connie Glynn

Undercover Princess

PRINCESS in Practice

CONNIE GLYNN

HARPER

An Imprint of HarperCollinsPublishers

Library of Congress Control Number: 2019944595
ISBN 978-0-06-284784-3

Typography by Jessie Gang
19 20 21 22 23 PC/LSCH 10 9 8 7 6 5 4 3 2 1
❖
Originally published in the UK in 2018 by Penguin Random House Children's
First US Edition, 2019

This is dedicated to anyone who ever made me a tea.
Thank you.

PART ONE
Family

✥ PROLOGUE ✥

IN THE DIMLY LIT DUNGEON beneath the Maravish palace a body lay sprawled on a thin mattress. The cells were bare, but they were at least clean—the royal family of Maradova could keep a prisoner here for weeks if they had to. The figure stretched out lifelessly; no one could have guessed that the cogs were turning furiously inside her head.

Every day Saskia San Martin meticulously plotted her escape, committing to memory the exact movements of each guard, the placement of the cameras, the gurgling of the pipes, and the overhead footsteps of members of the household. No detail had been overlooked. Still, she was running out of time. It had been seven weeks since her attempt to kidnap the Maravish princess had been thwarted. Soon her old classmates would return to Rosewood Hall for their next year of studies. She had not spoken a word of Leviathan's plan to any of the guards. She refused to open her mouth except to eat and to reiterate her one demand.

"I want to speak to my master, Anastacia Alcroft."

She knew by the guards' guilty expressions that no one

had sent for Anastacia. Now she turned onto her side to eye the clock on the wall. As each second ticked by, she felt a sinking dread. Thankfully, all that remained of Saskia's embarrassing defeat was a faded bruise around her eye and a cut on her jaw that would probably leave a scar. But still she was trapped.

Tick-tock, tick-tock.

Any day now, Leviathan would begin phase two of their plan. But if Saskia was stuck in this cell, she had no way of being sure Anastacia was safe. Leviathan had assured her that if Saskia joined their cause, then she would finally be free to be with her. The two of them would no longer have to hide from Anastacia's overbearing father—the man who was also Saskia's boss.

Saskia froze as an image flashed into her mind: Anastacia standing furious in the light from the palace hallway, her brown hair billowing around her. Then another picture came to her: Ellie, standing barefoot in a torn dress, brandishing a golf club in an attempt to save the princess from attackers. Except Ellie wasn't saving the princess. Ellie *was* the princess. It had taken Saskia weeks of incarceration to realize this. How could she have been so stupid? But with so much time to think, she'd finally been able to connect the dots. Ellie was a princess in hiding. Lottie Pumpkin was not the real princess of Maradova. She was a Portman, officially hired to operate undercover, *pretending* to be a princess to protect the true identity of the real princess. Saskia rolled onto her back and stared at the patches of damp on the ceiling. *I need to see Anastacia, to warn her about what's coming.*

A high-pitched beeping sound alerted her that someone was about to enter the room, so she scrambled to a sitting position. A tall, scarred man with an intimidating build unlocked the cell door and entered with a tray of food. It was Sir Nikolay Olav, the king's Partizan and the person she dreaded seeing the most of anyone.

He stared at her as he placed a tray of gray food on a small table in the center of the room. Nikolay carrying the tray down alone meant only one thing. Interrogation.

Nikolay sat on a plastic chair by the table and took a long, exasperated breath. He knew exactly how this would go: the same way it had every other time.

He rubbed the stubble on his chin, his fingers grazing the scar on the left side of his face.

"Saskia San Martin." He said her name with a low grumble. She didn't respond, instead spooning up gray lumps of food and letting them fall back to the tray. He ignored her actions. "You need to tell us everything you know about Leviathan."

She stared at him blankly. There was only one possible

1

LOTTIE WINCED AS SHE FELT the palace floorboards vibrate beneath her feet. The knowledge that Saskia was down there somewhere sent a prickle up her spine with every step. But Lottie couldn't dwell on that now. She needed to stay focused; she needed to stay poised. She needed to act like a perfect princess until this party was finally over. Then she could get back to Ellie and finish packing for Rosewood.

Lottie was being treated to a grandiose birthday soirée, attended by some of the world's most powerful people—and the press. She'd been on her feet for nearly two hours, smiling and shaking hands with royals who all believed she was the real Maravish princess. Thankfully the king and queen had imposed a strict no-photography rule to protect her identity. The palace's gallery had been adorned with jewel-encrusted streamers, and the marble pillars were encased with winding ribbons of rainbow colors. Frilly tablecloths covered tables that were piled high with offerings for the princess, each gift fighting to outdo the last.

Lottie was dressed in traditional Maravish garb,

including a dark embroidered sash that circled her long-sleeved jade dress. A silver tiara nestled in her curls, a gift from her mother on her birthday nine years ago. Well, *just over* nine years ago. This whole party was a charade, after all. It wasn't Lottie's birthday; hers had been five days before. Today, September 1, was Ellie's birthday. Lottie wasn't even really a princess—she was standing in for her friend. And that was a secret that none of the guests could ever be allowed to discover.

"Are you okay?" By her side, Jamie kept his voice low enough so that only she could hear. Lottie had been asked this question too many times over the past few weeks, and it always left a hard feeling in the pit of her stomach.

"Yes, of course," she said automatically, her eyes drawn to a figure approaching them. "Tall woman on my left."

Jamie glanced in that direction. "Olga Ulov, editor of the *Golden Sovereign*." The older ebony-haired woman wore a pristine silk suit as she strode through the colorful crowd. In contrast to all the other guests, Jamie was wearing a simple black shirt and trousers, his dark hair scraped back from his face. Lottie had tried to get him to relax, but he'd remained rigidly alert during the whole party, scanning the room, convinced something terrible might happen again.

Olga stopped in front of them and dipped her head in greeting. "Princess Eleanor Wolfson." She dragged the name out slowly, her eyes narrowing as her gaze traveled over Lottie. "It is my absolute pleasure to finally make your acquaintance after all your years of hiding."

Lottie had thought that she'd never get used to being called by someone else's name, but now she responded with an effortless smile. She wondered how Ellie would respond to this situation.

"Why, thank you, Olga—I can only hope it has been worth the wait," Lottie replied sweetly, doing her best to seem as humble as possible. Jamie gave a small nod of approval. Although they no longer had "princess lessons," Jamie still kept close to make sure she didn't slip up.

Olga's lips curved into something resembling a smile, but her eyes penetrated Lottie's as if she were trying to read her mind. Ellie had never had a good relationship with the media. Rumors had been spread about the reasons she'd been kept undercover, none of them true but all of them harmful. It was Lottie's job as Ellie's Portman to keep the rumors at bay by playing her role in public, being the most pleasant and modest princess she could be. The queen had decided that a birthday celebration would be the perfect opportunity to fix Ellie's image troubles. *Smile and shake hands*, Lottie had said to herself. *How hard can it be?*

Lottie just had to hope she could pull it off.

"Your Highness . . ." The words, coming from behind her, ended in a hiss. Lottie turned to see the king's advisor, Simien Smirnov, standing rigidly at attention, his arms behind his back. He gave a small bow to Lottie. "The artist Sir Yanovski would like to present his gift to you. Kindly follow me to join the king and queen." Simien gave a thin smile as he gestured for her to follow him.

"That sounds delightful." Lottie beamed back at him, happy to have an excuse to get away from all the snooping attendees. She followed Simien's lead, walking elegantly— she hoped—between the party guests. They passed a group of servants, each of them balancing a silver tray loaded with caviar and truffles. *I wonder what Saskia is eating now.* She quickly shook the thought from her head. It had been difficult to truly relax in the Maravish palace that summer. The deeper she got into her role as Portman, the more uncomfortable she felt. She wanted nothing more than to be back at Rosewood Hall, back at the academy where she felt like her true self. But no matter how uncomfortable she was, she had to get through this party first. She mentally repeated the mantra that her mother had taught her before she'd passed away: *I will be kind, I will be brave, I will be unstoppable.*

As they emerged from the crowd, Jamie gave a small cough, dragging her from her thoughts. She looked up to see they'd arrived at the far end of the gallery and were standing before Ellie's parents, the king and queen.

King Alexander and his wife, Queen Matilde, couldn't have been more different, but they suited each other superbly. The king stood motionless, his eyes dark as an abyss, strong and unreadable. Beside him, Queen Matilde appeared as light and delicate as gossamer, as though she might float away at any moment. Lottie was still taken aback by how much she herself resembled the queen. It felt like looking in a mirror sometimes—no wonder she'd been accepted as Ellie's Portman.

"You look lovely." The queen smiled at Lottie, gently drawing her over to stand between herself and King Alexander. Anyone who didn't know any better would assume that Lottie was taking her rightful place between her parents. The king gave a brief wordless nod to Lottie and then to Jamie.

On their left was a shimmering purple velvet drape, covering something huge. Whatever was hidden beneath almost reached the ceiling of the ballroom. It made Lottie a little nervous. Someone clinked a fork against a champagne glass, and the room slowly hushed into silence as the crowd turned respectfully to look. A round-faced man with colorful hair and quirky spectacles stepped forward. Lottie was sure she recognized him. *Where do I know him from?*

"That's Yanovski, the knighted artist," the queen whispered to Lottie, keeping her face trained on the mystery gift.

Lottie had been told that the princess would be receiving

an important gift—something not only in honor of her birthday but as a commemoration of her coming out into the world. Moments like these made Lottie feel especially odd about the Portman agreement. These gifts were meant for Ellie, *for a real princess.* Although, knowing Ellie, she'd probably hate this over-the-top display.

Yanovski approached and lightly took Lottie's wrist, bowing deeply as he kissed her hand.

"Isn't the princess simply wonderful?" He addressed the crowd, gesturing grandly to Lottie in a way that made her feel like a prized horse. Everyone in the room clapped, and voices rose in agreement. *"Just wonderful! The perfect princess!"* Instantly Lottie blushed, feeling a thrill of pleasure. No matter how much of a fake she felt like, she couldn't help enjoying being treated like a princess.

The king raised a hand and the crowd hushed again.

Yanovski cleared his throat. "Your Majesties, I'm sure I speak on behalf of everyone here when I say how delighted we are to finally meet your beautiful daughter." Lottie's heart squeezed. "She is a glorious representation of the Maravish family and a shining example of everything a princess should be." He paused for applause and gave a self-satisfied smile as everyone clapped and cheered. The queen's smile didn't falter, but Lottie noticed the king's mouth twitch. "You must be very proud," Yanovski continued. "It is my honor to present this gift to the princess on her fourteenth birthday, to commemorate her debut into society."

Two uniformed men walked over to the gift, and the crowd held its breath. The stewards snatched away the velvet, and a river of glistening purple flowed to the polished floor. Lottie arched her neck to gaze up at . . . herself!

A towering statue filled the room. It was an expertly crafted depiction of Lottie cast in bronze. It was, by far, the most extravagant gift she had ever received in her life. Yanovski had effortlessly re-created the dress Lottie had worn to the Maravish Summer Ball. She looked like a natural-born princess. The statue was wonderful, so wonderful that it took Lottie a moment to realize how entirely silly it would be for the king and queen to display a statue of *her* in their palace.

"Oh dear," she breathed through a forced smile.

Queen Matilde smiled grimly; the king stood in silence, his expression impossible to read.

"An uncanny likeness!" Simien clapped, laughing a bit too loudly. "Look! The royal family has been shocked into silence." The king threw Simien a look, and the laughter dried up on his lips.

"It's truly remarkable. This certainly looks like . . . a challenging piece?" The queen had found her voice. It must have been very unnerving for both of them to see a girl who wasn't their daughter cast in bronze as their princess forever.

"Why, yes, actually! This has indeed been one of my most difficult works, but worth every second for our princess." He gave Lottie an adoring glance and swept his arm around in a deep bow.

Lottie could almost hear Ellie howling with laughter from somewhere deep in the palace. What a joke! Lottie dared to glance at Jamie and saw him biting his lip, his shoulders shaking. He was trying to stop himself from laughing.

She stared up at the bronze reflection of herself and held eye contact with the statue. It made her feel dizzy. She blinked rapidly and shook herself. *Come on. Say something!*

"Thank you." Her mouth opened and closed as she struggled to find the right words. What would a princess say? Finally she smiled and gazed around the room at the delighted onlookers, the people who had to believe she was daughter to the king and queen. "It looks just like . . . a princess!"

2

"WE'LL SIMPLY HAVE TO PRETEND Lottie is the real princess forever. What a shame!" Ellie doubled over with laughter—again. As expected, she'd found the story about the bronze statue absolutely hilarious. "After all, we can't embarrass *the* Sir Yanovski."

"This is not a laughing matter, Eleanor," King Alexander said, slamming his wineglass down on the table.

Ellie rolled her eyes, exasperated. Over the summer holiday Lottie had been reminded how much Ellie did not like being stuck in the Maravish kingdom. She was clearly itching to get back to Rosewood just as much as Lottie was.

They were sitting in the powder-blue dining hall for an intimate birthday dinner, rehashing the details of that afternoon's party. This dining room was one of Lottie's favorite places in the palace, with its gold-flecked walls that cast the room in a honey-warm light. Although her birthday had been a few days before Ellie's, they had agreed to wait and celebrate together. The dining table heaved with all Ellie's favorite foods, as well as plenty of vegetarian treats for Lottie. On the table by the wall was the stack of gifts Lottie had accepted on behalf of Ellie, all expertly wrapped with an assortment of frills and bows. Each gift had been checked meticulously by Jamie and Sir Nikolay Olav, no safety measure overlooked after the incident at the summer ball.

Looking at the towering pile of gifts, Lottie worried that her own present for Ellie, a portrait she'd painted of her friend, might seem small and pathetic. She was relieved that she'd left it in Ellie's rec room rather than bring it here. She chanced a look beside her at Jamie, who met her eyes with his usual intensity. There was also a present for him, waiting with Ellie's—a book about Pakistan, his mother's home country, that had been meant for his birthday on July 26. She'd wanted to give it to him then, but Ellie had explained that, understandably, he did not celebrate his birthday, because it was the same day that his mother had passed away. Instead she'd saved the gift for today; this way it was like they all had a birthday together.

"At least we can agree it's a gorgeous statue," Queen Matilde said, looking to her husband, "and a wonderful way to honor Eleanor's Portman."

The king turned to consider his wife. "That is one way to look at it."

Lottie had spent nearly two months with Ellie's parents, and she was finally getting better at reading the tiny expressions on the king's face. Right now his eyebrows were only faintly furrowed, the left side of his lip twitching ever so slightly. He was either tired or annoyed—possibly both.

"But honestly," Ellie began, scooping some pâté onto her plate. "It's the best birthday present I could have asked for, a big statue of my best friend—I will cherish it forever." Ellie grinned over at Lottie, whose cheeks went pink.

Lottie subtly rubbed her temples. At the end of the soirée she'd had to remove her tiara. Its weight had given her a terrible headache, and although she was trying her best to enjoy their joint birthday celebration, the pain behind her eyes wouldn't budge. Before Ellie and Jamie had a chance to pick up on her mood, the door clicked open loudly.

"Happy birthday!"

The grand doors of the hall swung wide and a gigantic cake was wheeled in on a mahogany cart. White petticoat ruffles peeked out from behind the cart, but the servants' faces were obscured by the huge mound of chocolate frosting. Lottie got to her feet, desperate to get a better look. Jamie coughed quietly at her side and she hastily sat back down again, slightly embarrassed about her childish excitement.

The cart trundled to a halt and two maids peered out from behind the cake. "WAIT!" Ellie cried. Everyone froze, and Lottie sensed Jamie stiffen beside her. "Before we blow out the candles, I have to give Lottie her present."

Ellie leapt to her feet, her chair clattering behind her.

"Eleanor!" her mother called after her, her brow furrowed. Then she turned to the servants and forced a practiced smile. "Midori, Hanna, thank you so much for the beautiful cake. It looks simply delectable."

At her mother's voice, Ellie froze at the door and turned. Her bottom lip stuck out, which Lottie knew meant she was embarrassed. She could usually read her princess like a book, but she didn't understand why Ellie was in such a rush to open gifts. Then Lottie remembered. As a child, Ellie had barely known anyone beyond the palace. This was probably the first time Ellie had ever bought a birthday present for a friend.

"It's okay, Ellie," Lottie said in a reassuring voice. "We can exchange gifts after dinner. Let's just enjoy your cake for now."

"No, I wanted to give it to you *now* so—" Ellie was cut off by a low grumble, and it took Lottie a moment to realize it came from the king. He was pinching the bridge of his nose as if he had a terrible headache.

"Eleanor," he began, his voice low but commanding. "I think maybe this is what you're looking for." He gestured to Midori, who stepped over to the table of gifts and retrieved a box that had been concealed by Ellie's pile.

Lottie watched as Ellie's whole face lit up, then twisted into annoyance.

"Why is it down here, and not in my room where I left it?"

The king dismissed his daughter's question with a curt exhale before turning his gaze to Lottie. "We decided that it would be more appropriate if we presented this gift formally from all of us." The king's words must have had some significance, because both Ellie and Jamie turned to look at Lottie. Ellie's lips curved into an excited smile, while Jamie, as usual, remained impossible to read.

Lottie looked down at the silver box as Midori placed it in front of her. It was easily the least lavish item in the whole room, and yet it seemed so important. She looked up at the Wolfson family gathered around the table, their eyes bright with anticipation. Lottie swallowed hard. Whatever was in the box, she was determined to be worthy of it.

"Lottie, we want you to understand how much we value you being here with us." The queen leaned her chin on her hand, her gossamer sleeves floating across the tablecloth.

Lottie found herself turning to Jamie, who nodded at her to open the gift.

"Thank you!" she said, excitement sparking through her. She eased open the lid, finding it to be heavier than expected, and gazed down at the box's contents.

Nestled inside the blue satin walls of the box lay a small silver pendant on a chain. It was etched with the figure of a tiny wolf, the light catching it so that the creature's eyes glittered. The pendant was identical to the ones Ellie and

Jamie wore. Lottie's heart skipped a beat.

"Now you're part of the pack." Ellie grinned at her, her white teeth shining like pearls.

"This is . . . ," Lottie began, but the words stuck in her throat.

This was her official welcome into the household—now Lottie was not just a Portman, but part of the family. She felt tears prick her eyes and had to hold her breath to stop from welling up.

Part of the pack.

She was so happy to have found a family, but there was another creeping feeling struggling to take over her heart. It came from very far away, and it reminded her of the siren call of Rosewood. It wasn't that she didn't feel worthy. No. Lottie looked around at the smiling faces of the Wolfsons—her new family. She knew she belonged there. But all at once she knew what she was feeling.

Guilt.

What about her own family, her mother? Was she just going to forget about her?

"This is so kind of you," Lottie said sincerely, hoping her voice wouldn't crack. Clearly she didn't hide her emotions well enough, because she saw Ellie's excitement falter, her eyes darting to Jamie's as they shared a look of concern.

Ugh! thought Lottie. She hated when they did that.

"The food is going to waste," Jamie said, breaking the spell.

"Yes," Ellie added. "We mustn't ignore this amazing cake." She grinned at Hanna and Midori, who each bobbed in a curtsy. "Lottie, I'll help you put your pendant on after we eat."

Lottie watched as people began to pile their plates with cake. She smiled widely, refusing to let her happy face slip. But she knew she had to deal with the guilt she'd just uncovered. She had a favor to ask of the Wolfsons—one that could throw their lives into chaos.

3

THE PENDANT BURNED IN LOTTIE'S hand as they made their way to Ellie's rec room.

"Lottie, if you're worried about the pendant being too expensive, it was really nothing," Ellie began as soon as the door was shut behind them.

Ellie's rec room always took a little bit of time to adjust to. It was so different from the rest of the palace—a chaotic haven of neon colors with framed movie posters, video games, and comics lining the purple walls. Arcade games flashed bright lights and a giant TV took up half the back wall, hooked up to what Lottie had to assume was every game console ever released. The home theater was accessorized with a popcorn machine and cotton candy maker, both of which Lottie had overused that summer. In the center of the left wall was Ellie's pride and joy, a guitar that had once belonged to Joan Jett. The room was Ellie's fantasy come to life and was affectionately referred to as "the Vault" for the lack of windows.

"No, no. I love it, Ellie," she said quickly. "That's not . . ."

Lottie glanced over at Jamie, who was settling down on one of the sofas. Was she about to open a can of worms?

"Is that for me?" Ellie cut off her thoughts, gesturing to the gift that Lottie had picked up.

"Yes. I wanted to give it to you when it was quieter." Lottie held it out and Ellie smiled as she gently took the floral-wrapped box. Their fingertips brushed, making Lottie's skin tingle.

Lottie watched as her dearest friend opened the gift. Ellie was much more careful about tearing open the paper than she had been with any of the presents in the royal dining hall. Lottie felt her body sag with relief—she could tell this present meant just as much to Ellie as any of the others.

Ellie held up the square of stretched canvas and glanced between the portrait and Lottie's face. "You painted this?" she asked in wonder.

Lottie felt her cheeks go hot. "Well, yes. I was working on it over the summer so—" She scratched the back of her head, a nervous twitch she'd adopted from Ellie. She came to stand beside her and together they looked at the portrait. Lottie had painted Ellie in a traditional style, with oil paints that she'd found in the palace. The picture recreated one of her favorite memories of Ellie, a moment that captured exactly how Lottie saw her: the moment when she'd taken her mask off at the fencing tournament. Bold and beautiful in her pristine white gear, she was clutching a saber and looking every bit like the heroic prince who had rescued Lottie at the summer ball.

"Jamie, come look at this," Ellie called, holding the painting out for him to see.

He joined them to inspect the canvas, and Lottie held her breath as Jamie scrutinized her art.

Jamie raised an eyebrow. "We should get you to do Ellie's official portrait for the gallery," he said finally, a smile creeping over his lips.

Lottie lowered her gaze, feeling shy from the praise. She loved making art, but it had been a long time since she'd actually painted anything. Her stepmother, Beady, had never been particularly encouraging, quick to get annoyed by the tubes of paint everywhere. So Lottie had put her paint box and easel away, not wanting to upset her.

"You should be really proud of this, Lottie," Jamie continued. "Ellie's parents will love it, I'm sure." Lottie looked up at his words. His eyes were earnest, and she was reminded how intense he could be, her mind flashing back to that terrifying vision of him fighting Saskia at the ball. Cold and deadly. Lottie needed to be as strong as Jamie if she was ever going to be useful to Ellie, and that meant tackling this odd feeling that was taking over.

"I'm glad you like it, Ellie, but . . ." Lottie glanced down at the pendant in her fist, rubbing the pad of her thumb over the engraving of the wolf. "There is something I need to talk to—"

But once again, before Lottie could get the words out, she was interrupted.

"Is this also for Ellie?" Jamie held up the other wrapped gift suspiciously, clearly worried that it was some kind of dangerous item.

"Actually, that gift is for you." Lottie nervously pushed a strand of hair behind her ear. She knew Jamie didn't want to be reminded of his birthday. "I thought it would be sad if Ellie and I were both getting gifts and there was nothing for you. It's just a little something."

The suspicion on Jamie's face did not dissolve, and he stared down at the rectangular package in front of him as if he had absolutely no idea what to do with it. Had he never received a gift before?

"Okay," he said bluntly, putting it aside without any indication that he wanted to open it. "Now, what did you want to talk about?"

Lottie blinked, struggling to make sense of his strange reaction. Sometimes Jamie was too weird for her to even begin trying to understand him. She just had to hope he liked the gift when he finally did open it.

With everyone's eyes now trained on Lottie, she found herself unable to speak, too anxious about the trouble she might be about to cause.

"What's wrong?" Ellie asked, gently putting down the painting before taking a step toward her. Both she and Jamie had been keeping a careful eye on her ever since the attempted kidnapping. They were both convinced that Lottie had been permanently messed up—which was why she needed to sort this out now.

Lottie took a deep breath, pushing Jamie's reaction to her gift out of her mind. "It's just . . . Remember that promise you made to me before the summer ball?" Ellie glanced nervously over to Jamie. "We agreed that I could tell my friend Ollie the truth." Lottie surprised herself with how steadily she spoke.

"No" was Jamie's curt response, but Ellie gave him a sharp look.

She turned to Lottie. "I remember," she said softly, "but is that still something you want to go through with?"

"It doesn't matter if she wants to, Ellie. This is not a promise you should have made."

Ellie stared at Jamie, and Lottie could sense an argument brewing. *Not today. Not on Ellie's birthday.* She looked down at the wolf pendant again, not ready to put it on until she knew she could do this. She had to tell Ollie before they went back to Rosewood; she needed to.

"I don't *want* to tell him. I *have* to," she said calmly. "Don't you see? He's the only one left." Her voice caught in her throat, and her friends stared at her. "He's the only connection I have to my family."

"I see." Jamie softened. "But there are rules, Lottie. With this new threat from Leviathan, we can't take any risks." Leviathan took particular interest in the children of royal families—hence the attempted kidnapping by Saskia. They couldn't allow something like that to happen again.

Still, Lottie was determined. She had to convince Jamie. Yes, she yearned to return to Rosewood and get to the bottom of this Leviathan threat, but she couldn't enter the school gates again until she'd reconnected with something from her old life. With someone. With Ollie.

"He'll find out on his own, even if we don't tell him." Lottie gave Jamie a serious look. She knew this was the only way to persuade him, and it was true; it had been a worry of Lottie's for a while. "I can't avoid him forever. He's far less of a risk if I tell him myself and swear him to secrecy."

Jamie rubbed the bridge of his nose. "This is a terrible idea."

That wasn't a no.

Ellie grinned at Lottie, knowing that they'd won.

"Aren't we stopping at your hometown on the way back to Rosewood anyway? So that you can pick up some of your things?" Ellie reached for Lottie's pendant. "You can tell Ollie then. It just makes sense." Jamie grumbled but made no further protest. "Jamie, indulge us. Consider it your birthday present to us." Her eyes twinkled.

She unclasped the chain and moved behind Lottie to drape it around her neck. "There. It's perfect," she murmured.

Lottie felt the cool silver against her skin and heard the clasp snap into place, the wolf resting close to her heart. She reached up and stroked the silver. She was one of the family now. She wondered just how different her next year at Rosewood would be.

❦ 4 ❦

LOTTIE AWOKE THE NEXT DAY, the day of their journey back to England, with the strangest feeling that she was being watched. The sensation was subtle but unmistakable, like a ghost breathing softly on her skin. Her eyes shot open, half expecting to see her statue in front of her, but instead her eyes fell directly on a pink velvet box that lay open on her lace-covered bedside table, her crescent-moon tiara glinting rainbow light from within it. There was no one in the room but Lottie, and she felt silly for being spooked. She pulled the peach fabric of her bedcovers up over her head and snuggled herself into the material like a protective cocoon. The palace beds were far too comfortable, like sinking into a fresh pool of feathers every night. She never imagined in all her life that she could get used to this level of luxury. But as comfortable as her bed was, she could not let it capture her this morning. They were heading back to England today, and the king had requested an audience alone with her before they left. Reluctantly, she shoved back the covers and swung her feet to rest on the sun-warmed floor.

All her clothes had been washed, pressed, and placed in suitcases along with her other belongings. It was all in stark contrast to the excited packing she'd done on her own the year before. A pile of books by one of the pink cases had her mind drifting to the gift she'd given Jamie, wondering if he'd opened it yet. She hoped it would make him feel more connected to his family, to help close the distance that she herself so sorely related to.

Lottie nibbled at the half-eaten cupcake sitting on her desk atop a shimmering golden plate, a leftover from yesterday's birthday celebrations. The white icing left a sugary smear on her mouth that she caught sight of as she passed the gigantic framed mirror. She paused, taking in the reflection looking back at her, dressed in a pristine nightgown. Her belly and face had grown rounder, her hair longer and fluffier. She wiped the frosting off her bottom lip and licked her sticky fingers, thinking about the past few weeks.

Lottie and Ellie had spent most of the summer in Mara-dova in a hazy splendor. Lazy mornings in fizzy fits of laughter, auburn afternoons relishing sugarcoated delicacies with steaming hot tea, followed by blue evenings of reading and glowing silver screens. They'd shared everything that summer, every film they loved, every song they cherished, and Lottie almost believed their happy pretending. But, like the persistent twitch of Jamie's top lip and the phantom pounding of Saskia's heartbeat from the basement below, the slumbering threat of their mysterious enemy was impossible to ignore. All at once, Lottie was anxious to get going on their travels back to Rosewood.

What on earth did the king need to tell her in private?

Lottie threw on some comfortable but respectable clothes for the journey before rushing to the ground floor to meet King Alexander. It was impossible not to skid on the polished floors, and she had to make a conscious effort not to slide around like a child all over the palace, although she was sure she'd caught the maids Hanna and Midori doing it themselves a few times.

Lottie was surprised to find the king waiting for her in the hall. He was dressed in a golden robe that flowed over the marble floor. The king was a tall, sinewy man with thick light-umber hair and a permanently furrowed brow that gave Lottie the impression he'd read a lot as a child. Sometimes it was difficult to see the family resemblance between him and Ellie: where she was volatile, he was reserved; where she was rushed, he was measured. But occasionally she'd catch something wild in his eyes—the wolf, forever waiting, ready to strike.

"We can have ourselves painted however we'd like, yet almost every single one of us chose to sit on our throne and look bored." The king spoke abruptly, without even greeting Lottie. He gestured to the wall with an attempt at humor, but Lottie was too distracted by the paintings to register the joke. It was her favorite part of the palace; she had to stop and study the fine detail of each piece, all the subtle coloring and hidden symbolism in the background. Every previous ruler of Maradova was depicted in this endless hall, the many eyes of a centuries-old lineage glowering down at those who dared to walk by.

"There's so many of them," Lottie muttered, a strange sensation creeping over her as she met the gazes of these past rulers. "It's amazing to have such a strong connection to your heritage."

The king turned to her, his arms crossed as he scrutinized her. A hard lump formed in Lottie's stomach, and she wondered if what she'd just said might seem stupid.

"It's an endless, unbroken chain," he mused, but there was something melancholic in his eyes as he gazed at the second-to-last painting in the hall. "Almost," he added. Lottie's eyes locked on the pair of emerald irises that looked out from the portrait, its somber black frame marking its subject as somehow lesser than his gilded companions. His hair was darker than the average Wolfson, growing sleekly down to his shoulders, and he had heavily lashed eyes and a roguish smile. There was only one other Wolfson who bore any resemblance to this man: Ellie.

"My brother, Claude Wolfson. *Odin pravila volk haka olen pak ranit.*" The king spoke the old Maravish language with ease, and Lottie recognized the phrase. It was a say-ing adopted by the Wolfson royal family, which Jamie had taught her.

One bad wolf can hurt the whole pack.

Lottie knew little of Ellie's uncle Claude; they scarcely spoke his name. He existed only as a reminder of what happens should one abandon one's royal duties. She only knew about him from her princess lessons with Jamie and from this painting, the painting intended to be his corona-tion gift.

"My brother remains immortalized in this hall as a warning." The king gestured at the painting, his golden robe shining like liquid sun as it swayed with each move-ment. When he turned back to her she could see the lines around his eyes, set from a decade of frowning. "To fail the family is an unforgivable act. Do you understand what that means?"

Lottie nodded solemnly. She knew that Claude had run away from the responsibility of the throne and become a gloomy symbol of how seriously the Wolfsons took their family traditions. Gulping down her nerves, she took in King Alexander's hard expression and tried to picture Ellie in the same golden robes, that lump of guilt building up in her throat. How could she feel so troubled by her fam-ily worries when Ellie had so much more on her plate? What must it feel like to have the constant burden of duty weighing you down whenever you left the palace? She turned back to the glowing green eyes of the family traitor, the image blurring until it almost looked like Ellie's mischievous smirk was peeking out of the black frame. It was in that moment, locked in a staring match with the rogue wolf of the Maravish royal family, that someone silently crept up behind them.

"You wanted to see me?"

Lottie nearly let out a shriek, her mind tricking her into thinking that Claude had materialized behind them, but it was only Jamie, looking very serious as usual. He gave her a brief once-over, but his face gave nothing away. As soon as she saw him, curiosity flooded her; she was desperate to know what he thought of her gift.

"Ah, Jamie." The king signaled for him to stand beside Lottie, the two of them looking very small in the presence of his cascading robes. "Has Nikolay spoken to you?" There was a weight to his words that Lottie tried to decipher but couldn't.

"He has," Jamie replied impassively, without even a twitch. Nikolay, the king's Partizan, was a man with such a broad and powerful build that Lottie couldn't help being a little scared of him. He had trained Jamie since he was a child, and, as far as Lottie was aware, he was the closest thing Jamie had to a father figure.

"Good." The hall suddenly seemed to turn cold, the

sunlight disappearing, shadows emphasizing the dark lines on the king's features.

"At the summer ball, you both succeeded in preventing a true catastrophe," he began, his voice echoing. "Lottie, like a model Portman, you bore the burden of any danger intended for Eleanor." Lottie resisted the temptation to squeeze her eyes shut, not wanting the memory of that bone-chilling night to creep into her mind.

I'm okay, I'm okay, I'm okay, she repeated to herself, determinedly focusing on the king's voice.

"And, Jamie, you expertly protected both your princess and her Portman while keeping the spectacle to a minimum."

She let out a deep breath as he spoke, forcing the dread out of her mind. She wouldn't let Leviathan win.

"We cannot allow the Maravish monarchy to appear weak, especially now that we seem to be the target of an unknown enemy. I need you both to be extra vigilant this year. Nothing can be overlooked."

Lottie blinked up at the golden-robed king, not sure she quite understood what he meant.

King Alexander paused, peering at them both, before turning his attention directly to Lottie.

"Lottie Pumpkin"—he spoke her name as if it tasted strange on his tongue—"my daughter has clearly become quite fond of you." The tone was matter-of-fact.

"Y-yes," Lottie replied, unsure what was expected of her.

"I know you both understand that Ellie must come first," he began, his eyes never breaking contact with Lottie's, "but there may come a time when you will have to put Ellie second in order to put her first. I trust you'll understand should that moment arise."

Lottie didn't say anything because, quite frankly, she didn't understand.

"Do I have your word?"

"Yes, Your Majesty," Jamie replied instantly.

"Yes, Your Majesty," Lottie added hurriedly, acutely aware that she was lost and that Jamie could probably tell.

The king narrowed his eyes at Lottie, and she had the feeling he was trying to pluck information from her head—but what he was hoping to find, she couldn't possibly guess. Finally he looked away and she felt her shoulders relax, not realizing how tense she'd become.

"Excellent—you're free to go. Good luck this year."

And that was it.

Lottie watched, bewildered, as the king left them alone, his shining gold robes flowing behind him as the sunlight returned in beams.

Stay vigilant? Put Ellie second to put her first? What does that even mean?

Jamie let out a deep sigh, and she realized he must have

been holding his breath the whole time. "That's the first time I've heard you say that."

Lottie was surprised to see a smile crack his lips. "Say what?"

"*Yes, Your Majesty.*" Jamie made quote marks with his fingers, but there was nothing mocking about his tone. "Did it feel weird?"

"A little bit," she admitted, glancing down and feeling embarrassed that she might have sounded silly. When she looked up, Jamie's expression was thoughtful, and she could feel that there was something he wanted to say. "Jamie," she began, before he had time to speak. "Did you like your gift?"

His face turned back to its usual blank mask and she grew nervous, her hands shaking slightly.

"I understand what it's like to feel disconnected from your family," Lottie said, rushed, "and I thought you might like it, that maybe you could learn something—"

An unexpected harsh laugh boomed out of Jamie's mouth, the sound lacking any humor.

"I threw it away," he said. The words were casual, as if it were completely obvious that he would throw the gift in the trash like it were no more than a rotten apple.

"You . . . what?" Lottie wondered if he was trying to make a joke, then remembered Jamie did not have the capacity for jokes. "Why would you do that?"

Jamie didn't seem angry; he was acting as if this was all perfectly normal. Though she'd wondered if he had ever received a gift before, she'd never considered he would be this dense about what to do with one.

"We can't get distracted by things like that, Lottie," he replied, making as if to leave. "You heard what the king said; we have to put Ellie first."

"I know, but—"

"I know you didn't mean anything by it, Lottie." She was about to interrupt him, to explain how rude it is to throw away someone's gift, when his face turned cold, eyes clouding over as his stony gaze latched onto her. "But never do anything like that again."

And just like that his face smoothed out, so calm she thought she'd imagined that split-second moment of warning.

She had a million more things she wanted to say, but she swallowed them reluctantly, not wanting to cause any more trouble.

"Okay." Her voice came out a confused squeak, sounding more like a question than she intended it to.

Why on earth was he acting so weird about a gift?

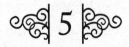

5

THEY TOOK THE WOLFSONS' PRIVATE jet from Maradova to England later that morning. Lottie had now flown more times on privately chartered flights than on regular flights; part of her felt uncomfortable with how quickly she'd gotten used to stepping onto a private plane.

"I still think this is a terrible idea," Jamie muttered now from his place in the passenger seat of the chauffeured black BMW. They passed through the narrow, winding roads of St. Ives, stone cottages lining their route. They were on their way to tell Ollie the truth about why Lottie couldn't come home, the truth about her new life as a Portman. But before that they needed to collect Lottie's belongings, and she couldn't fight her strange feelings about returning to that house.

The first thing Lottie noticed as she stepped out of the car was the familiar salty tang of the sea. She could hear the waves in the distance, pushing and pulling her back to her childhood and her mother.

She was home.

Although it didn't feel like her home anymore. The

street felt smaller, the cobbles harder beneath her feet. The colors of the scene seemed faded, as if she were looking at a memory. Too much had happened since she'd left, and she knew she could never look at this little seaside town in the same way again. The thought made her heart ache. Leviathan, Saskia, Portmans, Partizans . . . When she'd lived here, stories like those were exactly that: stories. Now they were all too real.

She was overcome by a wave of embarrassment about her old humble life as she watched Ellie step out of the other side of the car onto the tiny narrow street. It felt weird to see Ellie in the context of her childhood memories; she was so used to seeing her in luxurious surroundings. Lottie's hometown seemed too small to contain this princess. Lottie gulped as Ellie removed her sunglasses, looking up at the tightly packed, colorful buildings that crowded around them. She stood out in her black ensemble and oversize leather jacket.

Ellie peered at the dusty shopfront at 12 Bethesda Hill, with its faded blue paint and rambling wisteria. The bakery used to be called Ms. Pumpkin's Pastries, and it was the place Lottie had once called home. In the whole year since she'd been gone, it seemed her stepmother, Beady, had not once attempted to clean the windows or tidy up. Lottie doubted she ever would.

"We'll pick up the rest of your stuff and then we're off.

No need to stay longer than necessary," Jamie said matter-of-factly.

He nodded at Lottie and she returned the gesture. She wanted to get this all over with as quickly as possible so she could get back to Rosewood.

They stepped through the red door and up the wooden stairs leading to the apartment above the shop. Lottie was greeted by a note in the kitchen, scribbled urgently in unruly handwriting:

I've gone to Cuba to see Simon.
Your stuff is in the black trash bags by the stairs.
Beady
PS Don't make a mess!

She quickly scrunched up the paper and tossed it in the trash before either of the others could read it. Seeing her dad's name always made her feel weird, especially written in Beady's handwriting.

"So where is your dad anyway?" Ellie asked, inspecting a photograph of Beady with Lottie's father that was stuck to the fridge with a tacky magnet from Las Vegas.

"Cuba," Lottie said confidently, as though she hadn't just found this out herself a few moments ago.

Lottie stepped around the coffee table. The living room was littered with takeout boxes. It was clear that Beady had left in a hurry, and Lottie wondered if she'd gotten into trouble over money again. Although they didn't exactly get along, Lottie couldn't help feeling bad for her. Becoming her stepmother was never something Beady had wanted, and Lottie knew better than anyone what her dad was like. Lottie picked up a few pizza boxes and put them in the recycling bin.

Jamie walked through the doorway carrying overflowing black trash bags. "This your stuff?" he asked, raising one of them in the air. "It looks like they've been left for you."

Lottie reached to grab one of the bags, but it dragged her down with its weight, and she gave a small "oof" of surprise. How much stuff had Beady crammed in here?

Jamie smirked. "You'll have plenty of time to prove your strength when we start training at school. Until then"— he heaved one of the bags up effortlessly to emphasize his point—"let the Partizan do the heavy lifting." Lottie smiled despite herself. Maybe they were okay again; maybe he'd forgiven her for the gift.

Training was one of the reasons she was so excited to get back to school—she couldn't wait to start learning how to fight. Lottie was determined to meet the threat of Leviathan head on. She would not let Ellie be put in the same danger ever again. Lottie's mind conjured up an image of Saskia, and she felt her hands go shaky. She couldn't find herself unprepared again.

"Hey, Lottie!" Ellie's voice floated through from the hallway. "Who's this?"

Lottie poked her head around the corner to find Ellie staring intently at a small framed painting on the wall. She walked over to her friend's side and the two of them gazed at the portrait of her ancestor Henry. She'd never really noticed the painting before; it had hung on this wall as far back as Lottie could remember. Henry had a soft, amused expression. His hair was a muddy blond like Lottie's, but cut closer to his head than her own unruly curls.

"That's my great-grandfather Henry Pitkin." Lottie was surprised that Beady had kept the painting up. "Well, he's actually my great-grandfather times about ten, but I can't manage saying all those *greats*." Lottie smiled as she remembered the stories her mother had told her about him. "He attended one of the first classes at Rosewood Hall and became a teacher there when he graduated." She leaned forward to stroke the frame, recalling when her mother had handed her the tiara for the first time. She could almost hear her mother's voice now as she looked into Henry's eyes. "Apparently he lived an exciting and mysterious life. Henry's the reason I wanted to go to Rosewood so badly. He's the one who was first gifted our family tiara."

Thinking about the heirloom made her reach for it where it was nestled safely in her bag, which hung by her side. Her fingers found it, the silver warm against her skin, and a faint haunting melody whispered in Lottie's mind.

"Pitkin?" Ellie echoed.

A prickly embarrassment ran over Lottie's skin. "Yes. Pitkin was my mother's original family name. We, um . . ." Lottie looked down, a furious blush creeping up her cheeks. She absolutely hated talking about her name. "We had to . . . She changed it."

Ellie nodded slowly, sensing Lottie's discomfort. "Who painted it?" she asked to change the subject.

"I have no idea," Lottie said gratefully. "It's always been a mystery."

Ellie peered more closely, the tip of her nose almost touching the ancient cracked surface. "It reminds me of your painting style," she pondered. "There's something about it . . . It's like the one you did of me."

Lottie chewed her lip in thought. Was Ellie right? Did she paint like this?

"Okay, you two—we're all packed up," Jamie called up the stairs from the front door. There was nothing left to do, no reason to stay here. Lottie sighed and turned to leave, but Ellie reached out a hand to stop her.

"You should take this," she said. "You said you were worried about losing your connection to your family, right? It's clearly important to you, to have something to remember them with."

Lottie stared raptly at the painting. Henry smiled back at her. Maybe Ollie wasn't her last connection to her old life.

"You're right," Lottie said, warmth spreading through her. "This painting doesn't belong in this house anymore." *In fact,* she thought, *none of the Pumpkins belong in this house anymore.* There was somewhere else they fit much better.

"Okay, Henry," she told her ancestor as she lifted the portrait off its hook. She grinned as she held the painting at arm's length and blew the dust from its chipped frame. "You're coming with me. You're going back to Rosewood!"

6

IT TOOK LESS THAN FIVE minutes to get to Ollie's. His house perched on a cliff just outside St. Ives. It leaned dangerously to one side and looked as though it were ready to tumble into the sea at any moment.

The driveway was empty, which meant his mum must be at her studio. Good.

"Ollie's dog doesn't like strangers, so try not to surprise him," Lottie said as they approached the door. For some reason, she was suddenly reluctant to ring the front doorbell. She was nervous. More nervous than she'd been since walking down the palace's marble stairs to be officially presented at the Maravish Summer Ball.

Will Ollie even want to see me? What if he hates me now?

Ellie leaned over her shoulder and pushed the buzzer.

"Ellie!" Lottie hissed.

Ellie grinned back at her. "What? You seemed like you were having some trouble."

Lottie turned back to the door, anxiously smoothing down her skirt. She heard footsteps in the hallway and her heart palpitated. She held her breath as the door swung open.

"Lottie?" Ollie's voice cracked. His eyes were wide, as though he couldn't quite believe what he was seeing.

"Hey, Ollie."

All her nerves melted away. She felt her stomach do a little flip-flop as she took in her childhood friend's scruffy hair and golden skin. She hadn't seen him in a year, but some things hadn't changed. There was still dog hair all over his jeans, and his eyes still twinkled with mischief. But he was noticeably taller, and the baby fat around his face had turned into a jawline. He'd grown up.

There was a familiar pitter-patter of claws, and a shape hurtled down the hallway, pushing past Ollie to dive at her.

"Link!" She held out her arms to Ollie's dog, but before he could throw himself into her embrace Jamie stepped protectively in front of her. Lottie watched in astonishment as Link froze and let out a low-pitched submissive groan. He flopped onto the floor and rolled on his back, tummy exposed in a passive position.

"Sit," Ellie's voice commanded from behind her. To Lottie's amazement, Link complied, scrambling into a dutiful sitting position. He'd never even met Ellie before!

Ellie stepped in front of Lottie, holding out her hand so that Link could sniff her scent. Jamie had moved to one side and was watching carefully.

"Good boy," she told the dog, rubbing behind his ear and getting dog hair all over her sleeves. Lottie had never seen Ollie's dog behave so well, let alone with strangers. Ollie came by her side and together they watched as Jamie and Ellie made friends with the completely docile Link.

"Lottie," Ollie said, staring at her two royal friends, "who on earth are these people?"

The Moreno house was as colorful as its inhabitants. Patchwork rugs covered the floorboards, and patterned cushions were scattered across overstuffed sofas and arm-chairs. Garlands of dried flowers and bunting hung from the low-beamed ceilings. Ollie took them to the kitchen. The TV in the corner buzzed lowly, and the windowsill was crammed with brightly colored trinkets his mum had collected whenever she visited her parents in Brazil. Lottie smiled to herself as she remembered how much trouble Ollie used to have stopping himself from touching the tiny cacti.

Ellie and Lottie sat at the green-painted wooden table while Ollie made tea for them, spilling water all over the brick-red floor tiles as he heaved the kettle over to the counter. Jamie stood in the doorway, one foot propped up against the frame, looking totally out of place among the clutter. Ellie had made herself comfortable at the table with a packet of biscuits. Every now and then she would surreptitiously snap off a corner of biscuit and feed it to Link, who sat at her feet beneath the table. Ollie's dog was so much more docile than the ball of energy Lottie remembered from when she was a kid. Both Ellie and Jamie kept quiet and watched as Lottie and Ollie chatted.

"So," Ollie said slowly as he placed two chipped mugs on the table, "I guess you've decided you *can* talk to me again."

Lottie cringed. Ollie had every right to feel angry. Phones weren't allowed at Rosewood Hall, and in the past year Lottie hadn't visited Ollie once. She'd been so scared and unsure about her new life that she didn't know how to reach out to her old one. She'd decided that the best thing for everyone was for her to just stop being Ollie's friend. What a mistake that had been. But here she was now, about to tell him the truth. Would that be another mistake? The truth could expose him to the very dangers she'd been trying to protect him from.

"I came back to explain myself," Lottie said calmly, "even though this is probably a terrible idea."

"It is," Jamie said from the doorway. Lottie scowled at him before turning back to Ollie. He was spooning his third sugar into his tea, his eyes trained on her. Watching, waiting.

Lottie cleared her throat nervously. "Ollie, before I explain, I need you to promise two things."

Ollie's eyebrows furrowed. "Okay . . ." He sounded less than convinced.

"I need you to promise that you will never, ever tell

anyone what I'm about to say." Ollie's glance darted over toward Ellie and Jamie, who were trying their best to stay inconspicuous and failing terribly. He opened his mouth to speak, but Lottie cut him off. "And I need you to promise that you will under no circumstances try to get involved in any way."

"Well, that's no fun," Ollie said, laughing in Jamie's direction as if he expected him to join in. Jamie didn't even crack a smile, but Ollie did get a small chuckle from Ellie.

"I'm serious, Ollie. You have to promise me."

He rolled his eyes. "Fine, I promise I won't . . . do either of those things."

"I got a job," Lottie said. They were the first words that came to her.

"What?" Ollie's brow creased in confusion.

"I mean," Lottie started again. She just had to tell him quickly, like ripping off a Band-Aid. She let her breath out in one long go.

"Ellie is the undercover princess of Maradova." She glanced over at her friend, and Ellie nodded encouragingly. Lottie swallowed, her mouth suddenly dry. "During my first weeks at Rosewood, a rumor started that *I* was the princess. So Ellie and I decided to swap identities. I've been hired by her family as a Portman—someone who pretends to be a member of the royal family so that the actual royal can live a safe and normal life. That is, until they're ready to officially take up their role." Lottie took another deep breath as she finished speaking.

Ollie's teaspoon made a clinking sound as it fell against his mug of tea. "Is this a joke?"

Lottie shook her head.

"But you have different names. How does this work?"

Lottie had always been a little touchy about her name, but this time it had come in handy.

"Oh, well, very few people actually knew the princess's name, and, well . . . everyone assumed Lottie Pumpkin was a fake name, so they just thought it was part of the undercover-princess thing and—"

Ollie shook his head, trying to make sense of what he was hearing. "So you're telling me that after a lifetime of being obsessed with princesses, you actually became one?" He burst out laughing.

"Well, that's not quite how it works, but—"

"Now I understand why you abandoned me." His voice dripped with his trademark sarcasm, but there was an edge of genuine hurt in his words too. "Because I definitely don't fit into the world of princes and princesses." He gestured to his jeans, covered in dog hair.

"You don't understand," Lottie said gently. "It's dangerous for people to know. I couldn't get you involved. Ellie has to come first." But as she spoke, she realized how disturbing her words might sound to someone outside the world of Portmans and Partizans. Ellie came first—before everything? She felt a pain in her chest as Ollie's smile faltered.

"Lottie, what are you saying?" He gave Ellie a sharp look, then Jamie, who darted Lottie a glance that said, *I told you so.*

"He won't understand, Lottie," Jamie said, turning his back on the room.

Ollie scoffed, gesturing at him. "Okay, who is this guy?" He spoke to Jamie's back. "I don't know you, but I can tell already that you need to lighten up." He laughed, but there was no reaction from Jamie.

"Jamie is Ellie's Partizan," Lottie explained. "He's a personal bodyguard."

Ollie chuckled again. "He's what?"

"This is serious, Ollie. Don't make me regret coming here. This is dangerous knowledge for you to have, but I couldn't go any longer without explaining, and . . . Ellie was kind enough to give me permission to tell you." Lottie's words didn't have the desired effect. Ollie's face had turned serious. None of this was going the way she'd hoped.

"If it's dangerous AT ALL, you shouldn't be doing it. You're really going to lose yourself in some childish princess fantasy?"

Lottie narrowed her eyes at him. She resented being

called childish, after everything she'd been through.

"Ellie is my friend and—"

"All of you, shut up a second!" Ellie was staring at the TV, straining to hear with the volume turned down low. "Lottie, *look*."

A banner along the bottom of the screen read "Breaking News," and Lottie could hear the phantom clicks of cameras in her head as bulbs flashed on screen from photos being taken at the scene. Two kids around Lottie's age were being escorted through a crowd. One was a pale boy with dark hair and sunken eyes, the other a very pretty girl in a tan hijab who looked furious to have so many cameras around her.

"Who are they?" Lottie asked.

"Just wait," Ellie said, not tearing her gaze from the TV.

The image changed and two other figures appeared on the screen. Lottie recognized them instantly. Jamie stood behind Lottie's chair and stared at the TV, where two very solemn but familiar faces watched from the sea of ravenous reporters. With their pale white skin and bright red lips, they looked like human candy canes. Candy canes that Lottie had seen before.

Jamie gave a low whistle. "Would you look at that?"

Their friends Lola and Micky Tompkins were on the news.

7

"QUICK, TURN IT UP!" LOTTIE said, flapping her hand.

Ollie reached for the TV remote and increased the volume. A reporter appeared on the screen with the twins, Lola and Micky, and a man behind them in a wheelchair. The reporter spoke urgently into a handheld microphone:

"*Negotiations over who would take over Tompkins Confectionery began two months ago after Alfred Tompkins*"—the journalist indicated the man in the wheelchair, the twins' father—"*was declared too sick to continue running the much-loved company.*"

Lottie's heart sank. She'd had no idea Lola and Micky's father was ill.

"*The Butter Company had been negotiating a proposal to merge with Tompkins until two weeks ago, when Emelia Malouf and Percival Butter, the eldest children of the Butter Company's owners, vanished under suspicious circumstances. Negotiations were put on hold while their disappearance was investigated. There's now been a release stating that the disappearance was, in fact, a kidnapping for ransom. Thankfully both children have been returned safe and unharmed.*"

The camera panned back to the girl in the hijab and the tired-looking boy, presumably the hostages, Emelia and Percival. Lottie felt a pang of sympathy as they were jostled by the journalists crowding around them.

"Bunch of vultures," Ellie hissed. "Emelia should throw something at one of them—that's what I'd do."

Lottie's mind wandered back to the trouble Ellie had had in the past with reporters who had spread false rumors about all the wild antics she got up to. It was no surprise she hated them so much.

"Yes, that would help your reputation immensely," Jamie said drily.

Ellie snorted in response and turned away from the TV. "Yet another reason why Lottie is so invaluable." Ellie grinned at her.

The woman on the TV pressed her finger to her ear, getting more information through her earpiece, and the "Breaking News" sign flashed up again.

"We have news that, with the children safely returned, the Butter Company and Tompkins will be moving forward with their plans to merge. The rush may be an indication of Alfred Tompkins's deteriorating health."

Lottie felt herself welling up. "This is terrible," she said, her eyes brimming with tears. "I hope Lola and Micky are okay."

"Who are these people?"

Lottie jumped as Ollie spoke from behind her. She'd almost forgotten he was there. She turned to him, wiping her eyes. "They're friends from school and—"

Before Lottie could continue, the reporter started talking again, pulling everyone's attention back to the screen.

"The circumstances of the kidnapping remain unclear and, although we have received word that neither child has been harmed, they have no memories of the week they were missing, indicating drugs may have been involved."

The scene switched back to the newsroom, and the program moved on to the next story.

"This is bad," Jamie said, leaning for the remote to turn the volume down again.

"Do you think it's Leviathan?" Lottie asked nervously. The word caught in her throat as if it were a curse.

"We can't assume anything," Jamie replied, rubbing his chin in thought, "but if there are kidnapping attempts being made on children of important families, then we need to stay extra vigilant."

"We could have Nikolay ask Saskia," Ellie offered.

Jamie let out a short breath of impatience. "She's refusing to speak until she can see Anastacia."

"She still won't speak?" Ellie said. "So we don't know anything new about Leviathan?"

"Correct," Jamie said flatly.

Ellie shifted her gaze to Lottie, who looked unexpectedly troubled.

"We should tell Anastacia," Lottie said softly. "She has the right to know."

Ellie nodded.

"I'm sorry . . . what?" Ollie exclaimed. Link bristled at the sudden noise, and Ellie reached out to calm him. "I'm starting to get the feeling there's a lot more to this job of yours than just pretending to be a princess." Ollie looked accusingly at Jamie and Ellie.

"I told you it was serious, Ollie," Lottie said.

"Serious enough that you might get kidnapped?" Ollie snapped.

Lottie, Ellie, and Jamie fell silent. Finally Lottie let out a long sigh and turned to Ellie and Jamie. "Could you give us a moment alone?"

Ellie put her hands up in defeat and the two of them left the room, Link trailing behind.

"We'll be waiting in the car," Jamie said bluntly.

As soon as the front door shut, Lottie turned back to Ollie. "A lot of things happened over the past year, some of them not so pleasant, but I wanted to come back here. I needed to make sure I still had a connection to home and, well, you're the only connection I have left."

Ollie blushed and looked away, all his previous front vanishing into embarrassment. "Oh, man." Ollie struggled to look her in the eye. "Now I feel bad. But, Lottie, how dangerous is this job?"

"Well—" Lottie reached for the wolf pendant, concealed under her clothes, and she sighed again, unsure how Ollie would take the truth—"I *did* get kidnapped." Ollie's eyes grew wide, but she continued quickly before he could say anything. "It was a failed attempt, but that's why my role is more important now than ever. There's a dangerous group out there called Leviathan. We know nothing about them other than their name. It turned out that one of the girls at school was working for them. Saskia tried to kidnap me at the beginning of summer, thinking I was the princess." Ollie's mouth opened and closed a few times, struggling to form any words. Lottie pressed on. "So you see why I need to do this. Ellie is very special to me, and I don't want her to be in any danger."

At the mention of Ellie's name Ollie suddenly found his voice. "But if it's serious enough that you might get kidnapped, then you're at risk too. What would your mum say?" Lottie flinched and felt her tiara burning in her bag again, singing to her.

What would she say? What would she think of who I am now?

"My mum isn't around," Lottie replied stiffly.

Ollie stared at her as if she were a ghost. "Well, I am.

And I'm telling you this is too dangerous." His voice had turned low and serious.

Lottie felt fire building in her chest. She didn't like being told she couldn't do something, and she wasn't going to stop now, no matter what anyone said.

"You don't get to decide that. I know what I'm doing. I'm trusting you to respect that, not asking you for permission."

He blinked at her, then his shoulders sagged. "Do you really know what you're doing?"

The question caught Lottie off guard. Being Ellie's Portman made her happy, happier than she'd been in years. But she had to try to see it from Ollie's perspective. He was scared for her, and he was scared *of* her—the new her.

Be kind, she reminded herself. *This is all new to him.*

"I'm sorry, Ollie," Lottie said, placing a hand on his shoulder. He leaned in to hug her, something they'd done a million times in the past, but his body felt stiff. It wasn't the same, and she knew he felt that too. "I have to get back to Rosewood," she said, pulling away. That was her home now. She'd done what she needed to; it was time to go back.

Ollie stared at her, then forced a smile that didn't quite reach his eyes. "You look like your mum," he said. Lottie's heart skipped a beat. "Lovely," he added hastily.

"Thank you, Ollie," Lottie said with true gratitude, then looked over at the clock on the wall. "I need to—"

"Get back to Rosewood. Yes, I know," Ollie interrupted.

Lottie smiled at him, feeling the tiara glowing in her bag and the pendant warm at her chest. The two of them walked down the hall toward the front door.

"And, Ollie," she added, pausing in the doorway. She looked straight into his eyes. "I meant what I said. Don't try to get involved."

8

"LOTTIE, WAKE UP!"

She blinked slowly, emerging from an anxiety-fueled dream filled with sad little candy canes and terrifying serpents that wanted to eat them. Her chest felt heavy as she woke, so many problems popping into her mind and demanding to be heard. Leviathan was out there somewhere. What were they planning?

They would have to speak to Anastacia when they got back to Rosewood. They hadn't heard from her at all during the summer and had no idea how she would feel about them. There was also the awkward question of Binah, Ellie and Lottie's other closest friend at school—did she know that Ellie was really the princess? They still hadn't come up with a good way of asking her. And now there were Lola and Micky, whose father was ill. Lottie was already thinking about a million different ways to try to make their lives a little easier during this difficult time, but nothing seemed right.

Her eyes fluttered open to see the school walls looming over the car as they passed through the ornate cast-iron gates that bore the school's initials. As they drove toward the drop-off zone, all her worries melted from her mind like butter. The school was no less awe-inspiring than it had been the first time she saw it. She remembered how scared she'd been of disappointing this magical place. Lottie leaned against the window to take in the rose-lined path that led to the entrance of the school. She was desperate to scramble out of the car and step onto the path so she could properly bask in the lavender and rose scents of Rosewood. She turned to see Ellie gazing out at the school grounds, her body relaxing now that they were here at last.

"We're home!" Ellie grinned as Jamie brought the car to a halt.

Other students were piling their bags around them, looking as well-dressed and primped as Lottie remembered. She looked back toward the gates, at the students coming through in shuttle buses from the nearby railway station, flashes of their house colors—deep purple, red, and yellow tartan—bounding through the invisible barrier that separated Rosewood from the rest of the world. Still, Lottie's attention returned swiftly to Ellie; she was just happy to see her so comfortable again.

They made their way to the path that led to the main school buildings. As soon as Lottie stepped onto it, she felt as though all the pressure that had been building inside her was now released. A sigh of satisfaction escaped her lips.

She curled her toes inside her shoes.

Even after everything that had happened last year, Lottie felt more at ease under the gaze of the school's windows than she had all summer. The flowers were in full bloom, roses of all colors lining the pathways and filling the air with their rich fragrance. It had taken Lottie a while to adjust to the clouds of blossoms that enveloped Rosewood Hall; it was impossible to take even a few steps anywhere in the school without feeling as though you'd entered a Monet painting.

Jamie heaved their bags up the path and insisted on helping the attendant place them in the golf cart, something students were not expected to do. Lottie briefly wondered if he'd be okay settling back into student life. The school knew that Jamie was the princess's bodyguard, but he was also a student and was expected to behave as one. That detail became glaringly obvious during registration.

"Excuse me?" Jamie asked the Conch prefect as he took his purple welcome packet and schedule.

"I said," repeated the prefect, "your roommate will be arriving this evening."

Ellie and Lottie looked at each other, trying to hide their smiles.

"But I don't have a roommate," Jamie said. "I have a single room."

The Conch prefect rolled her eyes and opened her file,

holding it out for Jamie to see.

"Well, now you have a double room," she said, pointing to the line that read: *Jamie Volk—Room 310.*

Lottie glanced over her shoulder at the line of students behind them. Most of them were new and were awkwardly eavesdropping on the exchange.

Jamie narrowed his eyes dangerously. He opened his mouth to say something more when the prefect called "NEXT!" as she peered over his shoulder.

It took all Ellie's and Lottie's willpower not to burst out laughing until they emerged from the main entrance onto the path toward Ivy Wood dorm.

"She completely snubbed you!" Ellie howled, resting her hands on her thighs as she doubled over in a fit of giggles. "Your face!"

"This is not funny, Ellie." Jamie's irritation was clear. "And, Lottie"—he turned to her—"I would expect a more mature reaction from you." Lottie tried to put on a straight face, but Ellie stood behind Jamie and started mimicking his grumpy expression, making it impossible for Lottie not to snort with laughter.

"I see a year at Rosewood has helped neither of you to grow up," Jamie grumbled.

Ellie and Lottie were about to burst out into another fit of giggles when a familiar face appeared by the gate in front of them, a face that made them immediately straighten up.

"Something funny?" Anastacia's cool voice floated over, her eyes hidden by her trademark sunglasses. She looked almost exactly how Lottie remembered her—like a brunette Barbie doll with a million secrets.

"No. Nothing is funny," Jamie said flatly, giving Ellie and Lottie a warning look. "Anastacia." He said her name with a little nod of greeting.

She slowly removed her glasses. "Jamie," she replied.

The two of them seemed to have found some sort of begrudging respect for each other after Anastacia handled herself so well during the summer ball. It couldn't have been easy for her to find out that Saskia—her bodyguard and best friend—had gone rogue.

Anastacia turned to Lottie and Ellie. "I was hoping I might be able to speak to the princess and her Portman alone."

A group of new Ivy students ran through the gate and froze at the sight of them.

"No running on the paths!" Anastacia shouted across to them. They nodded nervously before slinking away.

Jamie turned to Ellie, who gave a small gesture, signaling that he could leave. He hesitated for a moment and leaned over to speak into Lottie's ear.

"Stay vigilant," he whispered before heading into the Ivy Wood dorm to find his new room.

They followed Anastacia to the pond at the center of the

Ivy garden, which was watched over by the bronze statue of Ryley the stag, the proud symbol of Ivy House. They sat on a bench by the pond, safely out of the way of the flood of new Ivy students. Lottie couldn't help feeling a little envious of them—they had no idea how much easier their first year would be compared to her own.

"Let's not bother with formalities," Anastacia declared, her French accent coming through stronger than usual. "You want to know what I know?"

Ellie nodded. "Yes, but also—"

Anastacia held a finger up to silence her. "*Arrêtez!*" she exclaimed. "Just let me speak, okay?"

Ellie grumbled, her eyebrows furrowing, but Lottie gave her arm a squeeze, reminding her that this wasn't easy for any of them.

"We're listening," Lottie said calmly, trying to ease the mood.

Anastacia took a deep breath. "It wasn't until I got back to Paris after the Maravish Summer Ball that I really started to consider some of the strange things that Saskia had said to me over the past year." She looked down at her hand, removing an imaginary fleck of dirt from her fingernails to avoid eye contact. "She was always telling me she'd keep me safe, over and over, saying next year would be the start of *interesting times*." She glanced up at Lottie and Ellie, who were listening intently. "I didn't think much of it at the time."

"Was she talking about the kidnapping attempt at the ball?" Ellie asked, turning to Lottie to check her reaction.

Anastacia shook her head. "She couldn't have been. This was before we even knew that you were coming to Rosewood." Lottie looked away, the word "kidnapping" dredging up terrible memories. She couldn't help wondering again if Leviathan had had something to do with those kids on the news going missing. "Anyway, I figured I should tell you both," she added flippantly. "Now we're even for you telling your parents that I didn't know anything about Saskia."

Anastacia turned to leave when Ellie grabbed her hand. She shrugged it off and gave her a furious look, cradling her hand to her chest.

"Don't you want to know what's happening with Saskia?" Ellie asked, ignoring Anastacia's furious glare.

"No," Anastacia replied, putting her sunglasses back on.

"But weren't you two . . . you know?" Lottie's words dried up. She wasn't sure what Anastacia would be comfortable with them knowing.

"She betrayed me," Anastacia spat out. "She betrayed me and that's that."

Ellie's fists curled up at her sides. "Saskia's refusing to

say anything." Ellie spoke urgently, as though she was hoping to change Anastacia's mind. Something was clearly bothering her.

"So?" Anastacia replied.

"There's only one thing she's said all summer. *'I want to speak to my master, Anastacia Alcroft.'*"

Anastacia went rigid, though it was impossible to read her expression behind the oversize sunglasses. "Why did nobody tell me this?" Her voice was cold, and Lottie could feel the ice coming off each word.

"We're telling you now," Lottie said, hoping to calm them both down. "It might be the only way to get her to talk."

Anastacia hesitated. "Well, I don't want to see her," she said at last, turning away again.

"But—" Ellie began.

Anastacia cut her off, scowling. "I don't want to see her! And you can't make me. I've told you everything I know. Now kindly leave me alone." She stormed off toward Conch House, and this time Ellie didn't stop her.

The second they got to their room Ellie let out a furious growl and collapsed onto her bed. The mattress was bare, the bed waiting to be made.

"Well, that was totally useless!" she huffed.

Lottie went straight to her bag and freed Mr. Truffles,

her beloved stuffed pig, from his cramped quarters, his squished little snout springing out as he emerged.

"It wasn't completely useless . . . ," Lottie said in an attempt to lighten the mood. She began making her own bed. "At least now we know something probably completely terrible is coming our way, and we have no way of knowing what it is." She tossed a scrunched-up gray pillowcase at Ellie with a smile.

"You sound like Jamie," Ellie groaned, snatching up the pillowcase.

Lottie paused from spreading out her bedsheet. Tomorrow she would start training with Jamie, something they had decided not to tell Ellie about. She had realized she needed to be able to defend herself with strength and vigor. Jamie needed to put Ellie first; Lottie couldn't have him worrying about her too. The only way to make sure of that was to learn how to fight, even if it made her nervous to think about it.

But there was more to her nerves than that. Ever since Jamie had acted so oddly about her gift, she'd started to worry she didn't understand him nearly as well as she'd thought she did.

"God forbid," Lottie replied, forcing a laugh. She was relieved to see a grin crack Ellie's face. "I think the world can only handle one Jamie." Lottie reached into her bag to pull out the box that contained her tiara. Yet again, Lottie was overcome by how heavy the tiara felt in her hand as she placed it on her bedside table. She didn't want to deal with those feelings right now.

"And you're *really* okay?" Ellie's question caught Lottie off guard, forcing her to quickly plaster a smile back on.

"Why wouldn't I be okay?" she replied cautiously. "We're back at Rosewood and can finally start getting to the bottom of everything." She slammed a fist into her palm, trying to look determined.

Ellie nodded slowly, fingering her pendant. "Okay, okay—I'll stop asking." She patted Lottie's mess of blond curls, ruffling her hair affectionately. "Let's just go and enjoy the fireworks for tonight."

"That's an excellent idea," Lottie replied, smiling sincerely this time. This was the first time Ellie would see the opening ceremony—she'd missed it the previous year. "We'll have plenty of time to start solving these problems tomorrow."

Little did Lottie know that their problems wouldn't wait for tomorrow.

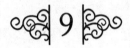

9

LOTTIE AND ELLIE MADE THEIR way toward the field. Even though it was a mild evening, Ellie wore her beat-up leather jacket and Lottie was wrapped in a knitted cardigan. The lights on the path flickered among the flowers, and as they walked across the flagstones Lottie looked forward to seeing all her Rosewood friends again. The heavy scent of the blooms enveloped them in a rich, expectant atmosphere. It was as if something had been sleeping in the air, waiting to emerge.

"Do you think Jamie's new roommate will come?" Ellie asked as they approached the outer edge of Stratus Side. The Stratus House tower loomed over them, obscuring the sliver of moonlight that hung in the lavender sky.

"I hope so!"

Both girls jumped at the familiar voice behind them and turned to see a huge pair of spectacled eyes peeping out from a curtain of dark ringlets. Binah was in her yellow Stratus uniform, but there was one very major addition to her usual pinafore and cardigan: a bright yellow sash that proudly professed that she was now the Stratus head of year.

"Binah, oh my God, you scared me!" Lottie choked, her hand rushing to her heart to stop it from jumping out of her chest.

"My apologies." Binah grinned, her teeth dazzling in the darkness. "I'm glad to see you both survived the summer holidays."

"Barely," Ellie replied drily.

Lottie gave a quick loud cough, hoping to drown out Ellie's words. They didn't need Binah asking questions.

"Congrats, Binah, that sash really suits you," Lottie said, attempting to change the subject. "Do you know anything about Jamie's roommate?"

Binah's expression suddenly turned troubled. "Absolutely nothing—I haven't heard a single tiny thing." She began quickly walking up the path toward the bridge that led to the field. "It's all very peculiar."

Ellie and Lottie looked at each other before silently following. Could Binah really have no clue? Lottie remembered how, on her first day at Rosewood, Binah had told her that she took it upon herself to know *everything* so she could help *everyone*. Lottie had soon learned how true that was. It was scary how much Binah knew. Her nose for knowledge had left Ellie and Lottie stuck in a serious conundrum—did Binah know that Ellie was the princess or not? They couldn't find out without directly asking her—but if they did that and she hadn't known, then they'd feel very silly indeed for having revealed their secret.

"Although I do wonder if maybe—" A group of Conch students ran past, and Binah seemed to remember herself, turning back to the two of them. "I suppose we'll just have to see."

Lottie knew not to take Binah's mysteries lightly. Last year Binah had created a puzzle for Lottie and Ellie that led them to question the identity—or possibly identities—of William Tufty, the founder of Rosewood. They had yet to get to the bottom of *that* mystery.

"I'm sure you heard about Dolores and Michael?" Binah asked. The names were not instantly familiar, and Lottie looked to Ellie in confusion. "They won't be coming back to Rosewood for a while, as I'm sure you can understand." Lottie suddenly realized who Binah was talking about, and sadness flooded over her. Dolores and Michael: aka Lola and Micky.

"I feel terrible for them," Lottie replied softly, feeling that ache crawl back into her chest. "I just wish there was something we could do to help."

Binah stopped in her tracks and turned to Lottie with a determined look. "I know you'll find a way to help them, Lottie. We'll solve this."

Solve what?

Lottie and Ellie were taken aback by Binah's sudden resolve. Her word choice seemed odd, and there was a twinkle in her eye that Lottie remembered from last year's fencing trials.

What does Binah know?

Ellie's lips were pressed together as she considered Binah with an intensity that Lottie recognized all too well. Was she about to ask Binah the one question that burned deep inside both of them? How much did Binah know? Ellie's mouth slowly opened, then—

"It's him!" she cried, pointing over Binah's shoulder.

"Excuse me?" Binah asked, clearly as confused as Lottie was.

"With Jamie—look!" Both Lottie and Binah followed the direction of Ellie's gaze to the bridge, where two dark figures leaned on the wooden railings. They weren't close enough to see the boys' faces properly, but Lottie could recognize Jamie's taut posture and dark caramel skin anywhere. The boy next to him had his back to them, but she could make out a mop of black hair. His posture was slightly hunched, as though he were shy and trying to hide himself. Jamie's new roommate, surely! A wave of excitement surged through her.

"Of course!" Binah exclaimed. "Prelingual otitis media."

Lottie blinked in confusion as Binah ran off to introduce

herself, and Ellie and Lottie followed behind, trying to keep up with her.

"Lottie, I think that boy is the one from the news this morning," Ellie whispered as they made their way over.

The boys turned as they approached, and Lottie finally understood. Those same sunken eyes . . . This was the hostage boy they'd seen on the news in Ollie's house! Now his glance locked with hers and instantly she was overcome by the scent of the flowers again, that drowsy feeling in the air swelling.

"So this is the mysterious roommate," Ellie said with a smirk as they joined them, effortlessly pretending she had never seen him before.

Jamie nodded at them in acknowledgment, his eyes narrowing for a moment at Ellie. Was he trying to tell her something? He gestured to the pale boy. "Everyone, this is Percy Butter, he—"

Jamie didn't have time to finish his sentence. An all-too-familiar American accent drifted their way.

"Jamie, my serious comrade." Raphael materialized beside them. His short-cut afro had grown out over the summer, making him look a little older somehow, and his chest was heaving as though he'd just been running. He wrapped an arm around Jamie's shoulder, then pulled away and ruffled his hair, something Lottie highly doubted

Jamie would be pleased about. Sure enough, Jamie quickly flattened his hair down and grumbled irritably, which only succeeded in making Raphael laugh. He glanced at Lottie and Ellie. "And the pumpkin princess returns," he said cheerily.

Lottie felt a strange pang in her chest at hearing the name. Everyone had assumed Lottie Pumpkin was a silly fake name she'd come up with to hide her identity. What they didn't realize was how accurate that really was. She swallowed hard, not wanting to think about her family and all of their secrets.

"Do you know how worried I've been about you all since the summer ball?" Raphael asked.

An awkward silence crept over the royal trio. It hadn't occurred to Lottie that they should contact Raphael. He'd attended with Anastacia, and they'd simply been relieved he hadn't been part of the conspiracy. "Not one of you thought to contact me and tell me you hadn't died horribly," he continued, pretending to joke. What was it with boys using jokes to hide how they were really feeling? She could tell they'd hurt Raphael's feelings. "I still have absolutely no idea what happened. It's hard enough getting anything out of Anastacia, but . . ."

There was a pause as Raphael became aware of Percy. He blinked twice, and Lottie noticed how very pale Percy looked standing between Raphael and Jamie.

"Hey, weren't you on the news this morning?" Raphael asked. "Something about a kidnapping?"

"Raphael!" Lottie found herself chiding him before she could stop herself, but he simply shrugged.

"What? I'm just asking. Seems like it would be terribly stressful to come straight to school after all that." He looked at Percy expectantly, and Lottie couldn't help being curious herself. It did seem odd that he would go immediately from surviving a kidnapping to starting a new school.

Percy stared at them all blank-faced, his sunken eyes turning to Jamie as if silently asking for help. He raised his hands and began quickly moving them in intricate patterns. Jamie watched intently and nodded.

A flash of understanding shot through Lottie. Binah's strange statement earlier made sense. He hadn't heard a thing . . .

"Percy is deaf, Raphael," Jamie said matter-of-factly.

Raphael's eyes widened. "Oh, I'm sorry, I—" His eyebrows furrowed as Percy continued to stare at him. "Hmmm." They were so used to seeing Raphael wisecracking that it was strange to see him stumped.

"I know ASL fluently," Jamie went on to explain, "but Percy uses BSL." Lottie watched in fascination as Jamie began moving his hands. She realized again that there was still so much she didn't know about him. She also found herself feeling sheepish and wondered why on earth sign language wasn't part of mandatory education. "Here"—Jamie turned back to Raphael—"move your hands like this."

There was something calming in watching Jamie demonstrate intricate hand and face movements, his fingers effortlessly shifting into different positions. "That's *'hello,'* and that's *'sorry,'* and this is *'can I help you?'*"

"*Hello*," Raphael signed, grinning with excitement over his newfound trick. Raphael may have lacked tact, but he was certainly charming, and it was easy to see why he was so popular.

Percy cracked a weak smile. "*Hello,*" he signed back.

It looked like they'd made a new friend.

10

THE GROUP FOUND A GOOD spot on the field to hear the speech and watch the fireworks, but Lottie was painfully aware that something was missing. Everything felt a little empty without Saskia, Anastacia, Lola, and Micky. She suddenly wished she could go back in time to when they were just a regular bunch of friends nervous about a new school year.

"I don't understand why Anastacia won't talk to me," Raphael kept saying. It was proving a true test of their strength to listen to it all without cracking. "And every text I tried to send to Saskia over the summer couldn't even be delivered. I thought something had happened to them at the ball, but then—"

"Maybe you should just leave her alone for a while," Ellie snapped, causing everyone to stare at her. "Maybe she's going through something and you bringing it up all the time is making it harder for her." Ellie's gaze shifted to Lottie as she spoke, and Lottie felt the pendant burning as she half guessed what was troubling her best friend.

Raphael stared at Ellie with his mouth wide open,

clearly not used to being spoken to like that. But Lottie's eyes were drawn to Percy. He was watching them with a pained look on his face—not one of confusion, but as if he could actually feel their emotions, even without hearing their words.

Before anyone could remedy the awkward silence, the lights on the stage went up and the headmaster appeared before them in a pool of yellow light.

With everyone's attention turned toward Headmaster Croak, Jamie took the opportunity to slink over to Lottie's side. "Is Ellie okay?" he whispered.

"I think she'd prefer if we didn't keep asking her that," Lottie replied, "and I think she thinks that I feel the same way."

"And?"

"She's right."

His lips pursed in consideration for a moment before he nodded. "The training will help."

Jamie was never one for motivational speeches, but those words were the most comforting thing she'd heard in weeks. She didn't want to be asked if she was okay all the time; she just wanted to get on with her life and face their problems head on. She looked over at Ellie, who was gazing up at the stage. Pushing forward was their way of dealing with the trauma of the summer ball. This is who they were. Unstoppable.

"Valued students of Rosewood." The gruff voice of Headmaster Croak traveled over the field. Behind him in a line, standing tall and commanding, were each of the house mothers: Professor Adina Devine, the Ivy house mother, a formidable Indonesian lady who was also the deputy head teacher; Dame Mercy Bolter, the Conch house mother, a tall ebony-skinned woman who regarded them all with intense fiery eyes; and Ms. Jo Kuma, the Stratus house mother, a large blond lady who had a penchant for bold patterns and even bolder jewels. Each of them was a hypnotic presence, sporting rose emblems in purple, red, and yellow, respectively.

"I hope you have all had a productive summer and are feeling refreshed and ready to take on a new year at Rosewood." He paused, gearing up for another one of his dull speeches. "Now, I know it can be difficult to adjust back into a routine, but here at Rosewood Hall we pride ourselves on rising to a challenge and . . ."

Lottie tried to stay focused on the headmaster's words but found herself distracted by a discreetly signed conversation between Jamie and Percy. They would pause every so often and rub their fingers, a version of an "um" or an "er," trying to bridge the gap between their two different sign languages. Lottie wished she could understand what they were saying but found it relaxing to watch the exchange. Percy suddenly looked up, his eyes locking on hers. All the while his hands continued moving, as if he were in two places at once.

"Righteous, resolute, and, of course, resourceful." The headmaster's words pulled Lottie away from Percy's dark eyes, but she desperately wanted to look back, convinced there was something he was trying to convey to her.

"These are the three pillars of—"

A loud shriek cut through the air—a gurgling howl that left thick acidic dread in Lottie's chest. Jamie instinctively moved toward Ellie, who tried to reach Lottie as the crowd looked around in confusion.

"Somebody help him," a girl's voice cried out.

Raphael looked to Binah as if hoping that she might have some insight, but she seemed as concerned as the rest of them. The headmaster peered out over the grounds before turning to Professor Devine, who marched forward.

"Students of Rosewood, please step aside. Quickly now. Hurry up."

Lottie watched with alarm as everyone scrambled out of the way to make a path down the middle of the field. Another scream cut through the air.

"Keep clear, everyone!" Dame Bolter shouted as the professor marched off the stage, accompanied by the science teacher Professor Duran. They disappeared into the crowd to the left, much too far away for any of them to see what the commotion was about.

Lottie felt her breath quickening, her mind sinking back to that claustrophobic feeling of being locked in the van, helpless.

"Ellie." The name came out of Lottie's throat as a choked whisper. The crowd had moved between them, cutting them off from each other. She glanced around wildly as she tried to find her princess. Another screech, this time more like a moan, drifted through the air, and everyone frantically strained to see what was happening.

Fingers curled around Lottie's arm and she almost screamed.

"Lottie, it's okay. I'm here." Ellie's voice calmed her as she pulled Lottie close.

"Where's Jamie?" Lottie asked, her glance darting about the sea of murmuring students.

"I told him to take care of Percy."

Lottie swallowed hard, realizing how much more bewildering this would all be for him, especially after what he'd just been through.

Another moan floated their way, closer this time.

"Give me a boost." Lottie was surprised by how commanding she sounded, but Ellie didn't miss a beat, leaning down and wrapping her arms around her waist to heave Lottie up to see over the heads of the crowd. And there—finally—she glimpsed where the panic was coming from.

Professor Devine was beating a path through the

students, holding up a redheaded Ivy boy as he sagged against her side.

"Good. One foot in front of the other. That's it. Easy, now." The professor guided the boy with an arm around his shoulder. On his other side was a blond Ivy girl wearing glasses. Her eyes were red and she looked as if she'd been crying.

Lottie recognized the boy immediately. It was Horace Silverton-Smith from year eight. A boy who liked to leave funny messages on the Ivy common room noticeboard. But he looked very different now. His skin was covered in a strange porcelain sheen, eyes bloodshot. He looked gaunt, yet his face was bloated, almost as though he'd been submerged underwater for a long time. His eyes rolled back in his head as he struggled to stay conscious. Something was very wrong.

Ellie gently lowered Lottie back to the ground, her feet meeting the damp grass. "What did you see?" she whispered.

Lottie shuddered. It wasn't the sight of the boy that alarmed Lottie; it was the smell. A thick, sweet fragrance that overpowered the scent of the flowers. It was a smell that was inexplicably familiar, but she couldn't place it. It somehow made her feel both calm and terrified at once. Her nose tingled.

"Something wicked this way comes," Lottie muttered to

herself. The sweet, rotting smell lingered, begging her to recall where she'd caught the scent before.

Binah was watching her closely, and Lottie wondered if maybe she had recognized the smell too. But before she could question her the crowd began to move again, and Dame Bolter stepped forward on the stage.

"Settle down, everyone!" she commanded. "Please remain calm. We will push on with the fireworks."

The students exchanged glances and murmurs.

Headmaster Croak wobbled forward on his walking stick. "Horace Silverton-Smith will be just fine—he is with the nurse. I'm sure he would want us all to continue with the ceremony tonight. Let us enjoy the fireworks and use this moment to practice our resilience."

Ms. Kuma came to stand beside him. "Please, let's look ahead to the new school year."

The staff left the stage, Ms. Kuma assisting Headmaster Croak. As the stage lights faded, Dame Bolter paused and looked out across the audience. Lottie saw her fists clench as she anxiously scanned the field. Then she too stepped down.

The first firework exploded in the air, dousing them in a fizzing orange-gold light. Lottie instinctively reached for her wolf pendant as she watched the hissing flashes of neon colors. She took a deep breath.

Be brave.

She couldn't let tonight's events rattle her; she had to stay strong for Ellie.

"Poor Horace," Binah muttered, appearing beside them with Raphael. A flash of blue reflected in her glasses. Lottie looked around, but Jamie and Percy remained hidden in the crowd.

"What do you think happened to him?" Raphael asked, obviously expecting Binah to shed some light on the situation. Lottie also hoped that Binah's magical knowledge of everything might extend to this strange situation.

"I couldn't say." This time purple flashed in the lenses of her spectacles. It was impossible to read her expression.

Lottie turned to Ellie, who looked equally inscrutable.

"Maybe it was food poisoning," Ellie suggested weakly, clearly not believing her own theory.

Lottie shook her head and turned back to the fireworks. "But that screaming, that sound. That was . . ." Lottie spoke slowly as they watched fresh explosions, sparks arcing down against the deep inky blue of the night sky. She chewed her lip, reluctant to remember the boy's tortured moans.

Another firework whistled above their heads, spewing out a cluster of toxic green light. The poisonous color caught in the whites of their eyes, the acrid smell of smoke filling their noses. Lottie looked over at the vine-covered wall separating Rosewood from the rest of the world and remembered what Anastacia had said about "interesting times."

Was this something to do with Leviathan? She quickly shook the thought away. Ellie had never seen the opening fireworks ceremony before, and she didn't want this evening to be completely soured. They'd have plenty of time to think about all this tomorrow.

"I'm sure Horace will be fine." Lottie gave her friends a thin, brave smile. "We'll all be fine."

Binah attempted a smile back. "You're right, Lottie. There's nothing we can do about any of this right now, so we'd best just try to enjoy the fireworks."

A reassuring grin spread across Binah's face, and Lottie instantly felt better. Ellie and Raphael gave each other an unconvinced look before he shrugged and turned back to the colorful display in the sky.

"Well, whatever was wrong with Horace, hopefully no one else catches it." Raphael's words sent an unpleasant shiver down Lottie's spine. Another emerald firework arced over the field.

Lottie caught sight of two sunken eyes that glimmered in the haze of smoky fireworks residue. Percy Butter raised his hand in a wave, a weak smile on his lips. Jamie stood by his side. They were a short distance away, and Lottie could see that Jamie was poised for trouble. Seeing this helped her relax a little, and she felt a surge of determination. She wanted to be just as calm and composed in any situation.

Lottie waved back to the peculiar solemn boy before going to Ellie and leaning against her, feeling a friendly arm drape across her shoulders and draw her closer. The scent of Ellie's leather jacket was familiar and comforting.

"Everything will be fine," she repeated in a soft voice as clouds of smoke filled the air around her.

She believed it. She had to.

11

LOTTIE STOOD ALONE OUTSIDE THE dorm in baggy sports clothes, her mass of blond curls caught up in a ponytail. Today was the day. She squinted and held up a hand to shield her eyes from the low morning sunshine. The grass shimmered with dew; Rosewood looked beautiful. It was hard to believe that anything horrible could have happened the previous night, but it had, and she couldn't shake the dark anticipation in the air. The petals on the flowers vibrated in the wind; it was as if Rosewood was anxiously waiting for more trouble.

Lottie had been violently awoken that morning from a nightmare in which Rosewood was infected with poison. It had choked the air, leaving her no way of finding out what was causing it or how to escape. She'd reached for her tiara and had tried to comfort herself with her familiar mantra:

I will be kind, I will be brave, I will be unstoppable.

But the words had fallen flat.

Now she conjured up the image of her tiara, how the crescent moon had twinkled, casting glittering lights over the portrait of her ancestor Henry, giving the strange impression he'd been winking at her.

"What do you want me to know?" Lottie asked into the empty morning air. She immediately felt very silly asking the tiara such a question and shook her head, marching off to find her new teacher.

It wasn't uncommon for students to rise early and step out into the school grounds for morning sports practices or exercise. If anyone spotted Lottie in her tracksuit, they'd assume she was doing the same.

Jamie stood to one side, waiting by the cast-iron gates that led to Ivy Wood. They'd arranged to meet here for her first training session. He was staring at his watch as if expecting her to be late, which was quite unfair, as Lottie was always very much on time.

"Did you sleep okay?" he asked as she joined him and they made their way up the small hill toward Stratus Side.

"Yes, surprisingly." She decided not to mention her tiara or her nightmare visions of poisoned gas snaking through the corridors of Rosewood. "How's Percy?"

"He's fine." His voice was strained, and she knew instantly that he wasn't being completely straight with her.

"Just fine?"

They had reached the wooden bridge that led to the field. She knew that as soon as they were on the grass Jamie would insist they start training. If she didn't ask now, the moment would be gone.

"Yes, just fine. What did Anastacia say to you both yesterday?"

Lottie was taken aback by the sudden switch in conversation but refused to let him sidestep anything.

"That Saskia had said that she'd keep her safe and that, quote, *'interesting times'* were coming. Goodness knows what she means by 'interesting.'" She paused. "Why are you being weird about Percy?"

"I'm not. Was this before or after school had started?"

"Before, and yes you are. I can tell."

Jamie let out a slow irritated breath as they reached the other side of the bridge. His hand met with the railings as he turned to face her, the sunlight catching in the dark hair that he could never quite tame properly. He came close to her—so close that she could see the flecks of hazel in his eyes.

"I would kindly ask that you remember I am in charge here."

Lottie clenched her fists at her sides. He was obviously avoiding talking about Percy, and she wouldn't be intimidated out of finding out why.

"We're supposed to trust each other, Jamie. No one's in charge. We're in this together." She rose on the balls of her feet, bringing herself level with him. "I demand that you tell me what's bothering you."

To Lottie's irritation, he laughed. "Oh, you *demand*, do

you? Do I need to also remind you that you're not a real princess?" He jabbed his finger into her shoulder, sending her staggering backward.

Lottie's cheeks exploded into a bright crimson blush. "That's not what—"

Before she could finish, he smirked again, his teeth glittering like a wolf's fangs. "Come on, enough dawdling. It's time to start your training." He turned to the field and signaled for her to follow.

She took a deep breath to calm herself. Clearly this training session was not going to be easy for either of them.

"Did I . . . do it . . . in time . . .?" Lottie bent over, leaning her hands on her thighs as clumps of sweaty blond hair fell over her shoulders. Breathing heavily and unevenly, she looked up at Jamie, sweat blurring her vision. She dragged a hand across her eyes and straightened up, wincing. Jamie leaned casually against the rugby goalpost, looking at his watch. He wasn't even out of breath.

"Two minutes, twelve seconds. Try again. Oh, and I saw you stop and walk those last thirty feet when you thought I wouldn't notice. Don't do that again."

She stared at him in disbelief. "You're kidding, right?" Her voice came out in ragged gasps. Sports had never been her strong suit, and she was feeling pretty proud of herself for running at all without passing out.

"You want to get stronger, don't you? First we need to toughen you up. You're too soft."

Lottie felt a pout forming. When they agreed to start training together she'd expected a gradual introduction, not military commands from day one.

"Well, maybe I like being soft?" she replied, finding it hard to hide her annoyance. She forced herself to stand up straight, a hand resting on her hip.

"You said you wanted to be stronger. You can't be soft and strong at the same time." He didn't even look at her, instead focusing on his watch again as he reset the timer.

Lottie considered his words for a moment, her chest still heaving. Her cheeks were burning from the morning's exertions.

"Well, I want to be both."

Jamie finally looked up, disbelief cracking his features.

"I'm going to show you there's just as much strength in being soft as there is in being hard," she told him.

There was a long pause. "Okay," he said at last. "Be soft, use that as your weapon. But you need something to back it up with." Lottie started to speak, but he cut her off. "By all means, lull your enemy into a false sense of security, but if you don't actually have anything to surprise them with, then it's useless."

She chewed her lip in thought. He was right—as always.

"And what exactly should I surprise them with?" she asked.

"Well, we can start with stamina. Then we'll move on to reflex and speed." He gave her a smile. "Now run around the track again."

After twenty minutes of continuous running, Lottie felt her lungs burning, every breath making her chest ache, and a thick metallic taste was swimming in her mouth. She did not feel good. *Does Jamie really do this every day before breakfast?*

"It'll be a long time before you make as good a running partner as Raphael." Jamie threw a pair of small rubber weights down. "Take these and follow this movement."

Lottie complied, following the sit-up routine and mirroring Jamie as he crossed his arms over his chest and lifted himself up from the ground over and over . . . and over. When would it stop? The mention of Raphael had put a strange feeling in her belly. She'd completely forgotten that Jamie and Raphael had originally bonded over a shared love of cross-country running. She couldn't help but feel a pang of jealousy.

"What do you two even talk about?" she wheezed between sit-ups. It was hard to imagine; they had such different personalities.

"Your shoulders are drooping." Jamie paused in his own

exercise to guide her back into the correct position before answering her question. "I was mostly trying to get information on the weird messages you were getting last year, but we also talked about his home in LA and what it's like having famous parents. Straighten your back."

Lottie continued the routine as Jamie's hands guided her through the movements. "Famous parents?"

"Yes. His parents are Marcus and Halle Wilcox. The actors. Lean back down."

"WHAT?" Lottie sat bolt upright, nearly whacking Jamie on the forehead.

How had she not known this? How had she known Raphael for a whole year and still knew nothing about his family? Three magpies flew overhead, perching on a small rowan tree at the edge of the field. They each took a different branch, nestling into the leaves, three points of a triangle. Lottie watched them, ignoring Jamie's confusion at her distracted gaze as they flew away.

"I never knew that . . ." Lottie trailed off. Come to think about it, she didn't know much about Binah's or Anastacia's families either. Family wasn't something she was very comfortable talking about, but she hadn't realized how much she'd been avoiding the topic. She remembered the look on Jamie's face when she'd asked him about the book of Pakistani history, how uncomfortable he'd been with it, and she suddenly understood his feelings a little better.

"Family can be hard to talk about." He concentrated on her posture. "Lean back."

"You're right," she said, and her mind wandered back to her tiara. "I thought seeing Ollie would stop me feeling so confused, but it didn't."

It was strange. Here she was, sprawled on the wet grass, covered in sweat, muscles aching. Not exactly the right setting for a sentimental moment. Jamie remained unreadable; the only indication he'd even heard what she said was a slow intake of breath. The ground turned cold underneath her, the damp grass icy between her fingers. She had been completely insensitive. All this time she'd been worrying about feeling disconnected from her family. She'd tried to fix her own feelings by . . . what? Giving Jamie a book? "I'm sorry, Jamie. I mean, for the book—for bringing up something painful." She stared down.

"You have nothing to apologize for." His voice came out as cold as the ground beneath her, and he wore a perfect mask of indifference. "I see you're still wearing your Wolfson pendant." He gestured to the wolf at her chest; it must have worked its way out from under her T-shirt with all her running around.

"So are you."

They paused for a moment, eyes locked, pendants dangling.

"And I always will," he said.

She couldn't look away from his eyes, that hazel color—so different from the rest of the Wolfsons because he *was* different.

She couldn't stop herself; she had to ask. "Don't you ever wonder about them? Don't you ever—" Lottie wanted so badly to know. Wasn't he ever curious about his parents, about his mother or Pakistan or who his father was? But she saw the look of furious warning on his face and swallowed hard. "I think it's time for breakfast."

Jamie removed his hands from her body. A low grumbling noise escaped his throat and his gaze softened. "I suppose we could head back now."

He made to stand up, but Lottie quickly grabbed his arm. "Wait."

It was too late, though. He hoisted her up before she could stop him.

"What now?" he asked, annoyed.

Lottie felt hurt at his flippant tone, but she couldn't blame him. He'd made it very clear he didn't want to think about his real family.

"It's just . . . before we go back, will you please tell me why you were being so cagey about Percy earlier?"

To her relief he let out a sigh of resignation. "He didn't sleep last night. I could hear that his breathing never steadied properly."

Lottie blinked. "You think he was watching you?"

"That's not what I said. I think he's just struggling to adjust." Jamie looked over to the main school building, as if he were conjuring a memory.

"I can see why."

And she could. It made sense that he would find it difficult to slip into normal school life after what he'd been through. "We need to look out for him," she said firmly. "Who knows what he's dealing with right now."

Jamie nodded, a lock of hair falling over his eyes. "But you need to look out for yourself too, Lottie. Stay vigilant." He walked away toward the bridge, leaving Lottie to make her own way back to Ivy House.

Vigilant.

There was that word again. Watching Jamie stride away, she was gripped with determination. She couldn't make the same mistakes she had made last year. She needed to be alert or she might miss something again. The only problem was . . . what exactly was she missing?

12

OLLIE STARED AT HIS COMPUTER screen, the glowing light from the monitor distracting him from how dark his room had become in the last hour. His phone buzzed with messages from his school friends, but he was too engrossed to answer them.

He should have been doing his biology homework. Instead he was finding out everything he could about the princess of Maradova. He'd promised Lottie that he wouldn't get involved, but what was the harm in doing a little research?

So far he'd found a string of slanderous articles from two years ago. An anonymous source had spotted the princess sneaking out to raucous parties and concerts and behaving in an altogether unprincessy manner. The online articles were badly written and sloppy—no one knew what the princess looked like or her name, so it was impossible to see how anyone could have spotted her at one of these events. But people believed what they wanted to believe, and people chose to accept that the Maravish princess was being kept undercover because she was *wild*.

But all that speculation had stopped this year—all because of one ordinary girl. Ollie stared in awe at a picture of his childhood friend in a flowing peach dress, the tiara he was so familiar with suddenly making sense on top of her golden curls. Lottie still had her round cheeks and big doe eyes, but in this picture it was undeniable that she was a princess.

Ollie clicked shut the tab he was on. It was all too weird.

Lottie was his smiley, artsy best friend who always had her head in a book and never brushed her hair. She obsessed over princesses and was always demanding he put on a Disney film. He'd pretend he didn't want to, but secretly he enjoyed indulging her. She was awkward and blushed all the time and snorted when she laughed too hard at his stupid jokes. She was just Lottie Pumpkin.

"I know what I'm doing. I'm trusting you to respect that, not asking you for permission."

The room's darkness crept up on him, jolting him back into the real world. Alone in his room, he felt something he'd not truly experienced before: he felt lonely. The type of lonely when you have absolutely no one to turn to, no one you can talk to about something that burns in your chest.

His mother's voice called up the stairs for dinner, accompanied by a waft of delicious smells from the kitchen. "Ollie, *o jantar está pronto*!"

"Just a minute, Mamãe!" He leaned over to shut down the computer, but another thought suddenly occurred to him.

"The empanadas will get cold," his mother shouted.

Usually the call of an empanada was too powerful for him to resist, but right now there was something even more alluring in front of him. He leaned over his keyboard again and typed in the names he'd heard on the news that day.

Percival Butter Tompkins Leviathan

His cursor hovered over the search engine results. He knew he shouldn't click any of them. Lottie had told him not to get involved, but he'd never been very good at doing the smart thing. The mouse clicked under his finger as he flitted through images and articles. There was no mention of Leviathan. It was all the same stuff over and over again: reporters, police . . . pictures of the tired-looking boy from the news and the white-haired twins.

"Huh?" His heart began to beat quickly in his chest. There was something odd about the last three images on the page; they set off a tingling feeling in the back of his head, like when you noticed the subtle changes on a spot-the-difference game.

"What the . . ." He squinted at a pair of dark-clad indi-viduals who loomed in the shadows, a girl with straight black hair and a boy in a cowboy hat, both of whom sent a shiver down his spine. Sure enough, when he flicked to the next image of the Tompkins factory, they were there again, almost hidden in the crowd. He went back to the last few images, and the same two faces popped up. A prickly feeling ran over his skin, as if the two unknown people could somehow see him. Why were they skulking around in all of these pictures?

This is too weird.

Throwing himself back in his chair, he wondered what Lottie would do.

She wouldn't let this go. She'd have to get to the bottom of the intrigue. What if those two people were important? What if he'd found some kind of secret conspiracy?

What would Lottie do? Come on! he thought again, frustrated.

He snapped on his bedside lamp, flooding the room with light. A pile of schoolbooks and pencils were waiting for him to do his homework. He grabbed a notebook and jotted down all the information he had before printing every photo he found containing the mysterious duo. When he was done, four different scenes lay in front of him with four sets of those menacing eyes.

"Ollie, *jantar*!"

He jumped. It felt as though his heart was going to thump out of his chest, but the sound of his mother's voice made him all at once feel very silly. He laughed to himself, running his hands through his messy brown hair. "Coming, Mamãe."

He grabbed his phone and made for his bedroom door, stepping over piles of dirty clothes. The smell of the food hit him as he opened the door and he instantly relaxed into the comforting aroma of his mother's Brazilian cooking.

They were just pictures. What could be so scary about a picture anyway?

13

ELLIE LET OUT A BIG yawn as she took a seat in the Ivy dining hall next to Lottie. It was in their usual spot at one of the dark oak tables by the second-story window, which had a perfect view of the statue of Ryley the stag. Her plate was piled high with all the greasiest and most sugary break-fast options. Jamie narrowed his eyes disapprovingly. Ever since their training session he'd seemed somehow more irritable than usual, and Lottie couldn't help feeling as though it were her fault. It didn't help that the atmosphere was already tense—all the students were acutely aware that Horace was still missing.

"What?" Ellie asked indignantly as he took in her piles of toast and chocolate spread. "I'm a growing girl."

Lottie giggled, delicately spreading jam on a crumpet. "She needs the energy," she said in her friend's defense. "We start our electives this morning." She couldn't dis-guise the excitement in her voice. She had a pile of books stacked in front of her—she was ready to study hard.

"Exactly," Ellie said through a mouthful of bacon. "I

have to be in tip-top condition for the Spearion."

"If you really want to be '*in tip-top condition,*'" Jamie said coldly, "you should be eating lots of whole grains and low-fat proteins and—"

Ellie rolled her eyes.

"What's the Spearion?" Lottie asked, hoping to prevent any arguments.

Ellie bit off a chunk of chocolatey bread and made an impatient motion with her hand as she swallowed it down and took a gulp of juice. "It's the international fencing tournament," she said. "It happens at the end of spring term, and it's being hosted by Tompkins this year." Ellie grinned. "I'm gonna win a trophy."

Lottie beamed back at her, not doubting for a second that Ellie could win this. "And I'll be cheering for you all the way."

"Why on earth is a fencing tournament being hosted by a confectionery company?" Jamie questioned, unconvinced by the whole thing.

"I don't know," she said, "something to do with Alfred Tompkins. Apparently fencing is his favorite sport, so he's sponsoring all the travel, accommodations, and equipment so he can watch one final tournament before he gets too sick."

Ellie realized the connotations of her words too late and

they hung cold and awkward in the air. It was starting to sound like Lola and Micky's father was preparing for the worst.

"Well, I'm glad to see you're both ready for your electives at least," Jamie said, gesturing to Lottie's pile of books in an attempt to change the subject.

Electives were one of Rosewood Hall's most exalted features—a program of extracurricular courses and activities to bring out the best in students, allowing them to pursue interests they were passionate about. Most electives were open to all, but a few were exclusive, like the Rosewood Lancers fencing team. They held tryouts, and Ellie had been good enough to make the cut. Lottie, on the other hand, had had to pick an open elective like everyone else, and now that she'd made her choice it sounded like a glaringly obvious one.

"Not gonna lie, Lottie, your elective sounds . . . kind of boring." Ellie made a face at the book pile and faked a shudder.

"Well, I think taking royal history is a very responsible idea. You should be taking notes, Ellie." Jamie tapped one of Lottie's books.

"Responsible, yes. Exactly my point," Ellie said, rolling her eyes again.

"I think it's exciting," Lottie said, trying hard not to sound defensive. "It's like unraveling a mystery. I'll be studying real-life fairy tales." *And it will also be very helpful in my role as Portman*, she added in her head. From the look on Jamie's face she guessed he knew that was exactly why she'd picked this subject—and it looked like he approved. "And I have a one-up on everyone in my class because of Oscar's diary." Thanks to Jamie, she'd already had a chance to read the leather-bound diary that had belonged to the Portman of Henric Wolfson, past king of Maradova—and Ellie's grandfather. She knew more about Portmans and the Wolfsons than most students. Lottie gave them a scheming grin.

Just then the hall fell quiet. Lottie blinked in confusion as she and the rest of Ivy House turned to see what had caused the sudden shift in mood.

The doors swung open and in walked Professor Devine and the new year twelve head of Ivy House, Alice Amari. But no one was looking at either of them. Everyone's gaze was fixed on the figure between them. Alice was leading a very shy-looking Horace to an empty seat at one of the tables. Although he seemed embarrassed by the attention, Lottie felt a flood of relief to see that he looked well.

Alice Amari was confident and poised, her sensible, neatly cut black hair emphasizing her orderly nature. Her bossy voice cut across the dining hall. "And you're absolutely sure you're ready to come back to class?" she asked, ignoring all the staring.

"Yes, I'm sure, thank you, Alice. Can I please go and join my friends now, Professor?"

"You may." The professor smiled at him and nodded for Alice to let him go. "But if you start to feel at all unwell again you must tell someone immediately."

There was something about Horace's big eyes and fluffy red hair, the way he always looked as if he'd just got some bad news, that set off people's protective instincts.

"Yes, Professor. Thank you, Professor."

Everyone watched as Horace took a seat next to the girl who'd called for help the night before.

The professor cleared her throat and made her way to the front of the hall with Alice, their shoes setting off echoes in the silence.

"Ivy students," she said, addressing the crowd. "I know you are all very excited to get off to your electives this morning, but we must stay vigilant." Lottie twitched at the word, feeling as if the universe were giving her some kind of sign. "If any of you are feeling ill over the next few weeks, you must tell someone right away. We can't have an epidemic breaking out in Rosewood, now, can we?"

Alice stepped forward. "If any of you do feel unwell at all, please come and tell the nurse right away. We don't want a repeat of what happened to Horace."

But what did *happen to Horace?* Lottie wondered.

"Now please enjoy your breakfast and have a good day,

everyone." The professor nodded at Alice and made to go, leaving the students to fuss over their newly returned house member.

"You should tell Percy," Lottie said to Jamie. Then a thought struck her: *Where is Percy?*

"He has counseling on Friday mornings," Jamie said, but he could barely tear his gaze away from Horace. He slowly turned back to both of them, his expression serious. "If either of you feel at all ill, you must immediately tell me. If you get so much as a sniffle, I want to know. Is that understood?"

Ellie looked like she was about to make a joke when her eyes darted to Horace again, remembering the awful sounds he'd made out on the field.

"We understand," she said quietly.

"Good. I'll see you both in the library after class."

Royal history was taking place in Room A-2, a small circular classroom on the top floor of the art department usually used for life-drawing classes. It was a testament to how few people had chosen the elective that they could all fit in the cozy room. The wooden desks had been arranged in a semicircle around a small table piled with old books and antique jewelry. Lottie, as usual, was the first one in the classroom and took the opportunity to carefully arrange her books in front of her, wanting to make a good first impression on the teacher. She'd been looking forward to the class ever since she'd picked it and was pleased to have a distraction from all the weird stuff going on in the rest of her life.

A few other students arrived—no one Lottie knew very well. Two Conch students, a girl with long red hair and an Indian boy with bleached hair, sat next to each other on the other side of the room. Next to arrive was an Ivy boy with large glasses and an artsy undercut, who took a seat on his own to the side, and then two Stratus boys who had book piles just like Lottie's. She smiled at each student as they entered, feeling awkward about not knowing anyone, but they all remained quiet. Clearly this was a popular elective among shy, studious types.

The door slowly opened and in walked their teacher carrying a large plate of biscuits.

Spiky red hair caught Lottie's eye and she almost choked. Adina Devine was the last person she'd expected to see—how could she not have known that her own house mother was the teacher for her elective? Before she had time to process this information, a tiny girl with a mane of frizzy hair walked in behind her, balancing a tray of pink rose teacups and a teapot. Binah!

Lottie felt like she'd entered some weird dream world. Was everyone she knew going to miraculously show up at the last minute?

"Good morning, class." The professor's voice echoed around the small room, her presence almost too large for the quaint circular space. "I know you were probably expecting someone from the history department, but there's been a last-minute change in schedules. I will be taking over royal history." She gently laid the plate of biscuits down on one of the spare desks and gestured for Binah to do the same with her tray. "Thank you for the help, Miss Fae. Please do take a seat."

Lottie could sense the other students squirming in their seats. The deputy headmistress could be very intimidating if you got on her bad side, and Lottie's intense desire to impress her became more urgent than ever. She carefully pushed forward one of her books but instantly regretted the attempt to draw attention to how prepared she was.

Professor Devine's lips twisted in a knowing smile. "I see some of you are prepared already." She took a piece of chocolate shortbread and dipped it in her tea. "Please, everyone, help yourself to tea and biscuits and"—she seemed to suddenly take in the very shy students—"would you all stop looking so terrified? This is an elective, not a prison sentence!"

Binah took the spare desk next to Lottie and gifted her with one of her wide, eager grins that always made people feel warm and happy. Maybe Lottie could use this class to get to know Binah better.

"Why are you taking royal history?" Lottie asked, leaning over to grab the teapot.

Binah shrugged, her big round spectacles glinting in the sunshine from the skylight. "It seemed the most mysterious option."

Lottie had never before heard anyone but herself refer to history as "mysterious." She had a sudden desire to grab Binah and jump up and down, screaming, *"YOU UNDERSTAND ME!"* Instead she coughed discreetly. "I feel the same way," she replied.

"Family," Professor Devine abruptly stated, taking a step into the center of the room. "Royalty is all about family."

Lottie sensed everyone watching her from beneath their eyelashes. After all, she was an actual princess, wasn't she? She squirmed.

"For every modern royal family," the professor continued, "there is a bloodline extending back hundreds, if not thousands, of years."

"But what about if the line gets cut off?" asked the Conch boy timidly.

"Or overthrown?" murmured the Conch girl.

"Ah, excellent points, Sanjiv and Orla. That's where it gets exciting, if I do say so myself."

From its place on the center table, Professor Devine picked up a gold necklace with an opal moon at its heart. The chain swung through a column of sunlight and the precious stone sparkled. Straightaway, Lottie was reminded of her family's tiara. Watching the item twirl in the professor's fingers, that strange feeling of displacement swirled in her stomach, and she felt the wolf pendant around her neck grow heavy.

"Who here has heard of the Mayfutts?" the professor asked, looking at her students.

Everyone shook their heads, even Binah. Lottie had seen the name in Oscar's diary but had yet to read any of those passages properly, so shook her head as well. The deputy headmistress smiled, delicately fingering the necklace.

"The Mayfutts were once as revered and renowned as the Windsors or the Wolfsons." Lottie blushed as the professor's eyes met hers for a moment. "The Mayfutts were the royal family of Albania for hundreds of years until one day"—the room had fallen silent, everyone leaning forward in their seats, fascinated—"their princess vanished."

There was a collective intake of breath from the students.

"What happened to her?" the Ivy boy asked, pushing his glasses up the bridge of his nose.

"Nobody knows, but it goes to show how fragile these royal lines can be. One weak link can break the whole chain."

"One bad wolf can hurt the whole pack." Lottie said it absent-mindedly and blinked when she realized everyone was staring at her. "Sorry . . . it's . . . it's a family saying." She flushed.

"What was her name?" Binah asked, preparing her pen to take notes and pulling the attention away from Lottie.

"Her name was Liliana Wilda Mayfutt, and from what little we know of her, she lived up to her middle name; she was rather wild." Lottie almost choked. *Wild* was what everyone called Ellie. Did Ellie know about Liliana? "How was she *wild*?" Lottie asked.

The professor paced around the center table as she spoke. "She never wanted to be a princess. She refused to attend any public functions; she wouldn't wear the dresses she was given or even show off the jewelry. Nothing that would mark her as royal."

This is all sounding very familiar, thought Lottie.

"One story states that a suitor made an inappropriate advance and she broke his nose." Lottie coughed, unable to cover up a laugh as she remembered when Ellie had broken Prince Ashwick's nose only a few months ago. Lottie was starting to wonder if the Mayfutts and the Wolfsons were somehow related.

The Conch girl smirked, pushing back a lock of red hair. "Sounds like a smart young woman," she said.

"Quite." The professor gazed again at the pendant she was holding up in the air. "Now, this necklace is one of the few remaining connections to Liliana and the Mayfutt family. They had no other children, and the line died out when she disappeared."

"Are there any paintings of her?" Binah asked, neatly writing everything down.

"I'm glad you asked." Professor Devine picked up a book from the table and paged to an illustration, the book's stiff leather spine creaking as she opened it. "This is the only image that remains of the princess. A self-portrait. I'd like you to pass it around." She handed the book to one of the Stratus boys, who scrutinized the picture. Lottie could feel electric anticipation building in her as she watched the book pass from student to student. She wanted so badly to see this princess. She *needed* to see this princess. In her mind she could only imagine her as Ellie, but that couldn't be possible. That strange feeling that she'd gotten from her tiara while she'd been in Maradova surged within her again, telling her she was missing something.

The book finally reached Lottie and she held out a trembling hand to take it. She felt nervous. Carefully she looked at the image of Princess Liliana.

The first thing that popped into her head was the painting she'd done of Ellie. The pose was so familiar. Liliana was also holding a saber and looking furious and fierce. But in appearance the two looked nothing alike—there was absolutely no resemblance to Ellie other than the look of ferocious determination. Liliana had dirty-blond hair that cascaded down her back in untamed curls. Lottie instinc-tively pushed her own blond curls back. The princess in the drawing was almost baby-faced, and yet the fire in her eyes made it clear she was not to be taken lightly. Lottie moved to pass the book to her neighbor but paused. *Stay vigilant.* Those words rang through her head again.

What am I missing?

She squinted at the image. There was a clue here, she knew it. And then it came to her, a spark igniting in her stomach that set her whole body alight.

Among Princess Liliana's dirty-blond curls sat a silver tiara. At its crest was a jeweled crescent moon. This was a royal adornment that Lottie would recognize anywhere—her most valued possession.

Princess Liliana was wearing Lottie's tiara.

🎀 14 🎀

THE ROOM CLOSED IN AROUND Lottie. Her mind was a blur of confusion. She spent the rest of the lesson in a daze, desperately trying to make sense of what she'd seen. She'd never really considered where her tiara had come from before it was her family's; all she knew was that Henry had received it when he taught at Rosewood Hall all those years ago.

By the end of the class her purple leather workbook was filled with sketches of Princess Liliana and the tiara, accompanied by bullet-point conspiracy theories.

- *Maybe it was a replica?*
- *Maybe the princess sold the tiara when she ran away?*
- *Maybe the princess was killed and the tiara stolen?*

Lottie shivered at that last one, struggling to imagine that the tiara could have come into Henry's ownership by such dark means.

Or maybe—a voice in her head that she barely allowed herself to listen to whispered—*your family has its own royal secrets.*

The professor's voice cut into her thoughts. "Your

homework is to draw your own family tree. I want you to get used to the process, as you will be drawing many more of them in this class." Lottie nodded distractedly, jotting down hasty notes in her book. She'd drawn the Wolfson family tree again and again in her princess lessons, but the idea of having to present it to the class put an unexpected hard lump in her throat. She swallowed it down.

"Well, this will be interesting," Binah said, laughing as they packed up their bags. "My family tree is immense. I have about forty cousins, and that's just on my mum's side."

"*Forty?*" Lottie choked in disbelief. "I don't even have *one.*" She was frantically putting away her workbook and pencil case, eager to get to Ellie and Jamie in the library and ask them about the tiara.

"Hmm, yes. It's true that the Maravish royal family is remarkably intimate."

Lottie paused, the twinkle in Binah's voice catching her off guard, and she realized the mistake she'd just made.

She'd responded as Lottie Pumpkin.

This is what happens when you think about your family too much, you silly girl. She remembered Jamie's flash of frustration when she tried to press him about the gift. It made more sense now. Just like Jamie had said, they couldn't get distracted—not even by their own families.

"Well . . . yes, that is, my uncle never had children, and

then he . . . so yeah. It's just . . . it's only me." *All the burden falls on Ellie.*

Binah nodded in understanding, and Lottie counted her blessings that neither she nor Ellie had cousins. This was not the kind of slip-up she could afford to make, especially not with Binah, who soaked up knowledge like a sponge.

"I've got to run, Binah—I'm meeting Ellie in the library." *And if I don't ask her about this tiara soon I'm going to literally explode.*

"Let me know if you two need anything." There was that twinkle again from Binah. *What* did she know? Lottie shook her head clear and without looking back she ran down the stairs, heading for the library.

It was no secret that the Rosewood Hall library was Lottie's favorite place in the school. The circular two-story white building was adorned with floral garlands—lilies currently—with glistening white roses in boxes studded along the walls. She had to force herself to slow to a walk as she entered the glass double doors. She spotted Ellie and Jamie in the cafe on the left side of the library, sitting on one of the cushioned benches. Ellie's dyed black hair was a complete mess from wearing her fencing helmet all morning, with tufts sticking up in different directions like antennae. A group of younger students walked past Ellie and Jamie, giggling. They smiled at the pair, then hurried away, as if embarrassed somehow. Ellie and Jamie were both wearing the Ivy shirt with the stag emblem and suspenders to hold up their trousers, but while Jamie looked professional and immaculate, Ellie wore her uniform with a rebellious edge. They always seemed to draw attention to themselves, and Lottie had had to get used to it.

"Ellie, you are *not* going to *believe* what just happened!" Lottie rushed over, fully aware how ridiculous she sounded—she couldn't hold it in any longer. Ellie looked up at her affectionately, a messy strand of hair falling over her face. "It was so strange," Lottie continued, her words bumping into each other. "I almost don't believe it, but—"

"This is a *library*, Lottie, even if we are in the cafe," Jamie said, without even looking up from his copy of *Hamlet*. His rebuke elicited an eye roll from Ellie, who leaned back against the wooden bench with her arms outstretched. They both had steaming cups of coffee in front of them— Jamie's black, Ellie's foamed with whipped cream.

"Do you have to ruin everyone's fun, Jamie?"

He met Ellie's raised eyebrows with a scowl. *What is up with him lately?* Lottie worried that he hadn't forgiven her for the book *or* the conversation on the field. He was often grumpy, but his recent behavior struck her as extra prickly.

"What's so exciting?" Ellie asked, smile back on her face.

"Look." Lottie slammed her workbook down on the

table in front of them and flung open the pages. They both peered over.

"That's a bunch of sketches of your tiara," Ellie said after a pause.

"Yes, right, but today in royal history we were learning about Princess Liliana and—"

"Liliana?"

"Yes, Liliana."

"As in the fall of Albania? The malevolent minx of the Mayfutts?"

"Excuse me?" Lottie blinked at Ellie's unexpected knowledge.

"She's the cautionary lesson they tell to all wayward princesses. Wasn't there even a poem, Jamie?" She clicked her fingers, trying to pluck it from her mind. "Jamie, recite it for me." The book in his hand thudded shut and Lottie saw his lip twitch. She held her breath, but a genuine smile spread across his face and he cleared his throat.

"Liliana took her crown,
tossed it on the dirty ground.
When they came to fix her up,
she bit and scratched, threw a fuss.

Because the princess never wed,
one night alone when in her bed,

the devil came and ate her whole
but left behind her rotten soul.

Liliana wanders round,
up and down the castle grounds,
Looking out for naughty maids,
any girl who misbehaves.

If you choose to disobey,
to talk back or go astray,
the princess will come for you
and eat you up as she was too."

A look of delight crept over Ellie's face as she listened. Lottie, on the other hand, struggled to see what was so funny. As far as she knew, she was in possession of a vengeful spirit's tiara. And as much as Lottie tried to persuade herself that she didn't believe in ghosts, she couldn't ignore the silly worry that maybe Princess Liliana was out to get her.

"Well, that was terrifying," Lottie said when Jamie drew to a close.

"Not to mention horribly sexist," Ellie said, cackling.

"But the poem completely backfired on you," Jamie said with a tut, and Ellie grinned even more.

"Like any sensible child," Ellie stated heroically, "I

thought the idea of a scary ghost was awesome and started misbehaving more in the hopes of summoning up the spirit of Liliana."

Lottie's mind conjured up the image of a young Eleanor Wolfson running around the palace causing mayhem in the hopes of finding a ghost. Though Ellie hadn't succeeded in summoning Liliana, Lottie couldn't help thinking about the link between her and this ancient princess—Ellie had certainly summoned someone.

"Okay, well"—Lottie raised her voice over their laughter—"the professor showed us a painting of her and . . . well, Liliana was wearing my family's tiara."

Ellie and Jamie went quiet and stared at her.

"I don't understand. Why would she be wearing your family's tiara?" Ellie asked.

"That's what I'm trying to figure out."

"And you're sure it's the same?" Jamie's tone remained distant, but she could see his interest was piqued.

"Yes, I'm absolutely sure, I—"

Suddenly there was commotion behind them. A plain girl with mousy hair in a Conch tartan pinafore had jumped onto one of the wooden tables in the cafe as a group of her friends desperately tried to stop her.

"Beatrice, get down! What are you doing?" one of the boys said, reaching up, but she batted his hand away.

The Conch girl—Beatrice—was laughing maniacally,

kicking all the elegant school plates off the table and howling as they smashed on the floor. Ellie and Jamie stood up sharply as everyone else scrambled to get away.

Beatrice began swaying in time to some music only she could hear. "Come and join me," she hooted. "Let's have a party!" She began mindlessly giggling again, holding her hand out and almost falling off the table.

"What on earth is going on in here?"

The cafe fell silent as Clark the librarian appeared, looking surprisingly intimidating for someone who practically lived among the bookshelves. "Beatrice Bartley, get down from there at once."

His fury was met with more hysterical laughing from Beatrice. "Why don't you stop being a boring old fart?" she replied.

"Oh my God." Lottie had to stop herself snorting; this was just too strange. Beatrice tried to break out into a dance again, but the table rocked beneath her and she stumbled dangerously to one side. The way she was talking, the way she was swaying . . . it seemed familiar, but Lottie couldn't place why.

"She's going to fall!" Ellie cried, and she ran over toward Beatrice.

Lottie moved to follow, but as soon as she did so she was assaulted by an overpowering saccharine smell—as sweet as baby powder, yet as sinister as poison.

"Ellie, wait—" Jamie made to stop her, but he too froze to the spot. As his face twisted, Lottie knew he'd detected the same scent.

Before either of them could call out any words of warning, Beatrice's expression grew serious. Her swaying stopped and she froze in what looked like a moment of terrified awareness. Then she threw her head back and screamed.

Her piercing howl cut through the library, a blood-curdling sound that sent an electric shock down Lottie's spine. A swirling, dizzy cloud overtook Lottie. Instinctively she reached out to steady herself against the table, her breath catching in her throat. She was plunged back into the memory of being thrust into the van by Saskia. Gulping in a breath, she forced her brain to repeat her mantra, reminding herself that she was safe, that she was okay.

I will be kind, I will be brave, I will be unstoppable.

Ellie rushed forward as the Conch girl stumbled backward, her feet close to the table's edge. Beatrice tipped over into empty air, her arms circling wildly as she tried to right herself.

"Help me!" she cried—too late. Her eyes rolled back in her head as she plummeted toward the hard floor.

Ellie dove behind the table, pushing a boy out of the way to catch Beatrice, pulling her into a protective roll.

Lottie felt her chest grow warm. The sickly, nervous feeling dissipated as she gazed at her fearless friend. Breaking out of the spell, she ran over to help, trying to ignore the overpowering sugary smell that had triggered this strange sense of dread. Beatrice's face, so alive a moment ago, was now pasty, as though a porcelain veneer had been painted over her skin.

"Pass her to me, thank you, Ellie. Tamsin, help me get Beatrice to the nurse." Clark began calmly issuing orders, and soon everyone was helping to clear up the mess. "Miss Pumpkin, would you kindly collect Beatrice's belongings?"

Lottie nodded, still dazed.

"This is getting serious." Jamie's voice was low, a deep growl that only Lottie and Ellie could hear. Not trusting her own voice to remain steady, Lottie didn't respond. She silently gathered Beatrice's things and piled them in her bag, when something made her stop. A half-eaten bar of Tompkins Confectionery popping-candy chocolate, the golden wrapping underneath glinting softly.

That smell.

Lottie stared at the chocolate bar with wide-eyed clarity. She finally knew exactly what that sweet, powdery smell reminded her of. It smelled like Lola and Micky.

❧ 15 ❧

LOTTIE FOUND HORACE SILVERTON-SMITH a few days later in a private study by the Stratus library, playing Dungeons and Dragons with a small group of other students. A large tapestry of the periodic table covered one of the walls triumphantly, very fitting for the house that so perfectly combined art and academics. The group was nestled in a corner by a window with yellow pyracantha pouring over the sill and were so intently focused on their game that Lottie felt bad about disturbing them.

She was sure there was something fishy going on with the Tompkins chocolate. It could be a stretch, but King Alexander had told her to stay vigilant, and that meant trusting her gut instincts. If this was something that could affect Ellie, she had to get to the bottom of it. It was her responsibility. But before she could take her theory to Ellie and Jamie, she needed to know if Horace had eaten any Tompkins chocolate on the first day of school. Lottie pulled a clipboard, a few sheets of blank paper, and a pen out of her bag, marching forward purposefully.

"Good evening, fellow students." The whole group turned

to stare at her, pulled out of their D&D trance by her awkward entrance. Lottie cleared her throat before continuing, "I was wondering if you could help me with something."

They all blinked at her, a herd of deer caught in headlights.

"Isn't that the princess from Marnovia?" a Chinese boy with bright blue eyes whispered excitedly to the blond girl with glasses next to him.

"It's Maradova," she hissed in response.

"How did you get in here?" another boy with brown freckles asked. "It's Stratus students only unless they're a guest."

"You can't ask her that; she's a princess." The girl with glasses bopped the freckled boy on the head with a rolled-up piece of paper, earning a grunt.

Lottie had no idea her princess status still had such an impact on people. She was used to the occasional whisper and stare, but these geeky kids were acting as if a celebrity had just walked up to them. She suddenly felt embarrassed. "If I'm disrupting your game, I can go—sorry to bother you." Lottie's cheeks instantly turned red.

"We haven't actually started yet," the girl in the glasses replied, placing a colorful screen in front of her, signifying that she was the Dungeon Master. "We're still setting up. We'd be happy to help." She gave everyone a sharp look. "Wouldn't we?"

They all nodded and murmured, eager to please the ruler of their game. It was very clear she was the master here in more ways than one.

"I'm Stevie. What can we help you with?" she asked. Lottie's gaze lingered over Horace, his blotchy face and doe eyes reminding her of herself. She was glad he was okay.

Lottie cleared her throat again, ready to begin her made-up survey. "Well, I'm doing a study for my biology class on food and memory," she began, holding out her clipboard as if it were all very serious business. "I was wondering if you could all tell me what you ate on your first day back at school?"

They exchanged glances before Stevie nodded and they all turned back to her.

"Hmm, I think I had porridge for breakfast?" someone offered in a squeaky voice.

Lottie dutifully jotted down the information. "Can you remember anything specific, like . . ." She pretended to think for a moment. "Like if any of you had any chocolate that day?"

"Um," another pondered, scratching his chin. "I guess we all had some of Horace's chocolate."

"Amazing!" Lottie exclaimed, sure that she was onto something. "And can any of you remember what brand it was?"

"I think it was Cadbury's, but we also had some

Tompkins," Horace chimed in, blushing as he spoke.

Lottie felt her heart rate quicken. "And did you all eat from the same bar?" she asked, struggling to contain her excitement.

Stevie raised her eyebrow suspiciously. "That seems like an odd question," she said bluntly. "I doubt any of us can remember that. We weren't paying much attention; we were sharing the chocolate when the fireworks started." She looked at her friends, and the rest of her party shrugged in agreement.

Lottie sighed, defeated. Without knowing for sure that only Horace had had the Tompkins chocolate, she didn't have sufficient evidence to prove that the bar was poisoned. She was about to give up and make an excuse to leave, when a shrill voice caught everyone's attention.

"I'm telling you I saw a GHOST!" A much older Stratus girl with olive skin and unbelievably long legs was pouting as she loomed over a Stratus boy, who clearly regretted whatever he'd just said. "I saw the ghost and that's how I passed my exam. It's the truth and you're just jealous because your wish didn't come true." With that, she strode out of the study area, leaving no room for argument.

The room broke into hushed whispers; it seemed even the Stratus students weren't immune to a bit of house drama.

"They're fighting about the Elwin statue superstition,"

Stevie said in a dark tone that caught Lottie off guard.

"The what?" she asked curiously.

"She's been going on about it ever since we got back to school," Horace said with a giggle. "Francesca Bennington in year twelve," he whispered. "She said that last year she sneaked down to make a wish at midnight and saw a ghost, and her wish to pass advanced math came true."

Stevie sniffed. "Yeah, but she said she saw a female ghost—and William Tufty was a man."

Lottie almost choked. Last year Binah had written a puzzle that led Ellie and Lottie to ponder the identity of William Tufty—and they were yet to find out the truth.

"I'm very sorry, but what are you talking about?"

They all turned to look at Lottie as if they had forgotten she was there. Stevie took a deep breath, making it clear she resented having to explain something so silly.

"Supposedly"—she interlocked her fingers, preparing to tell the story—"the Stratus namesakes, Shray and Sana Stratus, weaved some magic into each statue they made for each house. So if you pat the bird statue of Elwin the merlin three times and polish the *W* on his plaque, then you will have one wish granted, but only if you are visited by the ghost of William Tufty."

The thought of ghosts immediately conjured up images of Liliana again, the furious princess who would gobble up any girl who misbehaved . . . or stole her tiara. The very idea of it had Lottie shivering involuntarily.

"Fascinating," Lottie replied, gulping.

"Sorry we couldn't be more help with your study." Stevie adjusted her glasses again, the movement shattering Lottie's enchantment.

Lottie blinked, taking a second to realize what Stevie was talking about. She'd gotten so caught up in the thought of ghosts and wishes that she'd almost forgotten she was there on a chocolate mission.

Stop getting distracted, she told herself, and yet she couldn't keep the questions from rolling off her tongue.

"Could one of you maybe," Lottie started timidly, "show me how to make an Elwin wish?"

A girl with a mop of spider-silk hair lifted her head. "I'm Sunny. I will."

And so Lottie followed the girl back to the entrance to Stratus Side. Sunny whistled a strange but happy tune as they approached the merlin statue.

They paused in front of the small circular white staircase that curled around the statue of the merlin. The bird had been cast majestically in bronze, wings spread, a knowing twinkle in his eye as if he held all the secrets of the school.

"First you reach up and pat him three times," Sunny said, reaching up to demonstrate.

"Anywhere?"

"Anywhere, I guess, but I'd probably try his beak."

Stepping forward, Lottie reached up and patted Elwin's glittering head three times, then stepped back.

"Now you simply polish the *W* and make a wish."

"Do I have to say it out loud?" Lottie asked, feeling embarrassed that she was letting herself get caught up in this fantasy.

Sunny shrugged and simply said, "It's up to you," as she walked away.

Taking another step forward, Lottie brushed the *W* on the center of Elwin's name plaque with her white shirt sleeve. The letter was slightly larger than the others and infinitely more shiny.

I wish . . .

She paused, suddenly unsure what she was doing, unsure what she should want. She thought about Lola and Micky and Percy and what they must be going through, about Anastacia and Saskia, Ellie and Jamie . . . and then finally she allowed her thoughts to wander to Liliana. She wanted to help everyone, she wanted to be an unstoppable force of good, but how could she do that when she was riddled with so many personal worries? One last image appeared in her head: her mother's tiara. The wolf pendant felt heavy around her neck and she knew exactly what she wanted.

"I wish for a family."

ঙ্গ 16 ঙ্গ

ELLIE ALWAYS FELT A LITTLE on edge around Conch House, hyperaware that her purple tartan uniform marked her as different among all the deep red Conch outfits. Conch House was at the opposite end of the school to Ivy Wood, and it was rare that any non-Conch student would come this way unless they were part of a sports team.

It wasn't just the students—where Ivy Wood was covered in wisteria and filled with delicately stitched cushions and sheer curtains, Conch was bold, surrounded by red roses ready to prick anyone who got too close and filled with dark mahogany and deep-colored velvets, thick with the scent of expensive antiques.

Ellie stared up at Saxon, the growling bear statue that warned off intruders at the iron gates of Conch House.

"I hate this place," Ellie grumbled, receiving a side-eye glance from two Conch girls carrying designer bags. The walk through Conch was a small price to pay for fencing practice, but that didn't mean she had to like it. She swung her gear over her back, ignoring their staring. Ellie knew she stood out; she knew she didn't fit into the made-up cookie-cutter idea of how a girl should be. She didn't care. That's how she felt comfortable and she wasn't going to change.

Ellie entered the grand double oak doors of the main hall, the cold swirling in around her as she walked through the arch. Dame Bolter and Thomas, a fellow Rosewood Lancer, were already setting up for practice, and Ellie automatically began laying mats out on the floor to help.

"We need to work on the footwork for your lunges this week, Ellie," Dame Bolter said. Mercy Bolter was taller than anyone Ellie had ever met, with hair she kept shaved down to her scalp. Her whole presence was commanding, and Ellie had developed an intense respect for the Conch house mother.

Ellie smirked, eyeing Thomas. "Maybe we can also fix Tom's terrible grip this week."

Not missing a beat, Thomas sauntered past her with a mat and playfully kicked the back of her shin. "Don't call me Tom."

Ellie pushed him lightly and they finished their task. She felt like she'd found her people in the fencing team, even if she was going to destroy them all at the Spearion at the end of the year. There was only one member of the team who Ellie still couldn't see eye to eye with. As if on cue, the door heaved open again and there stood the perfectly groomed brunette Barbie doll that was Anastacia Alcroft.

"Ellie. Thomas." She nodded to each of them in a curt greeting before breezing past to place her kit on one of the benches. Nowadays, she and Ellie exchanged no more than a few words with each other.

Ellie couldn't understand why Anastacia didn't want to know anything about Saskia. How could she just not care about her anymore? They'd been so close; it didn't make any sense.

Two more team members, Riyadh and Marzia, showed up together just as they had last week. It was pretty clear to everyone that they were crushing on each other. Ellie refrained from making a gagging motion as the short brunet boy placed an arm around the pretty Italian girl, who, as far as Ellie was concerned, was way out of his league. Finally the last member of their team appeared, a boy from the year above named Aden Wong who'd taken over from Jacob Zee as head of the Rosewood Lancers after Jacob graduated.

"Okay, team. Let's get right into warm-ups today," Dame Bolter shouted across the hall. "Thomas, pair up with Aden. Ellie and Anastacia, you will go together, and Riyadh and Marzia, you too. Get to it, everyone."

Ellie froze, her fists tightening into balls. She didn't

know if she had the self-control to not bring up Saskia if they were paired together. "I want to pair up with Tom." Ellie's words were less of a request than a demand.

She was met with a severe gaze from Dame Bolter. "Miss Wolf, you will pair up with whomever you're told to pair up with. Now move." The sharp point of her finger made it clear this was not an argument Ellie could win. She took a deep breath and thought of Lottie and how disappointed she'd be in her if she got into trouble with the fencing team.

"Yes, ma'am," she said begrudgingly.

Dame Bolter nodded in return before walking off to the supply room.

Ellie didn't even turn around to look at Anastacia as she walked over to the saber stand. She couldn't stop thinking about Saskia. Saskia, who was still in the dungeon of the palace. Saskia, who Anastacia was supposed to love more than anyone. She pulled a saber toward her with a furious grunt, the force of the movement upsetting the stand, causing all the weapons to drop with a loud clatter.

"Come on!" She kicked one of the swords across the floor.

The rest of the class stared at her, shocked by her outburst.

Why do I always do this? She leaned down to tidy up the fallen swords. Why couldn't she be more like Lottie and think before she reacted? A hand reached out to help, wearing a perfectly pristine, immaculately white glove.

"You need to get it together," Anastacia said in a whisper.

"I don't need your help," Ellie snarled.

They all took their places on the mats, helmets on, a collection of white-clad figures poised and ready to perform. The doors of the studio locked out the cold. Ellie could feel the sweat building on her forehead already as she faced the almost identical figure in front of her.

Dame Bolter returned from the supply closet, eyebrows furrowed in irritation.

"It seems that someone has moved the footwork markers, so while I go to find them I want you all to practice those forward lunges. Aden will be in charge while I'm gone," Dame Bolter's voice called out as she left, but Ellie was hardly listening, too focused on the mask-obscured Anastacia in front of her.

Why won't you talk to Saskia?

She lunged but sensed immediately that her footwork was off. Anastacia easily swerved the move.

"Watch that left leg, Ellie," Aden called.

Ellie barked out a curse. She couldn't focus with the heat inside her suit building like a furnace.

Next it was Anastacia's turn. Her lunge was almost perfect, but Ellie noticed a subtle shaking where she held the saber, as if she was gripping too tight, scared to lose contact with the handle.

"Your hand is shaking," Ellie said bluntly, narrowing her eyes at her. Anastacia was clearly not as well-adjusted as she was pretending to be.

"I had too much coffee." Her words were muffled behind the helmet.

Ellie attempted another lunge, but again it was too forceful. She felt unable to center herself.

"*Imbécile!*"

Even through the helmet Ellie could hear the insult loud and clear.

"What did you just say?" She broke stance, marching up to the white figure in front of her.

"You're messy, Ellie. I can't practice with you." Anastacia didn't flinch, a white pillar standing its ground.

"Oh yeah? Let's see how messy I am, shall we?" Ellie held her saber out, preparing to parry.

"As you wish." Her opponent mimicked the stance, sword outstretched, and the duel began.

Ellie lunged forward, taking the offensive instinctively. "You'll need to speak to Saskia eventually."

"*Tais-toi!*" Anastacia swiped the saber out of the way instantly, the sound of metal on metal ringing out.

"People might be in danger." The heat inside Ellie's suit

rose with each word, red-hot lava running through her veins with every movement. Anastacia moved into her own offensive stance, taking control of the fight.

"I just . . . I can't do it," she cried, knocking Ellie's sword to the side again.

Ellie shook her head, pivoting to get another strike in. "I know you hate her now, but you can't just ignore the problem."

Anastacia faltered at these words, her shaky hands losing their grip, and Ellie's sword made contact with the side of her, surprising both of them.

"Hate her?" Anastacia quickly shook her head and regained her stance. "You really are clueless."

This time Ellie faltered and Anastacia took the opportunity to plant a hit. Ellie recoiled and her opponent desperately tried to remain in control, holding her sword out in a menacing pose. The two stood panting, trying not to hunch over with exhaustion. Ellie's sword hung from her hand as Anastacia's words sank in. She couldn't see Anastacia's face, but it was clear her shaking had increased. If she didn't know any better, she would think she was crying.

Something snapped and Anastacia slowly lowered her sword, shaky breaths emerging from her mask. "I'm not scared of hating her. I'm scared that I don't hate her, and that hurts even more." Her hand clutched her chest, and

Ellie could almost feel the pain in her own body, a piercing ache through her heart. Anastacia reached up and removed her helmet, a tear running down her cheek, masked by beads of sweat. "Imagine if it was Lottie."

A bolt of lightning ran up Ellie's spine at the sound of her best friend's name, and she reached up to remove her own helmet.

"What does *that* mean?" she demanded.

Anastacia's pained face turned into a snarl. "Oh please, just because Lottie's completely oblivious doesn't mean I can't tell how you feel about her."

"Lottie, she's . . ." Ellie had never found herself so lost for words before, but this mention of Lottie had her heart thundering so loud in her chest that she couldn't hear her own thoughts.

"You and Saskia are so similar sometimes," Anastacia said with a humorless smile. "But if it makes you feel any better, I'm pretty sure Lottie feels the same way. Although I doubt she has any idea what she's feeling at all; she's too busy distracting herself with work. Honestly—"

"Miss Alcroft, Miss Wolf." Dame Bolter's voice pierced the air, cutting off their conversation. "That is quite enough parrying and chitchat; I expect more from the two of you." They both froze at the furious voice of the Conch house mother. "If you don't hurry up and return to your practice, I'll have you running laps around the field."

The two girls slipped their helmets on. In her mind Ellie conjured up the image of Lottie. She was her little ray of light, a soft flower that she would do anything to protect.

"You and Saskia are so similar sometimes."

A flash of electricity ran through her chest at her sudden understanding. Anastacia's actions made perfect sense to her now.

If Ellie was just like Saskia, then Lottie was her Anastacia. And what would Ellie do if Lottie ever got hurt like that?

17

If ye doth seek to find the truth,
approach bronzed Elwin where he stands.
Lay thy hand upon the bird three times over;
tend to the W upon his name.
You will find your wish comes true,
but only if my spirit alights in you.

This was the poem that had spawned the superstition. Its words danced around in Lottie's head as she glanced around, cringing at the idea of spirits descending. She was already regretting her wish.

Lottie slammed the book of Tufty's poems shut, making Ellie look up.

Ever since she'd gone to Stratus Side and made that wish, she couldn't shake the thought of ghosts from her mind, no matter how much she told herself she was being silly. And to make matters worse, she'd gotten nowhere with her chocolate theory.

"Are you okay?" Ellie asked, her voice muffled by the pen sticking out of her mouth.

"Yes, I'm just procrastinating," Lottie replied, although it wasn't just her work she was trying to avoid. "What were we talking about again?"

Ellie rubbed her forehead in an attempt to bring herself back down to earth. It seemed to Lottie that Ellie was also in a total daze. As soon as they'd met up that night after fencing practice it had been clear that her head was somewhere else, and it wasn't helping to put Lottie's mind at ease.

"You were trying to tell me that you think Tompkins chocolate is what's causing people to have those meltdowns?"

The two of them were sitting cross-legged on the purple Persian rug on their bedroom floor, hair pushed back with bandannas, surrounded by piles of books and homework. Lottie pulled the family tree she was meant to be working on for royal history back in front of her. She was trying her best to fill it in, but it was only causing her more stress.

"Yes, right." Lottie shook her head, trying to push the poem out of her mind. "I just . . . I feel it in my gut."

Lottie carefully added some flourishes to the tree, hoping that if she made it as pretty as possible it would stop making her feel so odd.

"I believe you believe it, Lottie," Ellie added, "but like you said, you couldn't get sufficient proof, and"—Ellie leaned forward to fill in a line on her worksheet before continuing—"if the chocolate is causing these strange symptoms, then why isn't everyone who's eaten a bar of it having the same reaction?"

Shoving her colored pencil in her mouth to free up her hands, Lottie reached over for her school bag.

"Well, that's exactly what I was trying to find out. My theory is that it's only some of the bars . . ."

Lottie pulled out Beatrice's half-eaten bar of chocolate, which she'd picked up a few days ago from the library.

Careful not to touch the actual chocolate, Lottie neatly placed it on the floor between them as if it were a sacred item. "I swiped this from Beatrice's stuff. She was halfway through eating it when she . . . you know, went all weird." "Went all weird" seemed like a gross understatement for what they'd witnessed from Horace and Beatrice, but Lottie was reluctant to describe it in more detail.

The chocolate bar finally seemed to grab Ellie's full attention.

"Quick thinking, little princess." Ellie's mouth curved up into a side smile, and Lottie lit up at the pet name. The idea that she was being useful to Ellie made a warm feeling spread over her. It was the first time she'd felt normal in days. Thank goodness Ellie didn't notice her blush.

"We should go and tell Jamie your theory," Ellie said, peering at the chocolate.

"No, actually . . ." Lottie hesitated. There was still

something bothering Jamie. She didn't want to bring this chocolate theory to him until she was sure it was right. "I'd rather not tell him until I've proven it, if you don't mind."

Ellie nodded slowly, strands of her hair peeping out of the purple bandanna. "So you need to test it, right?" Ellie grabbed the chocolate to inspect it further, holding it up to her eyes as if trying to interrogate it.

"Correct."

"To see if this bar is one of the poisoned ones?"

"Exactly, but the only way to do that would be to try it, and—"

Lottie watched in horror as Ellie plucked off a square of the milky chocolate bar and began lifting it toward her mouth.

"Ellie!" Lottie cried.

Jamie's training suddenly kicked in and she dove across the floor, tackling Ellie and snatching the chocolate from her before it touched her lips. She threw it in the trash and turned back, furious, to face Ellie.

"Don't ever do that again." Lottie's voice came out in a horrified croak, nowhere near the tone of authority she'd been aiming for.

Ellie choked out a surprised laugh. "What's wrong?"

"Ellie, how could you do that? What if you had a reaction?" Lottie felt the pendant anchoring her, burning at the center of her chest as her heart thundered.

"I wasn't really gonna do it. Jeez. It was just a joke."

"No, Ellie, that was completely inappropriate." Lottie stared at her princess, refusing to back down.

"Wow!" Ellie blinked with shock. "Lottie, when did you and Jamie become the same person?"

Lottie flinched. "I'm not . . . I don't . . . What does that even mean?" She was tripping over her words.

A crashing sound pulled Lottie away from the stuttering in her mind. The painting of Henry Pitkin had fallen off her side table, clattering onto the wooden floor.

Ellie chuckled, turning back to Lottie. "Do we have a ghost? Maybe Liliana has come to get her tiara back."

Lottie barely heard her, frozen in fear as she stared down at the image of her ancestor.

"Lottie?"

Hearing her name brought her to her senses, and she rushed over to the painting and carefully picked it up, checking for any damage on the wooden frame. His eyes peered out at her, light blue, like her own, the color of the sky on a clear sunny day. A strange haunting melody whispered in her ears. Without knowing why, Lottie reached into the drawer in her side table and gently touched her tiara. Was the singing getting louder?

"Is it me or did it just get colder?" Ellie asked, looking around.

Lottie could feel it too, as if another presence were in

the room, a ghost from the past. She shivered, the Stratus superstition snaking its way back into her mind.

"Are you okay, Lottie?" Ellie's voice had softened.

"Yes." *Except I made a very stupid wish today and now I think I'm being haunted by it.*

She thought back to Jamie and how angry he was when she had brought up his family and how irritated he'd seemed recently. Is this what he meant when he said he couldn't think about things like this? Ever since she'd been thinking about her family, it felt like they were constantly haunting her, stopping her from focusing on Ellie and Leviathan. "We just need to get to the bottom of this; we can't get distracted by ghost stories." She placed the portrait back on the side table and closed the drawer.

Ellie's eyes narrowed at her, and for a moment Lottie was sure she was about to say something else. Instead she sighed, shaking her head clear.

"If that's what you want."

Ellie picked up her pen again and Lottie resumed her position on the floor next to her, hoping she wouldn't notice how shaky her breath had gotten.

"And no more jokes like that, Ellie, please. I would never forgive myself if something bad happened to you."

Ellie paused and the room became painfully quiet. "Sorry."

The word was so soft that Lottie wondered if she'd

imagined it. It was so rare to get an apology from Ellie that she almost expected it to burst in the air like a bubble.

"It's okay . . . We just need to find someone who can test the chocolate properly," Lottie added quickly. "Someone we can trust."

"But who?" Ellie asked. "And how?"

Lottie looked down at the family tree in front of her, rubbing her temples in silent thought. The family tree that was really Ellie's, the family tree that she'd be presenting to her royal history class tomorrow. A name popped into her head with such sudden clarity that it made her eyes shoot open in surprise.

"I think I have someone in mind." Lottie gave Ellie her best smile in the hopes of winning her over. "But it might be a terrible idea."

18

THE SMALL ART ROOM SEEMED extra quiet the next morning when Lottie arrived for her royal history class. Every creak of a floorboard and drafty rattle of a centuries-old window sent her into high alert.

She'd slept badly—dreaming about the ghostly figure of Liliana Mayfutt creeping through the Ivy dormitory, intent on retrieving her tiara and snatching Ellie away for not fulfilling her role as a perfect princess. There was one advantage to her insomnia—Lottie had arrived more than ten minutes early for class. She placed her wooden board with the family tree to one side of her desk and took out Oscar's old leather-bound diary. Why not see if she could learn anything more? She was flicking through the nuptial information when a short passage caught her eye. A throwaway entry on Ivan Wolfson, which she'd never taken much notice of, mentioned his original intended wife:

Lili was never assigned a Partizan or a Portman. She was considered too much work for a Partizan to contend with, and her family worried that a Portman would only encourage her reckless behavior.

Although few nobility were given the opportunity to meet her, she did become close to Ivan Wolfson. The family encouraged the two of them to exchange letters in the hope of a future marriage.

Ivan Wolfson never recovered from Lili's disappearance. I regret that I never was able to learn a notable amount about her. Other than a few existing portraits of the princess, there is little historical detail about her life. She has become a true enigma.

Lottie stared at the book, her breath coming in excited gasps. She bolted over to the table in the middle of the room, nearly knocking over her chair, and grabbed the book the professor had passed around the week before. Flipping through the pages, she reached the image of Liliana Mayfutt, that furious gaze locking with hers. Lottie traced the tiara on Liliana's head, the familiar crescent moon. Then she turned the page and began to read out loud, feeling the shape of the words in her mouth . . .

"'*Liliana Wilda Mayfutt, sole heir to the Albanian throne, remains one of the most mysterious characters from royal history. Named after the lily, the symbol of the Mayfutts, her name was often abbreviated to Lili—*'"

"What are you reading?"

Lottie hastily slammed the book shut. She'd been so

engrossed that she hadn't even heard Binah enter the room. Now her schoolmate took a seat beside her; she was carrying a massive wooden board similar to Lottie's that was intricately decorated with her own family tree.

"Oh, just about ghosts from the past," Lottie said, keeping her voice light.

The rest of the class began trickling in, and at last Professor Devine arrived with another tray of tea and biscuits, including some very fancy-looking Florentines.

"I see you've all been busy with your family trees," she said, raising her eyebrows at all the boards in the room. "Would anyone like to volunteer to show theirs first?"

Lottie looked down, desperately trying to avoid eye contact, but luckily Binah's hand had already shot up.

"Excellent, Miss Fae. Please come forward."

Binah's yellow head-of-year sash swayed as she took her place at the front of the semicircle of desks.

With a nod from the professor, Binah began to address the class. "Neither of my parents come from any form of nobility," she said. "My mother came from a large family in Kenya where most of the women became nurses. My father was from a long line of carpenters in Korea dating back to the 1800s." She pointed to a drawing of a Korean man at the top of the board.

Lottie stared at the beautifully drawn lines that led to each beaming face. The family resemblance was uncanny, particularly between Binah and her mother's Kenyan family. The huge comforting smiles mirrored the one she already knew so well. Looking at Binah's sprawling chart, Lottie realized to her own shame that she was jealous, an emotion that was very unprincessy.

But you're not really a princess, a voice in her head hissed.

"My parents met at a medical research facility in London, where they teamed up to discover and develop anti-TNF therapy, which has revolutionized the treatment of autoimmune disorders."

One of the Stratus boys across the room started clapping. Binah nodded at him in thanks before continuing to go down the line of her family, explaining all the names and occupations of family members, until every smiling face had been accounted for.

"Lovely, Binah. You've shown a thorough understanding of both your family history and the intricacies of legacy."

Binah took her seat, and the professor turned back to the class, her gaze coming to rest on Lottie.

Showtime.

Clearing her throat, Lottie picked up her own board and took her place at the front of the class. A thick lump of dread rested in her chest.

"Good morning," Lottie began, trying not to sound too nervous and reminding herself that she was meant to be a princess.

Be brave.

"I think most people at Rosewood are aware that Lottie Pumpkin is a faux name used to hide my identity as princess of Maradova. I thank everyone for continuing to respect my privacy."

The words left her mouth easily enough, but that strange feeling of displacement swirled inside her belly again. Murky-water images emerged in her head: her mother, father, Henry Pitkin. The origins of Lottie Pumpkin. She shouldn't have brought up the ghosts of her past—asking questions, digging into diaries. What had she been thinking?

I was born Charlotte Edith Curran-Pitkin, of no notable nobility. Her real family history unfolded inside her head, as though someone were whispering to her. But she couldn't let that distract her.

"My family tree spans back over six hundred years," she intoned, regurgitating the speech she'd rehearsed. "Generations of Wolfsons, stretching all the way back to Alexis Wolfson, who seized the throne from Roanov rule."

Pitkin was an old English name that we had to lose because my father tarnished it forever.

"My father, Alexander, the current ruler of Maradova, inherited the throne when he was twenty-four after my uncle rejected his role and left the kingdom."

My mother was a baker who ran a patisserie, and my

father was a gambler who lost all our money and had to leave the country.

Every sentence was like pressing on a bruise.

I shouldn't have made that wish; I shouldn't have made that wish.

"He married Swedish noble Matilde Hedin and they had one child—me."

Pumpkin is a silly name that a silly little princess-obsessed girl came up with when they had to run away to avoid the debts of her father.

"The Wolfson name bears a heavy burden. The name is symbolic of the wolf, loyal and fierce and forever devoted to the pack."

My mother died when I was nine, and my father returned with a new wife to look after me. Then he left again.

"The royal family of Maradova takes tradition very seriously, committed to keeping the line pure and strong."

I am the only Pumpkin left in the whole world.

Jamie was right. Family was hard. No matter how far you ran away from a bad feeling, you always took it with you.

"May I please sit down now?" Lottie asked faintly. The swirling feeling in her head made her worried she might not be able to stand up.

"Yes, of course." The professor gestured for her to take a Florentine on her way back to her seat. "Thank you for that brief Maravish royal history lesson. Very helpful indeed."

Lottie helped herself to a rosebud china teacup and some rose tea, allowing the pungent fragrance to wash over her and soothe her mind. It was difficult to concentrate on everyone else's family trees. It was difficult to concentrate on anything at all. How could she possibly expect to take on Leviathan or help anyone when she was being haunted by her own demons? She was useless like this. She couldn't avoid it anymore; she knew what she had to do.

The class came to an end and Lottie stayed in her seat, waiting for everyone else to wander out. She gave Binah a look, silently willing her to stay. Binah got the hint and took a long time packing her bag. Finally they were alone.

"Is something the matter, Lottie? Your eyebrows are more furrowed than usual."

"Binah," Lottie began, taking a deep breath, "we need your help."

A grin broke out on her friend's face, and she shifted her yellow-lined cloak to one side to place a reassuring hand on Lottie's shoulder. "I thought you'd never ask."

19

SURROUNDED BY A COLLECTION OF glass bottles brimming with colorful liquids and powders, the Bunsen burner flickered. Ellie, Lottie, and Binah were gathered around a table, each of them wearing an oversize white lab coat, the flame from the burner reflected in their protective goggles. Lottie was painfully aware of how silly they all looked.

She'd explained to Binah all her worries about the chocolate—that she thought it was responsible for the strange symptoms that had afflicted Horace and Beatrice. Binah hadn't questioned her logic at all, but instead had immediately suggested tests.

"If you need anything else, Binah, do let me know." Professor Duran carefully adjusted the wire gauze tripod above the Bunsen burner's flame. "I'm always happy to feed the curious minds of my best students."

"Thank you, Professor." Binah beamed at him. "Anything to help a fellow student."

Professor Duran was a balding man with thick spectacles and a contagious enthusiasm for science. Binah was clearly his favorite. She'd used that to persuade him to let them use the lab under the guise of tutoring the princess of Maradova, something he was more than happy to allow.

"Yes, thank you, Professor. My parents will be ecstatic to know I'm receiving extra tutoring." Lottie attempted one of Binah's knowledge-hungry grins, and Professor Duran's face shone with delight.

"Let your curiosity guide you," he said before leaving the three girls to their experiment.

As soon as the door was firmly shut behind him, a serious expression fell across Binah's features—though Lottie had to admit she still looked a little funny wearing the goggles on top of her glasses.

"Why is Binah so willing to help when she doesn't even know what's going on?" Ellie whispered in Lottie's ear. Binah didn't hear—she was concentrating on taking precise measurements, the tip of her tongue poking out of her mouth.

"I don't know," Lottie whispered back. "But let's just be thankful she's helping at all."

Ellie pulled a face as she peered over Binah's shoulder, and Lottie had to kick her shin to stop her from saying something. Ellie had been less than thrilled by the idea of asking Binah for help. Usually Lottie would agree that they shouldn't drag anyone else into their messes, but she'd promised herself she'd stay vigilant, and all these stories of ghosts and missing princesses were keeping her from concentrating. She needed help, and Binah had been happy to get involved.

"I see, I see." Binah squinted as she poured a small amount of pink powder over the melted chocolate. The powder stank of rotting fish guts. "That's peculiar."

"What is it?" Even Ellie leaned in to see.

"Well." Binah straightened up so quickly she almost knocked into the two of them. "The chocolate itself is completely normal, but it appears to be covered in a thin coating. Look." She sprinkled more of the pink powder, and Lottie watched as a glistening liquid with an intense smell shimmered across the chocolate before evaporating in a puff of smoke. Lottie knew that smell—she'd smelled it out in the fields when Horace had had his screaming fit and in the library cafe when Beatrice had danced maniacally on the table.

She knew the smell, but she didn't know what the substance was. Binah sprinkled more powder onto another section of chocolate, and the coating gleamed with a toxic rainbow of colors, like a dirty oil spill.

"Whatever it is, it's certainly not supposed to be in a chocolate bar," Binah stated, pulling her hair back into a tighter ponytail.

"Gross!" Ellie's nose wrinkled up, and she covered her face with her hand. "It smells horrible."

"Are you sure it's safe to inhale?" Lottie suddenly asked, panicking that they might have all exposed themselves.

"Quite safe," Binah replied, switching off the Bunsen burner. "Do you recognize it?"

Lottie gulped. She hated to involve Lola and Micky when they were going through so much, but it was undeniable that the smell was similar to their own baby-powder scent.

"Yes," Lottie said reluctantly. "It smells like a poisonous Lola and Micky."

Binah chuckled, reaching over to grab the rest of the chocolate bar. "That's quite a poetic description, Lottie."

Lottie blushed.

"But I have a theory," Binah continued, "that you might be missing something."

"What do you mean?" Lottie asked.

"The symptoms, and the smell—I wonder if there's something they're even more similar to." Binah pushed her goggles up, light glinting off the protective lenses. "Maybe something you're choosing not to remember?"

"I . . ." Lottie was about to say she had no idea what Binah was talking about when she caught another whiff of the chocolate. A niggling memory pushed at the corners of her mind. She remembered the way Beatrice had swayed on the table in the library, the way Ellie had raced to save her, and the person who had held back. The person who usually never faltered at anything.

"Jamie." Lottie's answer emerged in a low whisper.

It was the same smell that had been on Jamie's breath the night he'd passed out into the Conch House pool. The memory flooded back to her suddenly. A group of them had stayed at Rosewood over the Christmas break and had gone to a New Year's Eve party at Conch House. She remembered how hazily Jamie had been behaving and how she'd thought his drink might have been spiked—but there was also that strange sweet smell on his breath just before he'd fainted into her arms, plunging them both into the freezing water.

Binah looked up sharply from the Bunsen burner. "Is it the same?"

A low growl caught their attention, and they turned to see Ellie drumming her fingers on the table. Her eyes sparked.

"What are you two talking about?" she erupted, slamming her hand down hard and making all the bottles—and Lottie—jump.

Binah seemed completely unfazed by the outburst, but Lottie felt her heart beating wildly.

"My apologies," Binah replied calmly. "I have a terrible habit of getting carried away. Maybe it's time for an explanation."

"Yes, please, Binah," Lottie said quickly, trying to defuse

the situation. "I think Ellie and I are both a bit confused."

Binah nodded, her ponytail bouncing. She slowly took her goggles off to clean them on her lab coat as she began. "Last year, after I found out what happened to Jamie over New Year's, I simply couldn't accept that there wasn't any explanation. So I snuck into the nurse's office one night to find the file."

"You snuck in?" Ellie choked. Binah was normally such a perfect student!

"Well, of course! How else would I be able to get my hands on the file? I'm sure the two of you are perfectly acquainted with such nefarious but necessary activities."

Ellie and Lottie gulped in unison, remembering how they'd stolen into the library after curfew at the start of last year.

Binah continued to talk. "There was nothing particularly noteworthy. A file that detailed his pallid skin, a sweet smell on his breath, and incoherent speech . . . All strange, but nothing that helped me work out what had happened. That is, until the incident with Horace on the field." She paused, giving Ellie and Lottie a moment to take in her words. The room seemed to glow with the light in her eyes.

"I recognized it instantly. I've become very good at picking up on patterns and symptoms from watching my parents work."

Lottie thought about how Binah had watched everyone so closely on the field during the fireworks.

"However, it wasn't until you presented this chocolate theory that I had a lead. Very good job, Lottie. I'm so impressed."

Binah beamed at her with a dazzling smile that would usually have made Lottie blush with pride, but instead a resignation settled in her stomach. Lottie turned to Ellie; from the look on her face she knew she'd come to the same conclusion.

If the secret ingredient in the chocolate was the same poison that had affected Jamie, it meant that their worst fears were confirmed. It meant that the chocolate had something to do with Leviathan.

"And we have no idea what this secret ingredient is?" Lottie asked.

"Well . . ." Binah snapped off another square of chocolate and placed it in a petri dish. Then she gestured to Ellie to pass her a pot of dark yellow liquid from the other end of the table. "There's one thing we could try, but we'll have to be very, very delicate when—ELLIE, STOP!"

But it was too late. Ellie was already pouring the liquid over the chocolate. The whole dish began fizzing, huge bubbles appearing on the surface. Two distinct channels of liquid formed, hissing and popping as if they had turned into live snakes.

"Oops!" Ellie said, taking a step back.

"This is . . ." Binah shoved her goggles back on with lightning speed, leaning forward to watch the strange chemical serpent dance in the dish. "This is not what I expected at all."

"Looks to me like a double displacement chemical reaction, but combustible?"

Lottie nodded along to Ellie's words, trying to remember as much chemistry as she could.

Binah whispered something, as if she were nervous to say it out loud. "Give me one second." She stood up quickly and grabbed her bag off the floor.

"So do you know what it is?" Ellie asked, covering her nose from the smell.

Ignoring Ellie, Binah pulled out a tattered book with a faded title and opened it to the page she needed. The book was filled with scary pictures of people in gas masks and words like "toxic" and "fatal."

"Here!" Binah exclaimed, her voice coming out in a squeak of excitement. "It's called the Hamelin Formula, a mix of chemicals including sucratine and intoxico-tin." Binah was grinning now, thrilled by the discovery. "It's notorious for its use in brainwashing techniques. It's intended to put the subject into a state of sleepy delirium in which they will do anything they are told."

"After the Pied Piper of Hamelin?" Lottie asked,

catching some of Binah's excitement.

"Yes, exactly that! But what's fascinating is that the lead researcher, Hanz Thumann, never completed the formula; it was always a theoretical idea. The Germans attempted to finalize a version of it during the Second World War, but all the information was lost, and no one has attempted to re-create the formula since, what with it being so terribly illegal." She seemed to be smiling to herself, but Lottie couldn't find any humor in it.

"It sounds like a magic potion," Lottie breathed. *"Bubble, bubble, toil and trouble . . ."*

"So what on earth are remnants of it doing in a bar of Tompkins chocolate?" Ellie asked.

The severity of the situation was dawning on Lottie. When she had connected the smell to Lola and Micky Tompkins she had never imagined a conspiracy as big as brainwashing. This whole time she'd been sure that with enough training she could take on Leviathan, but now all she felt was afraid.

Be unstoppable! she told herself.

She put on her bravest smile. She could not let Ellie know how scared she was.

"We'll get to the bottom of this," she told the others, her voice shaking.

Ellie's features softened. "Lottie—"

"Right!" Binah interrupted. "The next logical step is to

put all our information together." She seemed so sure, so unaffected by their discovery. Binah's composure and confidence made Lottie feel a little better.

Binah began casually packing her stuff. "First, I need you to tell me exactly what happened to Saskia San Martin and everything you know about Leviathan."

Time slowed down as Lottie registered what Binah had just said.

Saskia? Leviathan? How did she . . . ?

Ellie and Lottie stared at her, mouths gaping, as she threw her backpack over her shoulder. All this time they'd wondered what Binah knew, if anything. And now they had their answer.

She knew everything.

20

JAMIE'S LEFT HAND FIDDLED WITH his wolf pendant absent-mindedly, the metal feeling cool to his touch. He stared at his copy of *Hamlet*, detached from the words, which blurred into unreadable symbols in front of him. A low moan escaped his lips as he realized, once again, he'd read an entire monologue without taking in a single word.

This was completely unacceptable.

He could see that Lottie was getting distracted, but he couldn't allow her to pull him down with her. He needed to be the strong one; he needed to bring her back up. Yet here he was, the book of Pakistani history that Lottie had given him burning a hole in the pocket of his bag. He knew he should have thrown it away, but something stopped him every time, something that begged him to pull it out and discover a missing puzzle piece.

"This above all: to thine own self be true." Raphael's charming twang pulled Jamie out of his thoughts. "What exactly does Polonius mean when he says that?"

Jamie briefly felt as if his mind had just been probed, but he quickly shook it off.

Electives had ended twenty minutes ago, but Jamie had promised Raphael that he'd help him with his *Hamlet* lines for their Shakespeare studies elective.

The Rosewood Hall theater was their preferred spot to practice lines. It was at the center of the school grounds, a robust dome with grand arches and ancient mahogany walls proudly displaying the creative achievements of previous students. The performance space had a dramatic look, with its dark-wood stage and tiered red-velvet chairs. Every word echoed in the theater, ringing against the walls and becoming trapped in every crack.

"He means what he says," Jamie replied simply, closing his own text with relief at the welcome distraction. "He is telling his son that the most important thing a person can do is be true to themselves."

Tight-lipped concentration overtook Raphael's face as he messily jotted down Jamie's words next to the line in his book.

Instead of going back to his own text, as he knew he should, Jamie took a moment to check on his fellow Shakespeare studies classmate.

Percy Butter sat curled up in one of the plush red velvet seats, melting into the soft fabric that seemed extra bright against his gloomy, tired face. He was clearly struggling to stay awake in the dimly lit theater, the siren call of slumber enticing him as Jamie watched him blink in and out of consciousness. He leaned forward then jerked awake repeatedly in a way that would have been funny to most observers, but Jamie knew there was more to his permanent exhaustion than simply a lack of sleep.

Jamie tapped Percy on the shoulder to get his attention and pull him out of his sleepy pattern. *"You need to talk to someone about your sleepwalking,"* he signed.

Percy looked up at him, blinking himself awake. *"It's fine,"* he replied.

"It's not fine. It's making you tired and it's waking me up every night."

Percy gulped sheepishly. Jamie felt bad about this, but he knew the best thing for him would be to talk to his counselor.

"I understand you'd rather not think about what happened, but you can't keep pretending you're okay."

Jamie felt his hands hesitate as he signed, his mind wandering to Lottie as memories surfaced, memories he wanted to bury. Her cherry-stained cheeks burned by the frost, facing danger she should never have been exposed to, that she should never have had to deal with. The memory was so clear it felt tangible, the cold from that horrible night creeping into his skin.

Percy looked wounded at his words.

"I'm not pretending. Maybe you should start taking your own advice," Percy signed furiously before grabbing his

books and storming out of the theater.

Jamie sighed deeply. This was exactly why he hadn't wanted a roommate. It shouldn't matter if he had any friends at Rosewood; he wasn't here to make friends. His eyes wandered to Raphael, who was still determinedly jotting down notes in his copy of *Hamlet*, mouthing the lines as he went over them. But as much as Jamie tried to tell himself that the only thing that mattered was his obligation as a Partizan, seeing the hurt on Percy's face and the value that Raphael placed on his help made him realize what he'd always been missing: companionship.

A memory flashed in his mind.

"Join us."

Saskia, reaching her hand out to him in her last desperate attempt to escape. Making him wonder . . .

No! Jamie shook his head, dismissing that memory. *What is this school doing to me?*

"Jamie!" The voice of his princess flooded his ears, snapping him out of his thoughts. "Hey! Jamie, are you in here?"

Ellie's voice echoed through the theater, as demanding as always.

"We're in here," Jamie called as Raphael looked up, but the troupe that entered stage left was not quite what either of them was expecting.

Ellie and Lottie walked in side by side with Binah trailing

behind them, her oversize book bag bouncing along with her curls. Binah seemed completely oblivious, but he saw Ellie and Lottie share a concerned look, and he instantly sensed something was off.

"What happened?" Jamie asked.

Both his princess and her Portman glanced at Raphael before exchanging another look. Something was definitely going on, and clearly Raphael could not be present for it.

"The pumpkin princess and her savage sidekick." Raphael smirked, not picking up on any tension. "What gives us the honor?"

Ellie responded by sticking her tongue out, which made him laugh more.

"Raphael, I think you may need to leave," Jamie said bluntly.

A weak chuckle escaped Raphael's lips, but then he took in Jamie's expression. "But you promised you'd help me with my *Hamlet* lines," he said indignantly.

Ellie shook her head at Jamie, making it clear that this was serious.

"Well, this takes priority." Jamie's tone was stony.

Raphael's cocky confidence was momentarily broken by a look of genuine hurt, but unlike Percy he quickly put his mask back on and turned to Binah. "So everyone's involved?" he demanded. "Everyone's keeping secrets. First Anastacia, and now all of you."

"Raphael, we're sorry, it's just—" Lottie looked genuinely upset by his outburst, always so desperate to avoid any conflict.

"Whatever." Raphael grabbed his belongings and stormed out of the theater, pausing briefly by Binah, who shrugged at him as if nothing particularly noteworthy had happened.

The side door slammed shut.

It had to be done, Jamie told himself. He couldn't put anyone's feelings above his princess's safety, no matter how difficult it was. As soon as Raphael's footsteps faded behind the door, Jamie turned to the three girls with a long-suffering sigh.

"This had better be good."

"So let me get this straight." Jamie tried to remain calm, but the atmosphere in the backstage greenroom was tense. The loud floral patterns on the walls and the pungent dusty air did nothing to help the claustrophobic feel. He stared at Binah. "You know about Saskia being a rogue Partizan?"

Binah nodded. "Correct."

"And you know about Leviathan?"

"Correct," she repeated, gazing steadily at him.

"And you think they might have something to do with Horace and Beatrice being poisoned?"

"Again, correct," replied Binah.

"And you are somehow aware of the undercover-princess situation?" Jamie's eyes flicked to Lottie as he spoke.

Binah removed her glasses to rub the lenses as she confirmed one of Jamie's greatest fears. "Correct."

A brief moment of darkness consumed him. He blinked slowly, trying to make sense of how this girl could know so much . . . and exactly what he should do about it.

There were plans in place for the discovery of the Portman arrangement between Ellie and Lottie—but this situation was clearly more complicated than a simple gag order could address.

A long breath escaped from Jamie, and he turned to his princess, eyes narrowing. "Exactly how long have you two been aware that Binah knows?"

The looks on Lottie's and Ellie's faces were answer enough. He couldn't help the low growl that crawled out of his throat.

"It's not that simple!" Lottie interrupted before he had time to chastise them. "We weren't certain. We just thought she *might* know . . ." Her voice trailed off at Jamie's harsh expression.

"And we only thought she might know that I was really the princess," Ellie added, stepping protectively in front of Lottie. "We had no idea she knew about Saskia or Leviathan or any of that stuff."

"I thought I made it quite clear that I knew you were

undercover," Binah interjected. "Hmm, maybe the William Tufty puzzle wasn't obvious enough," she added, muttering to herself.

"You should have told me," Jamie barked. It was impossible to mask his frustration at Ellie and Lottie. They should both have known better after everything that had happened.

"Told you what?" replied Ellie, anger vising in her voice. "That maybe, possibly our friend knew about our secret?"

"Exactly."

Ellie was unable to hide her own frustration. "So let me get this straight," she said, folding her arms. "We're in the wrong because we didn't tell you about something we didn't know about that may or may not have been happening."

But Jamie wasn't listening. He paced up and down as he spat his words out. "That's not the point. You and Lottie are constantly—"

She cut him off. "Lottie is never anything but loyal to me."

Jamie stopped his pacing and glared at them. "Maybe that's the problem."

"What?" Lottie spluttered.

But Jamie couldn't stop the words spilling out of him. "Maybe you both need to be more loyal to your roles and stop being so childishly concerned with each other." The two girls looked so shocked that neither of them could look at him. This made him irrationally annoyed.

Lottie finally spoke up, her words like a thorny stem squeezing his chest. "Jamie, that's an awful thing to say."

Now it was his turn to look away.

"Um . . ."

All three of them turned to Binah, who was carefully putting her glasses back on.

"Nothing in life is to be feared; it is only to be understood. Now is the time to understand more, so that we may fear less," she said matter-of-factly.

They all stared at her in bemusement.

"What . . . ?" Jamie began to ask.

"It's a quote from Marie Curie," she explained. She gave a smile and the tension in the room lifted ever so slightly. "I think, possibly, you're all a bit scared. And it's making you angry, and you're not sure where to direct that anger, so you're directing it at each other."

Jamie sighed deeply. Binah was right; this wasn't helping. What he needed to do was make sure nothing like this happened again.

"How do you know all this, Binah?" he asked.

Binah paused, considering her answer.

"Actually, I was wondering that myself." Ellie's hand rested on her hip as she turned to Binah.

Binah pursed her lips thoughtfully. "We used to be best

friends," she began in a quiet voice. A shadow of sadness passed over her face, but she quickly recovered. "That is, Saskia, Anastacia, Raphael, and myself. We were best friends all through our first years at Rosewood together."

Everything turned quiet, the dusty velvet texture of the room soaking up Binah's words as she told her story.

"Things were wonderful until the year before you all joined, but then Saskia became distant and secretive. I could see it was hurting Anastacia, but Raphael was oblivious." Her brow furrowed as she remembered. "It was them—Leviathan. They took advantage of the tension between Saskia and Anastacia. They seduced Saskia with the promise of money and freedom from her conservative parents."

The twisting snake of Binah's story curled through the air. Jamie could see Ellie squirm at the thought of a Partizan's betrayal. She turned to him, their eyes locking like magnets as her hands curled into fists at her sides. He shook his head slowly, willing her to trust him, to trust that he would always stay true to his Partizan duties.

Lottie stepped forward, coming between Jamie and Ellie. She looked from one to the other.

Does Lottie know what we're thinking? He quickly shook the thought from his mind, not wanting Lottie to distract him again. "So Leviathan is recruiting Partizans?" he asked.

"I believe that is part of their plan."

"And how do you . . . how did you find this out?"

A mischievous smile curled onto Binah's lips. "Why, I heard it in the tunnels, of course."

"I KNEW IT!" Lottie cried excitedly, then quickly covered her mouth when she saw Jamie's horrified face. "Sorry, I mean . . . the tunnels. I knew there had to be more tunnels."

"Tunnels?" It took all Jamie's willpower not to explode. *Is there anything these girls aren't keeping secret from me?*

"Like the tunnel you found that led us to the library?" Ellie asked Lottie casually.

Jamie was sure his eyes were about to bulge out of their sockets.

"There are underground tunnels and rooms all over the school grounds; I've barely explored half of them, but I know there must be more." Binah was almost giddy as she spoke, excited to have others to share her discoveries with. "William Tufty was a very secretive person. I can only imagine he had them built for a reason."

Lottie nodded, turning thoughtful. "Sometimes it feels like the school"—she hesitated, but plunged on—"it feels like the school is trying to guide you."

"Maybe it is," Binah replied, a twinkle glittering in her eyes.

"So you can hear people's conversations in these tunnels?" Jamie quickly cut them off, not wanting to get caught up in silly talk about the school's supernatural spirit.

"Oh yes," said Binah. "There's a brilliant tunnel by the art-supply cupboard near Stratus Side. Some of the secrets I've discovered while studying in there have been quite scandalous, if I do say so myself."

A tiny squeak escaped Lottie's lips at this information, and they all turned to her.

"You've been in that tunnel," Jamie said. From the look on Lottie's face he already knew the answer. "And you could hear people's conversations?"

"Well, actually, that's how I found out that everyone thought I was the princess." Lottie tried her best to smile, but Jamie didn't think there was anything worth smiling about.

He rubbed his forehead, half-frustrated and half-impressed. "This is all completely insane," he grumbled. He looked at the three girls. Ellie still seemed unsure, Binah was clearly excited, and Lottie was, as usual, determined. "However, the information you've acquired from the secret corridors could give us a distinct advantage over Leviathan." He took a deep breath, not quite believing what he was about to say. He turned his gaze on Binah. "We'd be glad to have your help."

Ellie erupted in a spluttered laugh of surprise.

"Excellent!" Binah proclaimed, stepping into the center of the room. "Now, with that out of the way, let's figure out how and why Leviathan are poisoning everyone with their copycat version of the Hamelin Formula."

Lottie hesitated, chewing her bottom lip in concentration. "How do we do that?" she asked.

There was only a moment's pause as Binah tapped her chin thoughtfully. "Well, first we need to keep a lookout for any more incidents and see if there's a pattern, and I think it's pretty obvious where we should start."

The royal trio stared at each other, stumped.

Jamie rolled his eyes, resenting having to take the bait. "No, Binah, please, tell us," he said in a dry tone.

Binah ignored the jibe. "The Halloween party's in five days' time," she told them. "Lots of food. Cotton candy, toffee apples, chocolate, that kind of thing . . ."

Jamie understood instantly. "Food that could be poisoned."

❦ 21 ❦

"YOU HAVE GOT TO BE kidding me."

Lottie couldn't believe it. She gazed at her reflection in their bathroom mirror. All her worst nightmares had come true.

She had been turned into a real pumpkin.

"You look adorable!" Ellie cackled from the doorway, looking effortlessly cool in her pirate outfit, complete with a plastic sword and fake hook.

It was the night of Halloween, and everyone at Rosewood Hall was getting ready for the party. Lottie's nerves were already strung tight from the Leviathan poison conspiracy; a school littered with creepily realistic skeletons, cobwebs, bats, and spiders was doing nothing to help.

Stupid pumpkins. Right now, she didn't need these reminders of her family. She had an important job to do tonight! It also didn't help that her outfit was ridiculous.

"Why do I have to be a pumpkin? This is discrimination," Lottie moaned, hardly able to lift her arms from beneath the inflated orange suit.

"Binah made these costumes especially for us, and I, for one, think they're great." Ellie stepped into the tiled bathroom, sauntering as if she were a real pirate captain.

"Well, of course you think they're great. You look amazing!"

"You look amazing too." She came to stand behind Lottie as they gazed at themselves in the mirror, the height difference accentuated by Ellie's heeled black boots.

"No, I don't. I look like a pumpkin."

"A cute pumpkin." Ellie grinned, resting her chin on Lottie's shoulder. Lottie pouted, her cheeks and hair matching her puffy outfit. "Besides," Ellie continued, raising an eyebrow, "since when does the ever-humble Lottie Pumpkin complain about a gift?"

Lottie froze. She hadn't even considered how rude she was being. Binah had made these outfits especially for them, and all she could think about was herself. That was certainly not princess behavior, and if she wasn't careful she'd end up becoming a cautionary tale about selfishness.

Kind, brave, and unstoppable, she thought, reminding herself of her mantra. She sucked in a deep breath, staring down her reflection in the mirror.

"A cute pumpkin?" she repeated, forcing herself to see what Ellie saw.

Ellie grinned. "The cutest."

Binah was waiting for them outside the Ivy gate, dressed as a flower fairy with a set of wings that quite literally glowed. Delicate patterns of colorful neon paint had been spread across the sheer fabric with glitter at the edges; it looked as if she were scattering fairy dust. Her dress was covered in hundreds of petals. Her hair was piled up on her head, tiny flowers and gems threaded between the dark curls. She beamed at them, her white teeth glowing along with her costume, and Lottie was struck by how completely natural it felt to see Binah dressed as a fairy.

"You two look perfect!" Binah clapped her hands together.

"Arrr! Why, thank you, madam. Now, let us young rapscallions away to dance a merry jig." Ellie tipped her tricorn hat at Binah before drawing Lottie into a one-armed hug as best she could around the pumpkin costume.

It felt good to have Binah with them, and it was a relief to have another person know about the Portman arrangement. It made Lottie's heart glow to see Ellie make another friend who knew her secrets outside the palace.

They made their way to the main hall, which overlooked the rose garden. The roses on the path drooped sleepily, but the thorns' points glistened, sharp. Dry ice flooded around them as they approached the building, red and green lights streaming out of the doors and music echoing around them. Two girls dressed as undead Rosewood students welcomed them. Lottie gave them a faint half smile. One of them grinned at her, and she realized it was Sunny, the sleepy girl from the Stratus library, almost impossible to recognize with all the scary makeup.

"Clever costume," Sunny said, smiling.

"Thanks. My friend made it." Lottie gestured to Binah, who proudly nodded. "Guys, this is Sunny. She, um, helped me with that biology study. Remember?" She widened her eyes at Ellie and Binah, hoping they'd get the hint.

"That's great!" Binah exclaimed without missing a beat.

"So," Sunny began, grinning, "did you see any ghosts?"

"Excuse me?" Lottie nearly choked at the question, and Binah and Ellie looked equally confused.

"You know, the statue of Elwin? Did you see a ghost?"

"You patted the merlin bird?" Binah asked, clearly familiar with the Stratus superstition. Ellie, on the other hand, looked completely lost. "What did you wish for?"

"I didn't. Nothing happened." Lottie licked her lips nervously. She hadn't told the others about wishing for a family, because how could she? A family wouldn't help her in her role as Portman.

Ellie raised an eyebrow slowly, noting Lottie's discomfort. "I want a toffee apple!" she suddenly exclaimed, and marched Lottie inside, with Binah trailing behind them.

Lottie knew that Ellie was shifting the attention away

from her, and she felt a wave of gratitude. "See you later, Sunny!" she called back.

The hall was packed with Rosewood students in terrifying, intricate outfits dancing wildly to pop music. Lottie wanted to join them, but she couldn't shake the spooky feeling the whole night was giving her. Ellie grabbed a toffee apple from a table—impressive, when she only had a hook instead of a hand—and surveyed the room.

"Everyone will be stuffing their faces with sweets tonight, so we need to be on the lookout for any symptoms of the Leviathan poison," Ellie said, preparing to take a huge bite out of her apple.

"Then maybe we should avoid eating any of the food ourselves, Ellie," Lottie chided, pinching the apple from Ellie's hook, leaving her mouth wide open.

"But if your theory's correct, then it should only be Tompkins chocolate that's the problem." Ellie reached for the apple again, but this time Binah stopped her.

"I don't think we should risk it."

Ellie let out a little huff but didn't try again.

As far as Lottie was concerned, apples were not to be trusted.

They looked out over the crowd and spotted a few familiar faces. Professor Devine, Dame Bolter, and Ms. Kuma were all dressed as witches, each sporting a pointed hat the color of her house. Anastacia was dancing with some fellow

Conch girls, who were all dressed as different classic Hollywood celebrities. Lottie felt relieved to see her enjoying herself. Raphael was looking both dashing and hilarious in a T-Bird outfit from *Grease* with his hair slicked back in a pompadour, and Lottie's heart nearly skipped a beat when she saw both Jamie and Percy dressed the same way. She highly doubted it had been either of their ideas, but she couldn't help thinking that Jamie looked great in a leather jacket. His eyes met hers and she was sure his smirk was because of her pumpkin getup.

Confound this ridiculous costume, she thought. A tomato would have been a better fit with the color her cheeks turned.

His gaze drifted past Lottie to Ellie, who waved at him enthusiastically with her pirate hook. He gave Lottie a curt nod before turning back to Raphael and Percy. She recognized the gesture: his way of telling her to stay focused.

As he moved, a glittering object at his chest reflected the red disco light, catching her eye and causing her hand to move instinctively to her own wolf pendant. Sunny's words pinged into her mind. *"Did you see a ghost?"*

How was she supposed to stay focused with these ghost stories following her around?

"Lottie, what's the matter?" Binah asked, scrutinizing the buffet.

"Nothing," Lottie replied quickly. Too quickly, apparently, because the girls shared a look that suggested they didn't believe her for a minute.

Ellie stepped in front of her, cutting off Lottie's view of Jamie. "Is this about what that Sunny said?" she asked.

"I didn't see any ghosts!" Lottie said defensively.

Ellie smirked, and Lottie realized that she'd been caught in a trap.

"Ghosts?" Binah asked, looking up from a piece of popcorn that she was now inspecting.

Her two friends stood watching her, the whites of their eyes glowing in the neon lights. Lottie took a deep breath, knowing she couldn't avoid this conversation any more.

"Okay, look. I did make a wish at the Elwin statue." Lottie sighed, feeling embarrassed. "And, ever since, I've felt as though I'm being haunted by a ghost or something." Ellie tried to interject, but Lottie rushed on. "I made a wish about family because I've been feeling like my tiara was trying to tell me something, and after seeing Liliana with the same tiara and realizing I don't know anything about my ancestors, especially Henry Pitkin . . ." Lottie paused, looking at Ellie's bewildered expression. "This all sounds really stupid, doesn't it?"

Ellie blinked at her, not even trying to hide her confusion. "You think you're being haunted by Liliana?"

A thorough throat clearing from Binah drew their attention. "I think what Lottie's saying is that she feels haunted by a disconnect to her family," Binah explained calmly.

Lottie noticed Ellie's glance flicker to her wolf pendant, and a wave of guilt swamped her. The whole reason she hadn't wanted to tell Ellie about these weird feelings was because of the pendant. As far as Ellie was concerned, Lottie was part of the Wolfsons, and Lottie didn't want her feeling like she was ungrateful.

"Lottie, is that true?" Ellie asked, all her usual bravado slipping away.

"Family is hard." Lottie repeated Jamie's words, knowing it would be too difficult to explain her feelings in her own words. Ellie was the opposite of her; she had an almost *too* intense connection to her family. She just couldn't understand.

"Well." Binah pushed her glasses up her nose. Lottie could see a plan forming behind her eyes. "We could try to contact your family, if you were so inclined."

"With all due respect, Binah, anyone in my family who I'd want to speak to has long passed."

That mischievous grin appeared again on Binah's face. "It's Samhain," she said. "October the thirty-first is a day of liminality, a time when the fabric separating our world and the other world is weaker."

"Binah, what are you saying?" Lottie asked.

"What I'm saying is . . ." The glitter on her wings sparkled as she flicked her hair back over her shoulder. "Have you girls ever performed a séance?"

22

BINAH STRUCK A MATCH AND touched the golden flame to the wick of a thick yellow candle. Light filled the room as she placed the candlestick on a wooden desk.

Lottie had tried to argue that they should stay at the party and look for signs of Leviathan poison, but Binah had been determined.

"If we don't do it now, we'll never have another chance!" she'd said. "And, besides, I've inspected the table. There's no Tompkins chocolate to be seen."

Ellie had agreed. "We can go back to the party once this is done. Lottie, let us help you. We'll still be close enough to hear any commotion." And between them they'd dragged her out, Lottie only half protesting.

Binah had led the way up the eerily silent path toward Stratus Side. It was only rarely that Lottie and Ellie got to visit the Stratus dormitory, and this was the first time either of them had seen Binah's room. It was not at all what they had expected.

Everyone knew that Binah liked to study; Lottie had just never expected to see the evidence laid out so obviously.

The floor was covered with books and papers, save for a low circular table surrounded by scattered cushions on varnished floorboards. Any surface that wasn't covered in reading material was occupied by plants that were flourishing, their tendrils dangling over the windowsills and surfaces. Lottie felt like she'd entered either a library or a greenhouse—or both.

Now they huddled in the center of the room, sitting on the cushions at the low table, their costumes feeling very out of place indeed.

"First, we need to light some sage," Binah said matter-of-factly, easing open a drawer by her bed and reaching deep within to pull out a bundle tied with string. She lit the end of the stems and began twirling the bunch in the air, letting the heavily scented smoke fill the space.

Then she reached under her bed to reveal a dusty box hidden by the blankets. Its lid was inscribed with the word OUIJA. She carefully blew away the thick layer of dust, and Lottie wondered how long it had been there.

Binah pulled off the lid and lifted out a wooden board that she placed on the table. She settled on a cushion opposite them, and they all stared at the board. A circle of letters ran around the edges of the board, and at the center were the words "Yes," "No," and "Goodbye."

Lottie gave an involuntary shiver. "Is this safe?"

"What could possibly be unsafe about it?" Ellie snorted.

"It's not real." She used the end of her hook to casually pick at a tooth, looking very much like the pirate she was dressed as.

Lottie wanted to agree. She wasn't quite sure what they hoped to achieve here, but she knew better than to question Binah.

"It's perfectly safe," Binah assured her, ignoring Ellie entirely. "All we have to do is rest our fingertips on the planchette and ask one of your ancestors a question. Once we've connected with a family member, they will guide our fingers to the corresponding letters or symbols on the Ouija board to form an answer."

Lottie listened intently as Binah explained the rules.

"Shall we begin?" asked Binah.

Lottie and Ellie shared a look before nodding. Ellie placed two fingertips on the planchette. Binah quickly followed suit, and then they waited for Lottie.

As her fingertips met with the polished wood of the planchette, a jolt of static raced up Lottie's arm, not an unpleasant feeling but certainly intense.

"We would like to connect with a member of Lottie Pumpkin's family," Binah intoned, her voice calm but commanding.

There was a pause of anticipation, and then the room went cold.

An undeniable chill crept into the air, their breath

turning frosty in front of them. Ellie shivered but tried to cover it up with a shrug. Something—or someone—was definitely present.

"Are you related to Lottie Pumpkin?" Binah asked in a respectful tone. None of them dared to breathe for fear of unsettling the room. But there was nothing—no movement, no sound.

"This is silly," Ellie groaned. But as she spoke, Lottie's fingers began to tremble. Lottie knew Ellie felt it too because she froze, her eyes wide as they darted back to the board.

It was a low vibration, the sensation almost tickling them as the planchette slowly began to move under their touch.

Lottie worried that it was their collective excitement pushing the object, but at the same time she didn't care— it was thrilling. She watched, enraptured, as the planchette approached the word "Yes," but then it moved right past it and headed toward the letters above.

"Someone grab a pen and paper," Binah whispered.

Keeping a finger on the planchette, Lottie reached over to the desk and grabbed the stub of a pencil and a sheaf of paper. Not taking her eyes off the board, the tip of her tongue sticking out in concentration, she scribbled sightlessly as their hands moved across the board, from letter to letter.

"*L, A, T, I.*"

They all said the letters out loud, and Lottie noted them down.

"*F, U, L, I.*"

Lottie's eyebrows furrowed. She allowed herself a quick glance at her scrawled notes. It was just nonsense. Ellie looked equally puzzled, but Binah was undeterred, focusing intently on the board.

"*T, Y, M.*"

At that last letter, something curious happened. The planchette quivered over the *M* and then slowly guided their fingers in a clockwise circle around the letter.

A smile erupted on Binah's face. She beamed at Lottie as she gestured to the board with her chin. But Lottie didn't quite understand what had just happened. What was she missing? The letters were all a jumble.

A jumble . . .

The chill in the room vanished as the three girls stared at each other. The vibration in their fingertips disappeared as quickly as it had started. Binah swiftly moved the planchette to the "Goodbye" part of the board, and they were done, just like that.

They crowded around the pad of paper and stared at Lottie's scrawled characters.

The letters swam before her eyes. They didn't make

any sense, but maybe if she rearranged them . . . A picture came into her head of the woman who'd been haunting her.

"Let's see . . ." she whispered. "*L-I-L—*"

Ellie caught on as Lottie wrote the letters in the new order and shouted out, "*I* . . . Lili! Then: *M-A-Y—*"

"*F-U-T-T!*" continued Lottie. "Lili Mayfutt!" She whispered the name, scared to say it out loud.

Why Lili? What does she want?

The room turned hazy as she looked at the jumbled letters again and muttered to herself, "Wait . . . I can see something else . . ."

"What is it, Lottie?" Ellie raised an eyebrow in concern as Lottie resumed her scribbling.

Lottie stopped writing and held up her paper in confusion. "Look—we can also get 'Tufty,' but we're missing the *W* for William."

At that, Binah started. "Lottie, remind me what the Elwin statue superstition is again."

Lottie blinked at her but knew better than to question Binah's instincts. "You pat his head three times, then polish the *W* in the middle of his name and make a wish. If you see the ghost of William Tufty, your wish will come true."

"Funny that the superstition talks of seeing the ghost

of our school's founder, and yet you've been haunted by a wayward princess," Binah mused, packing up the Ouija board and moving to blow out the candle.

The moment the flame vanished, a memory erupted in Lottie's head. She wasn't the only person who'd been haunted by the wrong ghost; so had Francesca Bennington in year twelve. She couldn't believe she'd missed this before. It had been right in front of her nose the whole time.

"*William* Tufty! Of course! The board was telling us to flip the *M*! Oh my God." Lottie's hands flew to her mouth. Suddenly the familiarity of Liliana and the painting of Tufty with that knowing glint in his eye made sense.

"What is it, Lottie?" Ellie asked, her glance darting between the two girls.

"*If ye doth seek to find the truth*"—Lottie recited the words from the poem—"*You will find your wish come true . . .*" The hairs on her arms stood up as she realized the mistake everyone had made. "Binah, it's not your own wish that gets granted; it's the wish to find out the truth about William Tufty."

She didn't even question whether Binah knew the poem. *Binah knows everything.*

Lottie stared at her princess. Her best friend, who was living a dual life, desperate to escape from the trap of her royal duties. Like Liliana Mayfutt—the original owner of

Lottie's tiara. The runaway princess . . . William Tufty's true identity . . . Lottie felt the pieces slotting into place.

"I think we just found out who William Tufty was."

"And," Binah added, snatching up a bag from the floor, "I think I know where they'd been hiding."

❦ 23 ❦

"I KNEW THERE HAD TO be more secret passages." Binah was practically singing as they crept downstairs to the merlin bird statue. But Lottie felt more anxious than excited. The decorative strings of bats and cobwebs made her feel as if they were entering a tomb.

She was doing exactly what Jamie had warned her not to, exactly what she'd told *herself* not to do: distracting everyone with a silly side quest when they should be focusing on the real enemy—Leviathan.

Yet she didn't stop them. The mysterious call from within the school had hold of her, and she knew she wouldn't be free of it until she met it head on.

They approached the bottom of the stairwell, their footsteps echoing. From beyond the door they could hear the faint sound of the Halloween party still in full swing. They came to a halt before Elwin, the symbol of the resourceful, the puzzle solvers, the creative thinkers. It made sense that if you were going to hide your secrets anywhere, you'd hide them with the Stratus students.

Lottie's hands began to tremble as she gazed into the

eyes of the all-knowing bird. He'd been untouched by the Halloween garlands, the students considering it disrespectful to decorate him. But somehow the lack of gaudy decor in the grand echoing room made it far more intimidating than anywhere else in Rosewood. As she stood and stared, the feeling only grew.

She knew it was in her head, a strange ache buzzing away where her tiara would usually sit. It felt like the sensation was coming up from under the floor, vibrating beneath her feet through her body to her crown. And, as if from a distance, she heard a whisper of a melody. She turned to Binah and Ellie, but neither of them seemed to hear anything.

Binah began inspecting the statue, but Lottie found she couldn't follow. Her hand moved to her chest to try to muffle the sound of her heartbeat.

"Hey, little princess," Ellie leaned to whisper in Lottie's ear. "Do you want to hold my hand?" She must have picked up on how Lottie was feeling. There was absolutely no sarcasm in her voice, only that comforting side smile as she offered her free hand to Lottie. "Yes, please." Lottie slipped her hand into Ellie's and felt her courage return.

Be brave.

"Look!" Binah cried, turning to them with a huge grin. Lottie felt Ellie's hand squeeze her own, and they went to where Binah was, near Elwin. "The *W*!" Binah traced the initial in Elwin's name plaque with her finger. "As the Ouija board suggests, it could also be an upside-down *M*. See?"

Lottie could hardly believe it, but if Binah was right—then this had been Lili Mayfutt's hiding place.

"So . . . what do we do?" Ellie asked.

Lottie peered at the initial and pressed her palm against the plaque hoping that something—anything—would happen. Nothing.

Binah drew closer and tried to do the same, but still nothing happened.

"Leave this to me." Ellie pulled her sword out of its holder, a mischievous glint in her eye. Lottie wasn't sure what she was expecting her friend to do with a plastic sword, but then Ellie let out a war cry and began to swipe and slash the sword's blade at the statue over and over, her arm flashing through the air.

"You. Are. Going. To. Open. You. Stupid. Secret. Room!" she roared. Predictably, nothing happened. "Liliana Mayfutt, you open this door right now." Ellie brought the sword down in one final blow.

Click.

Ellie quickly stepped backward, grabbing Lottie's hand again.

"What was that?" Lottie asked, squeezing her friend's fingers. No one said a word as they watched the *W* slowly turn around on the statue, hidden mechanics groaning as the initial swiveled around to become an *M*.

"*M* for Mayfutt!" Binah cried with satisfaction. She was right—she was always right.

There was a grinding noise and the statue of Elwin began to rise up, its wings towering above them as it ascended toward the winding stairs. The statue's eyes glinted as they met the moonlight from the window above, reflecting silver light into the room below. Where the merlin had once stood on a plinth, a hollow archway was revealed with stairs leading down, down, down to a dark unknown space beneath their feet.

Ellie whistled as she gazed down into the stairwell. "This school is completely nuts."

Binah, ever prepared, pulled out two flashlights from the bag she'd grabbed from her bedroom.

"Come on, quickly." She handed them each a light. "We don't have long before the party ends." She didn't have to tell Ellie twice, and she marched forward to join her, pulling Lottie by the hand.

And, once again, Lottie found herself heading straight down the rabbit hole.

There was a lever on the tunnel wall, just inside the door that had slid open. "Ah, so this door can be activated from the inside," Binah murmured, peering at the brass lever. "Interesting. We had better close this to avoid discovery."

With that, she pulled the lever and slowly the door was hidden, drowning them in darkness as they made their way down the stairs.

Lottie clung to Ellie's arm, and Ellie gently squeezed her back. The buzzing and the haunting melody in her head were getting louder with every step they took. She knew they had to see what was down here.

"This is it!" Binah called, jumping down the last step and scattering glitter behind her as if she were a real fairy.

They emerged into a cavernous circular space lined with stone walls that were cold to the touch. A wooden easel stood in the center of the room opposite a red velvet love seat, covered in dirt. Stacks of oblong shapes were propped against the walls covered in dust sheets. Ellie reached out her hook and lifted a corner to reveal a gilt frame.

"Paintings," she whispered.

Other canvases were bundled on the floor. The veneer of a stunning mahogany desk glowed in the light from their torches. Papers spilled out of every drawer.

They were looking at an artist's studio.

"This must be where William Tufty—or Liliana— came to work." Ellie paced the room with Binah, the two of them picking up items and putting them back down again.

"What's this?" Ellie's hand met with a leather-bound book on a dressing table, the pages so frail and discolored that it looked as though it might crumble in her fingertips. The three girls stood beside each other, gazing down at the tattered object in rapturous silence as Ellie, afraid to even breathe for fear of turning the words to dust, delicately turned the pages.

There was no room left for doubt; the words in front of them confirmed everything.

"This diary belongs to Liliana Mayfutt," stated Ellie.

Dates, names, and countries flashed before them in elegant handwriting as Ellie continued to flick through the diary.

"*1643 . . . Albania . . . Japan . . . Kou . . . 1646 . . . Rosewood . . . Edith . . .*"

A tumbling onslaught of hidden history was laid bare in front of them. It was all there: the story of how a young princess ran away and assumed another identity, and all the adventures that eventually led to the opening of a school. The very school they were standing in right now.

"Well then," Ellie declared, very carefully shutting the diary as if it were a sacred text—but Lottie could barely hear her. She could hardly register what they'd just found, her mind consumed by that strange melodic feeling in her head.

Something caught her eye: leaning against the desk was a gold-framed painting partly covered by a dust sheet. Beneath it Lottie glimpsed a soft smile that filled her with warmth. Enchanted, she approached the painting and pulled away the sheet so that it fell to the floor with a ghostly sigh. When the rest of the painting was revealed, Lottie immediately began coughing and spluttering—not because of the dust, but because of the person looking back at her. She stumbled backward into another pile of paintings, and their dust sheets slid off to reveal more gilt frames and more images of the same face. She ran to the next painting and the next, pulling off sheet after sheet in a frantic circle.

"Lottie, what's the matter?" Ellie said, running to her side to calm her down.

The pumpkin costume suddenly felt suffocating. Lottie frantically pulled at it, dragging it over her head and throwing it to the ground until she stood in nothing but her black slip. She pointed an accusing finger at the first painting and the cloudy-blue eyes that she knew so well. Eyes that were just like her own.

"All these paintings . . . ," she began, struggling to catch her breath. "They're all of my ancestor Henry Pitkin." She could barely comprehend what she was seeing.

Why on earth would William Tufty have painted so many images of him?

"Well, that is peculiar," Binah said, pondering. "How can you tell?" She moved to the desk and picked up one of the many folded pieces of paper scattered there, raising the sheet to her owlish eyes to inspect the handwriting.

"Can't you see it in his face?" Lottie panted, pointing at the image. "We have the same eyes. And it's the same painting style as the portrait that I have. They must all have been done by the same person."

"You think Liliana painted your ancestor over and over again?" Ellie asked, peering at the painting.

Lottie didn't have time to answer before Binah materialized behind her, the piece of paper still in her hand.

"I think she may have done more than paint him," Binah said, stifling a giggle as she handed over a handwritten letter, "although this kind of sentiment has always eluded me slightly."

Lottie hardly heard her. Her hands shook as she took the paper and flattened it out, holding the flashlight up so she could see the words better. A bittersweet ache started up in her chest.

To my beloved Vixen, Liliana,

Every morning I awaken with joyous anticipation to gaze into the rosy face of our beautiful Edith.

She is getting quite fat now, and I'm sure if you could see her round little belly your mouth would water with a temptation to gobble her up. She is causing quite the stir around the household, delighting in giving her nurses chase around the grounds. She is just as loud and demanding as her mother!

But it is her eyes that remind me most of you, that

forget-me-not blue. She is truly a creation of love and out of love she will bloom.

From your ever-besotted mouse,
Henry

"They were in love," Lottie breathed, clutching the letter to her chest, wanting to absorb as much of the tenderness weaved into the words as possible.

When she'd wished for a family, she never imagined she'd find it hiding in the heart of Rosewood.

"What? Who?" Ellie peered over Lottie's shoulder, shining her flashlight on the secret love letter.

"William—I mean, Liliana—and my ancestor Henry Pitkin." Lottie looked down at the letter again, her eyes turning misty. "They had a baby together—Edith."

Lottie carefully folded the letter and realized that the melody in her head had stopped. It was as if the music had guided her to the truth and now was needed no more. She had found what she was looking for. She'd thought coming to Rosewood had meant turning her back on her family— but instead the school had brought her closer to her loved ones than she could ever have imagined.

"So that's how I got my middle name, Edith," she said, hiccuping back a tiny sob. She wasn't sad; she was elated. All this time she'd felt the call to Rosewood, all this time she'd known her tiara was special. Together they had led her to the one thing missing in her life.

Thank you. She closed her eyes as she silently said the words, a sweet ache in her heart.

"So it *is* Liliana's tiara?" Ellie asked, unable to hide her thrill at seeing a real piece of her childhood idol's jewelry.

"Yes," Lottie said, smiling. "Now it truly is my family tiara."

To know that her tiara had once been Liliana's filled her heart with joy. This heirloom, this legacy, had not simply been gifted to Henry Pitkin; it had *belonged* to her ancestor Liliana, Henry's beloved wife. The fact that Liliana had renounced the throne—to run away to find freedom, to find love, and to take on a whole new identity as a man in order to set up a school—only strengthened Lottie's belief in her mantra: *Be kind, be brave, be unstoppable.* Liliana had been all these things, and Lottie believed she could be too.

The girls headed back to their dormitories before the party ended, sliding the secret door shut and waiting for the statue to lower itself back down to ground level. Then they turned the *M* back to its upside-down position.

"What about the Leviathan poison conspiracy?" Lottie asked as they walked. She'd climbed back into her pumpkin costume before they'd left the secret room. After all, they didn't want any awkward questions.

Binah stretched her arms above her head, yawning.

"Well, we haven't heard any cries of terror or hysteria, so I guess we're safe for an evening."

Lottie nodded, but she knew that they needed to get to the bottom of this before more people got hurt.

The three of them made their way back to their rooms, agreeing that William Tufty's studio would remain their little secret.

It was, after all, Lottie's legacy.

When Lottie climbed into bed that night, she wondered if she'd already been dreaming. Liliana Mayfutt had run away and set up Rosewood Hall under the guise of William Tufty—this had turned out to be a truth no stranger than the existence of Portmans and Partizans. Lottie thought she understood—her own research had shown her that it had been difficult for female members of the royal family to do anything other than simper, marry, and have children. If Liliana had truly wanted to live free in such a time, to be able to make her own choices, maybe she'd had no choice except to go undercover as a man. Lottie stroked the tiara on her bedside table, imagining how many times Liliana, Henry, Edith, or her mother would have found comfort in the same way.

Kind, brave, unstoppable.

Knowing where the tiara had come from made these

words feel even more powerful now.

This world of royalty just kept getting more magical, and Lottie understood a little better why she felt she was meant to be here.

"So you have royal connections to Rosewood." Ellie's finger drew small figure eights above her head as she lay back in her own bed, meditating on everything they'd discovered.

"I guess I have," Lottie replied, squeezing Mr. Truffles. She still found it hard to come to terms with.

"And we both have royal blood."

It was not a question, but Lottie answered anyway. "That doesn't change anything," she said quickly, picking up on Ellie's sad tone.

"Lottie, why didn't you tell me how you were feeling about your family?" Ellie asked suddenly, almost cutting her off.

Lottie wriggled around onto her side to look at Ellie. She hesitated before replying, not sure how to articulate how she felt.

"Your parents have been so kind welcoming me into the Maravish royal family. I didn't want to be ungrateful by worrying about my own family."

Silence fell over the room again like a soft mist.

"I'm glad you've found your home, Lottie," Ellie said at

last, the words coming out slow and deliberate.

Lottie couldn't help laughing, though she tried to stifle her giggles.

"No, Ellie, don't you see?" She couldn't believe Ellie could miss it, but then she never had been great at picking up on subtleties. "Henry and me. Liliana and you. It's history repeating itself. I think I was always meant to be connected to you." Ellie turned to face her, their eyes locking. "The Wolfsons, the Mayfutts, Rosewood . . . Ellie, they're not my home. You're my home."

Ellie's lips parted, her eyes widening at Lottie's words. Finally she smiled. "I guess there's a tradition of wayward princesses becoming smitten with kind little pumpkins."

"Wha—" Lottie's nose twitched as she took in what Ellie had said, and her cheeks grew hot in a way she couldn't explain.

"Good night," Ellie said, turning over in her bed and pulling the sheets up to her chin, leaving Lottie to mull over exactly what she had meant.

PART TWO
Friends

24

LOTTIE FELT GOOD. HER BODY was light, her mind clear as crystal, and for the first time since all the Leviathan stuff had started she actually believed it when she told herself it was going to be okay.

She practically danced out of bed that morning, eager to get to her lessons with Jamie. Her tiara glittered on the bedside table, a warm reminder of how far she'd already come this year; it was her legacy, the proof that she was the heir of Rosewood, that she belonged here.

"Liliana . . ." Lottie nearly jumped out of her skin at the croaky dream-drenched voice of her best friend. Ellie's eyes fluttered a few times in her direction. Lottie stayed very still, terrified to make any sound, but Ellie slowly drifted back to sleep.

All night, having discovered how deep her connection to Rosewood really was, she'd felt a profound responsibility for the school settle over her. It was as if every student were part of her family now, and it was her duty to make sure they were all safe and happy. That responsibility meant her training with Jamie was even more important.

She was determined to stop Leviathan, but to do that she had to be strong.

It was particularly cold that November morning as she walked toward the field; the air was still and quiet, and the scent of the flowers was softer as they prepared to sleep for the winter.

"You're five minutes late." Lottie faltered at Jamie's unexpectedly harsh tone. Was he still mad about something?

"Sorry, Ellie slept in so I had to tiptoe around. Though that girl could sleep through a hurricane." She attempted a smile at him, but to her dismay he didn't even crack a smirk. There was none of his sarcastic humor, just a look of irritation.

"Don't be late again," he said coldly, turning around and leaving her to follow him.

Lottie felt her heart sink. She really thought that they were okay, but he kept switching between friendly and prickly, and she couldn't figure out what she was doing to cause it.

"Okay," she replied in defeat.

He walked her to a spot on the side of the field, a little closer to Conch House than she was used to, and threw two weights at her feet. "Start with those exercises I taught you last week, then we can practice self-defense."

She sighed, not entirely sure what she could possibly say to warm him up, when to her surprise he pulled out his own set of weights—much larger than hers—and moved to stand next to her.

"Oh!" she said dumbly. "I didn't know you'd be joining in."

"Is that a problem?" he asked, pulling off his hoodie. He lifted his weights and began punching the air with them easily.

"No, it's just—"

The words caught in her throat as she watched him aggressively attack the chilly air; he was somehow both deliberate and manic at the same time, as if he were suppressing a feral fury. "It's distracting." She said it without thinking and immediately covered her mouth. "I didn't mean that . . . I just meant . . . you know, because you're so good at this, it makes me feel silly." She wanted to kick herself for being so rude. This definitely wasn't going to lighten his mood.

"Yeah, well, you're distracting too," he replied without missing a beat.

"Excuse me? I don't know what you think—"

"There you go again, distracted *and* distracting. Pick up your weights," he huffed, still violently punching the air.

Reluctantly she held her tongue and picked up her own weights.

Distracted and distracting? That was pretty much the opposite of how she was feeling since discovering the truth about her family.

"You're wrong," she said.

"What?" Jamie stopped his air punching and she began attacking the empty space herself. Each violent movement hissed through the air, and she didn't stop. Jamie's attitude was discouraging her, and it was the last thing she needed right now.

"I've worked so hard," she said, "and faced things I didn't want to think about so that I could stay vigilant and stop being distracted. I don't know what I've done that's been putting you in such a bad mood, and I don't know what to do to put it right, but don't for a second accuse me of being distracted. I've confronted my demons, Jamie, which is more than I can say for you."

She dropped the weights on the ground, catching her breath, hardly believing what she'd just said. A hank of hair escaped from her ponytail and fell in her eyes. She blew it out of the way, but it simply drifted back down in front of her face.

She turned back to Jamie and froze at his expression. He looked pained, and it reminded her so strongly of how he'd looked at her that night by the pool. Abruptly, he reached out to brush her lock of hair behind her ear, his eyes making such intense contact she couldn't look away.

"Lottie," he began, his voice soft. But then he shook his head, his expression turning cold again as he pulled his hand away. "All you do is drag me down."

Lottie was almost too shocked to speak. A sour feeling rose up in her chest, the cold in the air twisting around her. It was one thing for him to accuse her of being distracted, but how dare he say she was dragging him down? She was doing everything she could to stop Leviathan, working her butt off to face things that terrified her, though he refused to see that.

"In what way am I dragging you down?" Her hand rested firmly on her hip, channeling as much of Ellie's don't-test-me attitude as she could.

"I need to put Ellie and the crown first, and you—"

"I *always* put Ellie first; she means everything to me. Don't you dare doubt that. That's the whole reason you agreed to train me, so we can both put her first and not worry about each other." She took a step closer to him, not letting his disapproving look deter her. "Stop making it my problem if you can't do that, or be honest about what's really bothering you."

Something she said must have gotten to him, because the air around them suddenly felt thick, as if their frustration were radiating into the atmosphere. Unexpectedly, and with more aggression than necessary, Jamie threw his dumbbells aside, but Lottie didn't flinch. She was tired of his attitude and she was tired of him making her feel responsible for it. She had enough to deal with already.

"Training you twice a week eats into my own training.

This is my job, Lottie, and somehow you keep getting in the way of that. I should never have agreed to teach you. I can't."

"*Can't?* I don't understand, I thought—"

"No, you don't understand. You never understand anything." He raised his voice louder than Lottie was comfortable with, and she took a step back.

What on earth was she doing to upset him so much? She thought they were past all this.

"What's wrong with you, Jamie? Why are you being so—" She hesitated over the word because it almost felt silly. "So mean?" She desperately rubbed at her face to fight back the tears, but she couldn't stop them staining her cheeks.

"Lottie, I—"

A high-pitched whistling pierced the chilly air, and they both turned to see Raphael jogging toward them, a backpack bouncing behind him and sweat glistening on his mocha skin.

Lottie quickly rubbed her face again, trying to compose herself before Raphael made any assumptions.

"I didn't know the pumpkin princess was the one who'd taken my jogging partner away from me." Raphael chuckled as he approached them, but he had to lean forward on his legs to catch his breath, throwing his backpack on the ground, clearly at the end of his pre-class run. He blinked up at them, taking in their expressions, and Lottie panicked that he might ask why she was crying. "I truly didn't think your cheeks could get any redder." He smirked, his perfect pearly teeth glittering at her.

Lottie blinked at him, knowing she should be offended at his jibe, but all she felt was relieved that he hadn't picked up on the negative energy.

"It's not red, it's rosy, and it just shows how hard I've been working, thank you very much," she replied, crossing her arms and instantly slipping into the mask of someone who was completely fine and hadn't just had a possible friendship-altering argument.

"And what's Jamie's excuse?" he asked, gesturing toward the glowering Partizan.

Lottie glanced in Jamie's direction. He was still staring at her, chest heaving as he towered over her. It was clear from the way his jaw clenched that he wanted to say more, but he would have to keep his lips sealed with Raphael around.

"I'm fine." He dragged his gaze away from her, letting out an abrupt breath like an angry bull.

"Seriously?" Raphael's tone shifted to what seemed to be genuine concern. "Jamie, in the nicest way possible, you look terrible." Lottie had to hold her breath to stop from choking at his bluntness, but she hardly had time to think before Raphael said something that changed everything.

"Is Percy still keeping you up with his sleepwalking?"

Percy's been sleepwalking?

Lottie cut him a look, almost not believing that Jamie had kept a secret from them after all his lecturing, but he refused to meet her gaze.

"I said I'm fine, Raphael. I'll see you later."

Raphael shrugged in defeat, turning to leave before pausing. "Oh yeah! Jamie, you left something in the bag of *Hamlet* notes you lent me."

The air fell still again as Raphael reached for his backpack, and Lottie watched as Jamie's expression turned to confusion, something she very rarely saw on his face.

"I was gonna swing by and drop it off when I saw you guys." Raphael unzipped the side pocket. "It's a history book or something," he added casually, and Jamie's confusion turned into horror.

The air changed again, an urgency took over Jamie, and with the lightning speed of a Partizan he grabbed Raphael's arm as it emerged from the bag. But it was too late. There was something Lottie never dreamed she'd see again. The book. The book of Pakistani history that he said he'd thrown away over a month ago. The book that she now realized was still haunting him.

Jamie snatched the book from Raphael and shoved it in his own bag without saying a word to either of them.

"Thank you, Raphael," Jamie said smoothly, trying not to let any hint of his discomfort show. Raphael stared at him, bewildered.

"Okay . . . ," he said slowly, eyes shifting between the two of them. "I'll see you both later."

They watched him jog off toward Conch House, gradually becoming a little dot as he moved farther away, no idea of the impact he'd just made.

"Jamie . . ." Lottie turned to him, not even sure what she should say. She felt as if she'd witnessed something very private. "I'm sorry," she said at last, the words coming out in a choked whisper.

"We should stop this," he said calmly, moving to pack up the weights. "This is my mistake. Let's just focus on school and our responsibilities. Both of us." A final look in her direction let her know how serious he really was.

She thought back to the beginning of summer when he'd agreed to train her, about how much she'd felt they understood each other. How could she have messed it all up so badly?

Not able to look at him, she hung her head. "I really wanted to help," she said.

A humorless breath escaped Jamie, but he didn't seem angry. "I know."

She finally looked him in the eye again—that dark

hazel, hidden beneath thick lashes, always so hard to read. He wasn't angry; he was sad. A deep well of loneliness was hidden behind his cracked mask. She sensed it would be a long time until they would be this close again.

❧ 25 ❧

As November trudged on a thick fog settled over the school, and with it an eerie hush. It was not the calm, studious hush Lottie remembered from last winter, but an anxious quiet, as if Rosewood knew that something sinister was lurking within the grounds.

Lottie, Binah, and Ellie were in their new "secret base," Liliana's studio. They had decorated the space to make it their own, filling it with fairy lights and wall hangings, turning it into a twinkling, cozy grotto to study and plan in.

"So there have been two more cases of people affected by the ersatz Hamelin Formula," Binah announced. "Rory Martin in year seven during a math class last week, and Alice Amari, year twelve head of Ivy House, during lunch break two days ago." Binah had been taking note of the exact times, dates, and circumstances of every poison incident. A pattern was definitely forming. There had now been ten incidents in total, each one causing the same symptoms and leaving that same baby-powder smell behind.

"One every week," Lottie said solemnly, her chemistry

study guide spread out on the desk in front of her. She was theoretically the heir of Rosewood; she had to keep the students safe. That meant figuring out what Leviathan was planning—and figuring it out now.

Ellie grunted, collapsing onto the love seat, which Lottie and Binah had covered with a new quilt. "It just doesn't make any sense. How is it once a week? And why?"

They didn't have the answer. There was no more information to go on, and it was starting to feel like they'd reached a dead end. Lottie glanced over at one of Liliana's paintings, imagining her ancestor's fury, remembering that that same fire was in her blood.

Be unstoppable.

"We'll figure it out," Lottie said, closing her book and giving Ellie one of her best reassuring smiles. They couldn't let Leviathan win; they'd pass their exams and they'd thwart the Leviathan plan . . . whatever it was.

"One every week." Binah repeated the words softly, almost in a whisper. "Are those your chemistry notes?" she asked out of the blue, her eyes going wide in that owlish way they did whenever she had an idea.

"Um, yeah? You want to see them?" Lottie held the notebook out, but Binah ignored it and pushed her glasses up her nose, her brow furrowed in concentration.

"One every week . . . ," she repeated to herself, staring at Lottie's chemistry book: *Modern Experimental Biochemistry*.

Her face lit up as something clicked into place.

"It's an experiment!" She grinned at the thrill of her new discovery. "Leviathan is experimenting."

"And the Rosewood students are their test subjects!" Lottie chimed in, leaping up out of her seat with excitement.

"They must be trying to perfect the formula," Binah theorized, pen tapping away in her notebook as she jotted down the new information.

"I just can't figure out how they're sneaking the poison into the school. Who could be doing their dirty work now that Saskia's been captured?" Lottie said, pacing the studio. Someone, or something, had to be regulating the supply—someone within the school. Faces flashed in her mind: the headmaster, the teachers, the students . . . *The students?* She paused, and suddenly Percy Butter, the traumatized boy who shared a room with Jamie, flashed in her mind.

"I think we should tell Jamie," Binah said, as though reading her thoughts. She glanced around the room like she was only just realizing he wasn't there, and that he hadn't been there for a while. "Where is he, anyway? Did something happen?"

Binah turned to Lottie, who felt her palms go damp, a lump forming in her throat. She had been giving Jamie the space he'd wanted, and he'd been doing the same to her.

They met up to discuss Leviathan and to have breakfast, but other than that . . . he didn't seem to be interested in the secret studio even when they'd told him about their discovery, and the looming exams had become a great excuse to avoid each other. She had to admit she was getting an extraordinary amount of work done because of it.

"Jamie and I—" she started, when Ellie abruptly sat up as if a jolt of lightning had shot through her body.

"Can you hear that?" Ellie's ears physically pricked up, her nose twitching, as if she were a wolf picking up on a scent.

"Hear what?" Binah and Lottie exchanged a look, staying as quiet as possible.

Ellie jumped to her feet. "Someone's crying."

They barely had time to grab their stuff as Ellie made for the exit.

"Ellie, where are you going?" Lottie called, nearly colliding into her as she came to a stop at the bottom of the stairway.

Ellie paused for a moment, listening intently before taking off again. "The sound is moving."

"Well, then, let's follow it," Lottie said, gesturing for Ellie to lead the way.

They crept out of their secret hideaway, listening carefully to make sure that no one could see them when they opened and closed the concealed doorway. The dreary weather had most of the students burrowed away in the study halls, leaving the school feeling extra creaky and quiet. They followed Ellie through the mist-covered grounds all the way down the path lined with roses, trying and failing to hear what Ellie had heard. The Ivy Wood dorm flashed past as they hurried to the edge of the Rose Wood, a place that was out of bounds to students.

The first thing Lottie noticed was the song. An odd, haunting melody drifted out of the woodland so dreamily it almost felt as if it were coming from inside her own head. Before she had a chance to cling on to it, the melody abruptly stopped.

Did I imagine it?

But when she looked down, she saw that there, at the entrance to the gloomy woods, lay a trail of tiny golden specks disappearing between the trees, as though to guide them.

"Are those . . . breadcrumbs?" Lottie asked, not believing what she was seeing.

Binah leaned down and pressed the pad of her finger against some of the crumbs, then lifted her fingertip to her nose. She sniffed. "Biscuit crumbs, actually."

"There! Can you hear it?" Ellie went very quiet as she stepped into the woods.

They followed her lead.

"I thought I heard a melody," Lottie whispered, but as she concentrated harder she heard what Ellie was chasing. A faint whimpering, muffled by the fog. The unmistakable melancholy of a girl crying.

Not crying, more like wailing. Thoughts of banshees filled Lottie's mind, of grief-stricken fairies running into the woodland to mourn. She reached out to Ellie, weaving their fingers together to quell the sudden ache the sound created in her. The two of them looked at each other before nodding. They took a step deeper into the shadowy and mysterious Rose Wood, following the biscuit crumbs.

Less than a year ago, Lottie had run into these woods on the anniversary of her mother's death. Now the three girls clung to each other as they trudged onward. Twisted oak trees blocked out most of the light, and the relentless fog that had settled over the school hung thick in the gloom.

"There!" Ellie breathed, pointing to a bloated oak tree in a mossy clearing. It was the same tree Lottie had found herself under all that time ago. They all held their breath, listening to the pained moans.

I will be kind. I will be brave, Lottie repeated to herself.

"Hello?" she said.

The crying abruptly stopped, and they cautiously skirted the tree so as not to scare the person away.

The yellow tartan of a Stratus uniform poked out from

behind the trunk. The unmistakable scent of baby powder hung in the air.

And there she was. Sitting under the cover of the great oak tree was Lola Tompkins, sobbing uncontrollably as she stuffed her face with a packet of biscuits.

26

THE FOG AROUND THE SCHOOL was becoming a nuisance, and Jamie couldn't help succumbing to its sleepy song. Everything was exhausting him, and the worst part was that he couldn't blame it on Lottie anymore. She'd kept her promise, behaving like a perfect Portman and a model student, and she'd miraculously gotten Ellie to behave herself too. Whatever had been haunting her was gone, and it would be pigheaded of him to keep blaming her for his distraction. And yet that's exactly what he'd done.

It had taken only a week of avoiding her to realize that she wasn't the problem. He was still distracted, he was still making no progress on Leviathan on his own, and he was still thinking about Lottie.

Since he couldn't blame her anymore, he blamed everyone and everything else.

"Jamie, did you hear me?"

Jamie looked up at Raphael, who was waving a hand around to grab his attention as they headed to the library.

"Yes, Raphael, I just don't know how many times I can

explain to you that I don't care which Avengers character would be my best match." Jamie rolled his eyes, knowing that Raphael was not going to drop the conversation.

"You always strike me as a Bucky kind of guy. You're both so tormented and serious." Raphael stared at Jamie as though he were about to read his future. Jamie stared back at him with a disapproving look, which only succeeded in making Raphael laugh.

"Yep!" Raphael snorted. "You and Bucky would be perfect for each other."

They walked past a group of Ivy students, who giggled and blushed as Raphael winked at them, and Jamie had to stop himself from scoffing. He'd gotten used to the effect that he and Raphael had on the other students, but he hated himself for being so flattered by it. He smiled at one of them. As expected, the girl blushed furiously and whispered to her friends. Vanity was yet another weakness this school had brought out in him.

They entered the arched doorway of the library where they were supposed to meet Percy. It was extra quiet today with everyone getting ready for the winter exams. Jamie found the atmosphere unsettling, like something evil was waiting beneath the calm surface.

Then the smell hit him.

Sweet, like baby powder. That unmistakable scent could

only mean one thing. Jamie instantly went on high alert, ready to move swiftly into action the moment someone showed the effects of the Hamelin Formula. Instinctively he put his arm out in front of Raphael, blocking him from any possible danger. His mind filled with images of Lottie in trouble, of Lottie being poisoned, of anyone he cared about coming to harm under Leviathan.

A growl escaped his throat. *You should only be thinking of Ellie.*

Raphael pushed his arm out of the way as the source of the scent came into their line of vision.

Micky Tompkins. He was sitting talking intently to Percy. It was odd to see Micky without Lola. He and Percy were signing to each other. It shouldn't have surprised Jamie to see that Micky knew sign language; Micky and Lola had grown up with Percy, their families tied closely through business. What did surprise him was the topic of their conversation, easy for him to read as their hands flew through the air.

He picked up on three key words. *"Dangerous"* . . . *"Puppet"* . . . *"Help."*

But it was the last sentence they exchanged that had Jamie most concerned. Percy glanced up and spotted Jamie looking. He lowered his hands, trying to hide his message, but it didn't work. Jamie saw what his roommate signed to

Micky: "*Stop. Jamie knows sign language.*"

They both froze, turning to Raphael and Jamie as they approached as if nothing unusual had taken place at all.

"Micky! We had no idea you were back." Raphael barreled forward, affectionately ruffling Micky's hair. "Are you okay? Where's Lola?"

Micky beamed at them both, his expression so sweet Jamie could practically taste it. "Hello, Raphael, Jamie. I'm perfectly well."

Micky always had an odd way of talking; he was a boy of few words. But even for him this response was curt, despite his smile.

"Where's Lola?" Jamie repeated, forcing his voice to stay light. He didn't want Micky to pick up on any of his suspicions.

Micky turned to him, his icy blue gaze piercing Jamie's heart. "I'm sure Lola is okay without me."

Lola was definitely not okay. Lottie had never seen someone so upset. It hurt to even look at her in so much pain.

"Lola?" Lottie asked softly.

Lola flinched at the sound of her name and quickly wiped her eyes in a desperate attempt to hide her tears. It didn't work, of course; her eyes were puffy and her nose had turned nearly as red as her lips.

"Are you okay?" Ellie asked stiffly, not sure how to comfort her.

"I'm totally fine." Lola attempted a smile that made Lottie's heart sink. Lottie herself had perfected the fake smile years ago.

Ellie pulled her jacket off and without a word wrapped it around Lola. Taking her lead, Binah and Lottie took the other side of Lola until they'd made a warm cocoon around her. She seemed shocked for a moment but soon relaxed into them, letting the tears fall freely down her cheeks.

"We didn't even know you were back," Lottie whispered softly.

"I got back this morning," she hiccuped. "How did you find me here?"

"We followed your trail of biscuit crumbs," Binah replied, laughing warmly.

"Oops." Lola blushed as she gave her own little half laugh.

"What's wrong?" Ellie asked. "Do I need to hurt anyone?" Ellie punched a fist into her palm to emphasize how serious she was. Lola almost smiled but quickly shook her head.

"No, no. It's just that everything's falling apart." She twirled a lock of white hair around her finger. "I worry we've come back to school too soon, but we had to get out of that house."

Lottie knew that feeling far too well, the vicious circle of wanting to be there for your sick family member but finding it hard to see them so weak.

"I understand," Lottie said softly, wishing she could open up to Lola about her real family life. "We heard about your dad on the news." Thankfully Lottie could feel that Lola was calming down.

Lola took a shaky breath and began to tell her story. "My dad is so ill. He's been sick for ages. Richard Butter has been helping with the business, but this year Dad got so much worse." She had to take another moment to collect herself, and Lottie felt Ellie's hand reach around and squeeze Lola's shoulder. She carried on. "With the merger with the Butter Company there's been strange people around the manor, and we never get any time alone with him." Lola scrabbled for a tissue in her pocket and blew her nose.

"What kind of people?" Ellie asked.

"Like the interns to Richard Butter—Ingrid and Julius." She looked very serious, as if remembering something unpleasant. "They scare me a bit," she whispered. "But it's my dad who's really scaring me. I think he's losing his mind. He keeps trying to play our mother's old piano from before she passed away, but his fingers are too damaged from the arthritis. And then Micky's been so worried about Percy. I know it's hard for both of us, but he won't talk to me about

it at all. We've never spent this much time apart. I just . . .
I'm very . . . I'm sorry, I—"

"It's okay, Lola." Binah patted her hand soothingly. "We
can simply sit here if you want. You don't have to talk."

"We're just happy to have you back," Lottie added, but
she wasn't sure Lola saw her comforting smile through all
her tears.

"I feel like something's not right at home. Like it's
been"—she crinkled her nose, as if smelling something
rotten—"poisoned."

Lottie felt herself stiffen. She glanced at Binah and
Ellie. Their faces told her they felt the same. The cocoon
had been broken. People's lives were in danger.

"Lola," she began, "we need to ask you something, but
please don't feel like we're accusing you of anything."

They all turned, forming a diamond shape on the mossy
ground where they sat.

Lola looked at each of them and nodded.

"Are you at all familiar with a group called Leviathan?
Or do you know why some Tompkins chocolate bars are
poisoning people at Rosewood?" Binah managed to get
straight to the point without being intimidating. Unfortu-
nately Lola stared at them blank-faced. The fog seemed to
thicken and grow more dense around them.

"Poison? Tompkins chocolate? I—I don't know anything
about this." Lola hung her head, pressing her palm into

the dewy grass beneath them and leaving a darkened handprint. "I'm sorry . . ."

Ellie began chewing her lip, dark hair falling over her eyes as she picked at the grass.

"That's okay," Lottie quickly interjected, trying to lighten the mood. She reached a hand out to Ellie in a way she'd done a million times. They were all damp from wandering through the mist, and everyone was starting to shiver. "We'll find out what's going on with the Hamelin Formula, don't worry."

Lola's eyes widened. "Did you just say 'the Hamelin Formula'?"

"Yes," Lottie said slowly.

"How on earth do you know about that?" Lola sat completely upright, knocking against the trunk of the tree so that a shower of dew fell over them.

The three girls looked at each other.

"Well, we have reason to believe that it's a variation of the Hamelin Formula that is poisoning people at Rosewood." Binah cleaned the lenses of her glasses with a corner of her yellow Stratus sweater and put them back on. "Do you know something about it?"

A sudden wind picked up, and the fog seemed to swirl around Lola, strands of her silken hair floating delicately so that a sugary-sweet smell filled the air.

"It's not a nice story," she said at last, looking much

older. Lottie caught Ellie's eye as Lola continued to speak. "My great-grandfather was the key researcher, Hanz Thumann. He was a very bad man." The words came out thick and heavy like dark molasses. "He abandoned the project after realizing how, um, evil it was. He hid all the research and ran away to England, where he changed his name." She looked down at her lap. Her hands had turned cherry red in the cold, and two perfect rosy circles had appeared on her cheeks. "That's how we became Tompkins."

Before any of them could respond, Lola reached for her bag and pulled out a delicate white music box. "This is all that's left of Thumann," she said, her voice almost a whisper as she carefully lifted the lid. It was painted with a whimsical scene—white birds flitting around and nesting in pink bushes on the cream-colored wood. As the lid came up, out popped a small china dove, dancing in a merry circle as the music came to life.

Lottie instantly recognized the haunting tune; it was the same melody that she'd sensed at the cusp of the woodland.

In beautiful cursive writing on the inside of the lid were words Lottie couldn't translate.

Um diese erinnerung festzuhalten, musst du sie zuerst zerstören.

"He gave this to our mother, and she handed it down to us," Lola continued. "It's very special. Our only connection to the past." Her hands cupped the precious item close to her chest, knees bent beneath her as if she were kneeling down in prayer.

Lottie had never realized quite how similar she was to Lola. They'd both had their family change their last names, they'd both lost their mothers when they were small, and they both had cherished items to remember them by. Lottie had her tiara, and Lola her music box.

Lola shut the box with a delicate thud and the music dwindled to nothing.

"This is wonderful news." Binah clapped her hands together, and the fog seemed to miraculously clear around them. "Leviathan must be looking for the research to perfect what they have."

"How is any of this good news?" Ellie said, her eyes bulging.

"Because," Binah continued, getting to her feet, "if Lola's great-grandfather abandoned his work, it means Leviathan doesn't have the information they need. That's why they're running experiments on Rosewood students. Don't you see? They're still testing. And we still have time to stop whatever they're planning."

Lottie felt a wave of relief wash over her. This was huge.

If they were right, then that meant Leviathan wasn't quite the threat they feared—yet.

"Did I help?" Lola asked in a little squeak, her usual honeyed demeanor returning.

"In more ways than you know," Lottie replied.

⚜ 27 ⚜

To Her Royal Highness, Lottie Pumpkin,

I have deliberated over whether or not to send this to you for MONTHS! But I've finally decided to do the right thing and show you what I've found even though I am absolutely sure you'll be mad at me for "getting involved." But remember that I am your childhood best friend and my mum makes your favorite meal, AND, if that doesn't help, try to picture my butter-wouldn't-melt smile and how it always used to win you over.

So without further ado—I found these images online while researching some of the names you said and they, understandably, gave me the creeps. I thought I should send them your way in case they have something to do with that "Leviathan" thing you mentioned.

Hope being a princess isn't too stressful.

Your very nice friend, who truly didn't intend to get involved and oops it really was an accident,

Ollie

PS DON'T BE MAD AT ME.

Lottie stared at the handwritten letter, unable to stop her teeth from grinding. She was on her own in the library. Binah was running a study session with some lower-year students and Ellie was at fencing practice.

You absolute muffin.

This was the one thing she hadn't wanted Ollie to do. She also knew, deep down, that what she was really mad about was that Jamie had been right—again.

He'd warned her that telling Ollie would be dangerous for him, that she shouldn't bring other people into their world. Now Ollie was stumbling around the edges of the Leviathan conspiracy, and there was little she could do to stop him. Lottie and her Rosewood friends had a lot of information now. They knew that Leviathan was trying to perfect the Hamelin Formula. They knew that they were experimenting once a week with bars of Tompkins chocolate. And they knew that something fishy was happening in the Tompkins Manor with the Butter Company.

But they still didn't know how Leviathan was getting the poison into Rosewood, what their end goal was, or where the research they were after was hidden. Lottie took a deep breath and picked up Ollie's letter again. A shadow fell over her, long and dark. Her heart rate picked up. Without even looking up, she knew exactly who it was.

"Hello, Jamie."

She tried to keep her face straight. The shadow moved

around the side of the table, and she heard the scrape of a chair being pulled out as he came to sit opposite her. She could see his tan hands on the table, fingers interlocked as he leaned forward.

"Lottie," he began, his voice low. "I think we should talk."

Lottie chewed her lip. Suddenly, facing him in this moment, she couldn't remember why they had been so distant.

Because you distract him, an irritating voice in her head reminded her.

"If that's what you want." She still hadn't looked up from Ollie's letter.

"Lottie," he repeated. This time his voice was more urgent. "Won't you even look at me?" She could hear the hurt in his voice. She glanced up, despite herself, and was shocked to see how tired he seemed. His wild, dark hair was more unkempt than usual, and she had the urge to push a lock back off his face. "That's better."

"What's the matter?" she asked instinctively, then wanted to kick herself because she knew he'd hate being asked that. This whole predicament had started because he felt like he was putting his emotions above his job.

He took a deep breath. "I wanted to tell you how pleased I am with the information you've uncovered." She started spluttering, but he held up his hand to stop her talking.

"And I'm impressed with how well you and Ellie are doing in school. You've really stepped up to your role."

It took all her mental energy not to gape at him. She couldn't believe it. Had Jamie actually sought her out to praise her? Was he actually impressed?

"Thanks . . . ?" She was sure his lip twitched at the disbelief in her voice, and for the first time in a long time she felt that perhaps they could go back to how they used to be.

"Yes, well . . . maybe it was a good thing we spent some time apart."

"Maybe . . ." She wanted so badly to apologize again for giving him that book, for causing him to think about things he didn't want to think about, but she knew better than that now. Those burnt-hazel eyes narrowed at her. It was the first time he'd really looked at her since their fight on the field. "Does this mean I'm forgiven?" she asked apprehensively, her heart thundering in her chest.

Jamie let out one of his long-suffering sighs; she couldn't help smiling. "You've changed so much," he breathed, not breaking eye contact. There was something melancholy in the way he spoke that made Lottie's chest ache. His words were so similar to Ollie's, but she wasn't afraid of them anymore. Since finding out about Liliana and her connection to the school, she was comfortable with who she was. She wished Jamie could find the same relief one day.

"I should hope so," she replied as casually as she could manage. "You've known me for over a year."

He pushed his hair back, his hand momentarily obscuring his eyes. When he lowered his hand, she saw a smile playing across his lips. "The longest year of my life."

She smiled back at him, though the gesture didn't quite reach her heart. It was clear he was pretending too; she could recognize a mask by now. He was glossing over what had led them here as if it had never happened at all. Lottie had seen Ellie do similar things, but the difference with Ellie was that she always found her own way of dealing with her issues. Lottie wasn't so sure with Jamie—he was too caught up with maintaining a facade.

Why won't you face your demons, Jamie? she wanted to repeat, but instead she continued to smile. Lottie had always prided herself on being kind and helpful, like the princesses from the fairy tales her mother had read to her as a little girl. But now she understood. You couldn't help someone who didn't want to be helped, and if you weren't careful, you'd do more damage than good.

"What's that?" He gestured to the letter in front of her, and she knew she'd lost any chance of untangling him in that moment.

She shook herself. "It's a letter from Ollie. He says he's found something he thinks I need to see." There was no point in skirting around it, and Lottie quietly anticipated

Jamie's disapproving expression.

"What kind of *thing*?"

"A *thing* he thinks might have something to do with Leviathan." Sure enough, Jamie's eyebrows knit together, any humor melting away.

"Go on." He gestured for her to show him the letter.

She carefully picked up the envelope, but as soon as she went to open it a wash of dread swept over her, the same wispy dread she'd felt last year when they'd found, under her mattress, a drawing of the Wolfson House sigil overlaid with a death mark—put there to scare the princess of Maradova. She'd known by the way her hands trembled that night that something sinister was lurking beneath the mattress, and her fingers were shaking now as she pulled out the images. But what emerged from the package was unrecognizable to her.

Four images lay in front of her, each with a red circle drawn around the same two dark-clad people in each picture.

Scrawled on the back of each image was a date and location in Ollie's handwriting. The same two faces popping up over and over. First at the press conference about Percy's disappearance, then again at Percy's recovery, the Tompkins and Butter Company merger, and finally at the Tompkins Manor.

"There's been strange people around the manor." Lola's

words echoed in her head. *"They scare me."*

She stared at the mystery boy and girl. They couldn't have been much older than herself, but there was something sinister about them, as if even looking at them in a photo might be dangerous. The boy wore a cowboy hat in every photo, which cast a dark shadow over his face, but the girl's eyes were bright and shone out of the photos as if she could see everything.

"Do you recognize these people?" Lottie asked, quickly sliding the papers across the table to Jamie, wanting to get as far away from their gaze as possible.

Jamie scrutinized each image, his eyes piercing the photos so intently she thought he might burn a hole through the paper. A frustrated huff of air escaped his nose and he slid them back. "No."

Picking at her lip, Lottie stared down at the two strange people again. There had to be something there that could give them a clue, something she was missing.

Her eyes narrowed over a tattoo on the girl's arm. If she could just . . .

"Jamie, pass me a pencil quickly." She held her hand out without looking away from the photo, locked on the small detail that she was determined to catch.

Jamie complied, leaning over her shoulder as she hurriedly began sketching in the back of her math workbook. Her fingers moved like lightning, as carefully as they could, forging the symbol onto the paper.

She pulled away, satisfied. In front of her was an unfamiliar symbol, pieced together from the four images. It was an infinity mark, like two all-knowing eyes staring out of the empty space, with a double cross beneath it with thorns at the edge of the lines. The whole image sat within a wreath of hydrangea flowers. The eyes of the infinity mark glared at her, watching her, spying on her.

"Lottie, where did you see that?" Jamie's voice was urgent enough to drag her out of her mesmerized daze.

"It's on the girl's arm, look."

She pointed to the third photo, but Jamie was barely paying attention as he snatched the paper and stood up to inspect it closer to the light.

"Jamie, what is it?" She moved around the side of the table to look at the drawing over his shoulder. "What's wrong?"

She tugged at his sleeve and he turned. His expression left a sunken feeling in her gut. He didn't seem scared or thoughtful. He seemed upset, as if he'd discovered something he didn't want to.

"I've seen this symbol before," he said solemnly.

"What? Where?"

Jamie handed the paper back to her. She noticed a muscle working in his jaw.

"It's on all the mail Percy receives," he said, almost in a whisper.

Three thoughts suddenly clicked together in Lottie's mind.

One: she should never have ignored her instincts about Percy.

Two: someone was sneaking the poison into school every week.

Three: Percy was a sleepwalker.

This was more than a coincidence. They'd found their next lead.

❦ 28 ❧

PERCY.

Jamie had been so distracted he'd missed what was right in front of him.

It had seemed completely normal for a recently kidnapped boy to have trouble sleeping. Jamie had been far more concerned with trying to help Percy feel comfortable than with considering that something more sinister might be happening.

"I need you both to be extra vigilant this year."

The king's words had been so simple. At the time Jamie, stupidly, had thought the message was meant for Lottie. How wrong he had been.

Jamie had been part of the royal Maravish household since he was born, and he had been taken in and graciously given a role within the palace. So why was Lottie, an ordinary girl, flourishing in her position as Portman while he floundered to meet his expectations as Ellie's Partizan? He should be the one solving the mysteries. He should be the one keeping everyone safe.

These were the thoughts that brought him to this

moment. Sneaking out of his dorm in the middle of a freezing December night to follow Percy Butter. He had climbed into bed wearing black clothes, pretending to fall into a slumber until he heard Percy move. He'd waited until the very last moment to creep out of the window and follow his roommate. Percy was deathly silent as he made his way across the grounds, expertly avoiding all the guards as if he'd been trained in the art of stealth like Jamie. This was not regular sleepwalking.

As they approached the bridge, Jamie was sure he heard a soft voice mumble from the brush. But he couldn't see anyone other than Percy, so he shook the thought from his head. *You must be hearing things.*

"Oh, pretzels!"

Micky Tompkins dove behind one of the bushes in his candy-striped pajamas and fluffy down coat, narrowly avoiding the flashlight beam of an approaching school guard. He was used to being pampered; so why would Micky, the coddled heir of Tompkins Confectionery, sneak out of his plush four-poster bed in Stratus Side to brave the harsh December night? The only thing that could possibly get him to do something so outrageous was the sleepy smile of his childhood crush, Percy Butter.

Lola and Micky had grown up with Percy. Micky had never dealt well with noise or big groups; Lola had had to do most of the talking for them. But with Percy it was different. Percy was quiet and spoke with his hands. Micky adored him. They'd sit in silence reading or drawing for hours, never needing to talk. Other than Lola, Percy was the only person he felt truly understood him.

Micky had known instantly that something was wrong when he saw Percy at the end of summer, and he'd been desperate to get back to Rosewood and help him. Percy trusted Micky—he told him he'd been sleepwalking and had asked Micky to find out what he was doing when he was unconscious. Micky swore to uncover what had been done to his friend when he was kidnapped, even if that meant following Percy across the school in the middle of the night.

Lola Tompkins watched in horror as her twin brother made his way down the hidden path by the English block and toward the field. She knew he'd been acting weird. She knew it, knew it, knew it. But sneaking out? That seemed too wild for someone who loved nothing better than curling up under a blanket on a cold night.

"Oh, pretzels!" she cursed as she lost sight of him for a moment, but he quickly reappeared heading across the bridge toward the field and Conch House.

What are you doing, Micky?

An owl hooted from somewhere behind her, making her jump. She turned to give the creature her best grumpy look but couldn't see anything.

"Shhh, I'm trying to be sneaky," she scolded into the dark before turning back to pursue her brother.

"One, two, three!" Anastacia thrust the sabcr on the beat of each number. "One, two . . . three!" She repeated the sequence over and over, turning the steps into muscle memory.

She'd started sneaking out to the Conch House gym at night, determined to get one up on the other fencing team members before the Spearion. She only had one goal. She had to win.

"One, two—"

She faltered, losing her footing and nearly gasping as a vision of Saskia appeared before her, as if to keep her from falling. The invisible opponent she'd been fighting morphed into a vision of her ex-Partizan. She furiously swiped at the apparition and watched Saskia's stupid charming smirk vanish, a phantom laugh echoing in her head.

No matter what she did, she couldn't get Saskia out of her head. It felt like she was going mad. Half of her wanted to scream at Saskia and never see her again . . . while the other half felt desperately lonely without her. She missed the way Saskia braided her hair, and she wanted to curl up next to Saskia and stay there forever.

"Argh!"

Anastacia let out her best war cry as she swiped her blade through the air again. This time another figure appeared—and this one wasn't an apparition. She froze in fear as she watched it glide past the gym's glass wall. Whoever it was looked like a zombie. Pale-faced, eyes half closed, but gliding past so smoothly it was like it was drifting on ice. The figure inclined its head to one side and she quickly hid behind a punching bag as the mystery person came into view.

She couldn't believe what she was seeing.

"Percy?"

What on earth is he doing?

It looked like he was heading toward the gym cafeteria. She dropped her sword and grabbed her bag to follow him. This was definitely a welcome distraction from thinking about Saskia.

The moon was so bright it practically burned a hole in the sky. A crescent-shaped tear in the midnight gray, striking out against the darkness. Raphael Wilcox had always been a bit of a drama queen, and he thought the moon looked especially poetic that night.

It's a symbol of clarity, he thought. *Of how everything is going to come out in the open finally.*

Because tonight Raphael was following Anastacia, determined to discover where she had been sneaking off to every other night. He was going to find out why everyone was being so weird.

He missed Saskia; she had always been so straightforward and laughed at his jokes. It felt like all his friends had either vanished or been replaced by sad, grumpy versions of themselves this year. It was definitely more than hormones causing it. Jamie thought he hid it so well, but anyone with eyes could see that something had happened between him and Lottie. He had been like a sad puppy for months, moping around, gazing gloomily at Lottie when he thought she wasn't looking. Raphael knew he wasn't always the most tactful, but even he knew that it would be completely useless to ask Jamie what was wrong. So instead, he was taking matters into his own hands. He was going to confront them all head on, starting with Anastacia.

He wasn't worried about getting caught as he sneaked into the rear entrance of the Conch House gym. He could charm his way out of anything! But what he hadn't expected was to spot three other people dressed in black sneaking around in front of him, one of whom had a very recognizable mass of black curls. It looked like he wasn't the only Rosewood student spying tonight.

"Binah?" he called.

Yet again, Lottie, Binah, and Ellie were sneaking around the school when they weren't supposed to. At least this time they weren't in Halloween costumes.

Ever since Jamie's reaction to the infinity symbol, Lottie knew what their next mission had to be. To follow Percy Butter.

There had been a time in Lottie's life when the idea of sneaking out past curfew would have been inconceivable. Now such behavior was practically second nature.

What has Ellie done to me? she thought. She couldn't help but smile thinking about how much she'd changed.

Ellie and Lottie had taken turns waiting up at night to spy out of the balcony window in the hope of spotting Percy. It had taken three nights for him to finally appear, almost invisible as he slinked down the path in a dark robe. Lottie hadn't even been surprised; she was certain her theory was right.

When they reached Stratus Side, before the bridge, they sent out an owl call that Binah had taught them. The sound was their signal for her to sneak down and join them. She materialized behind the two girls, making Lottie jump. Binah held a finger to her mouth to warn them against making any noise. They were all dressed in head-to-toe black, with voluminous hoods covering their heads. Binah's hood didn't quite manage to cover her glossy black curls.

They followed Percy all the way to the Conch House gym, trying not to trip over each other as they stumbled through the pitch darkness and between a set of doors.

"Did you hear that?" Ellie grabbed Lottie and pulled her back. "There's someone else in here."

The unmistakable creak of a door's hinges came from behind them, and they all held their breath. A million thoughts burst into Lottie's mind.

We're going to get in trouble; Ellie's going to get expelled; I'll lose my job as a Portman. How could I have been so stupid?

But as the panic rose in her throat a familiar voice called out. "Binah?"

"Raphael?" they all said at the same time, pulling their hoods down.

"What the heck are you guys doing here?" He gently shut the door behind him.

"What are *we* doing?" Ellie choked. "What are *you* doing here?"

She finally let go of Lottie's arm, but as Raphael moved toward them there was a loud clanging sound from the next room followed by a sweet little voice that they all recognized.

"Oh, pretzels!"

"Was that . . . Lola?" Lottie asked, wondering if maybe she'd never woken up and was actually just dreaming this whole weird scenario.

She tiptoed to catch up with Binah and Ellie, who were already peeping around the wall. And indeed, it was Lola, sprawled on the floor wearing a fluffy black cloak, desperately trying to pick up some weights that she'd knocked off a shelf.

"Are you sure we're awake?" Lottie whispered.

"*It seems to me that yet we sleep, we dream,*" Binah said, giggling and earning a snort from Lottie and Raphael.

Lola abruptly turned around at the sound of Binah's laughter, dropping one of the weights she'd just picked up. Lottie spoke first.

"Lola, what are you doing here?"

She stared up at them, eyes wide. "I was following Micky." She came over to join them.

Is Micky following Percy too? Lottie suddenly thought.

Raphael gaped. "Micky's here too?"

"Why are you all here?" Lola asked.

"We were following Percy."

"You were following Percy?" Raphael echoed, downright baffled.

"Yes, aren't you?" Binah was grinning; she clearly found the whole situation funny.

"What? No, I was following Anastacia. She keeps sneaking off to the gym every other night."

"I knew it!" Ellie hissed. "That little cheat is trying to get a leg up on everyone."

Lottie barely acknowledged Ellie, realizing that they might be running out of time. "Lola, where did Micky go?"

she asked, not bothering to hide the urgency in her voice.

Lola pointed off to the left. "He went into the cafe."

They all tiptoed to the double doors at the end of the gym.

"So why exactly are you guys spying on Percy?" Raphael asked as they pushed through the swinging door.

"We're not exactly sure yet," said Lottie as she crept toward the panel that screened the sandwich counter from the door, "but we—*ARGHH!*"

She tripped over someone crouching behind the door. Two pairs of hands reached out to grab her. The first pair belonged to Ellie, who tried to pull her back to standing. The second reached out to steady her as she stumbled. This bit of help was from someone she very much did not expect to see.

"Jamie?"

Before he could respond, the three of them went tumbling backward onto the tiled floor. Ellie cushioned her fall, but pain shot through her legs, and she immediately knew it was going to leave a bruise. But there was another, more urgent problem. Lottie was trapped in an Ellie-and-Jamie sandwich. The wolf pendants lined up like a spear through all three of their hearts.

Jamie easily righted himself, but when they all tried to sit up at the same time Lottie found her legs tangled with Ellie's.

"Let me just . . . Hang on." Jamie leaned forward to help her up, his face dangerously close to hers. She could feel his breath on her cheek.

"Wait, I need to get my arm free—" Ellie grabbed Lottie's waist to right herself, her breath hot against her Portman's neck.

Blood rushed to Lottie's cheeks as they tripped over each other. Jamie growled, grabbing Lottie and Ellie and pulling them both up as if they weighed nothing.

"*What* are you all doing here?" he huffed, rubbing his hand over his forehead. She couldn't see him properly in the dark, but he seemed flustered.

But before she could respond, Lottie spotted exactly what it was that she'd tripped over. Micky Tompkins was crouched on the floor, wincing and nursing the spot where Lottie had run into him. However, he seemed distracted by something on the other side of the panel by the sandwich counter.

"There he is," he said in a muted tone.

Everyone fell silent and went over to peer around the panel as Percy sleepily made his way across the cafe, eyes glazed over as if he were in a trance.

He approached the stand of candy in front of them, and then he did the one thing they were all dreading. Out of his pocket he pulled a single bar of Tompkins chocolate, and carefully he placed it on the stand.

It was him. He was the one planting the poisoned bars.

Somehow Percy Butter had been conditioned to infect the school with the test Hamelin Formula.

Binah, Ellie, and Lottie all looked at each other.

"Well, I guess we have our answer," Jamie said.

Poor Percy, Lottie thought, clenching her fists.

Micky looked distraught, reaching out wordlessly to grab Lola's hand.

A snarl escaped Ellie's lips. "They'll pay for this," she growled.

"We'll make sure of it," Lottie added, surprising herself with the conviction in her voice. No one messed with her Rosewood students and got away with it.

"Um, guys?" Raphael's twang tore them out of their thoughts. "Is that Anastacia?"

"Hey," Anastacia called furiously, grabbing Percy by the shoulder and turning him around. His eyes flickered with recognition.

The friends watching didn't have any chance to react—at that moment the panel they'd been leaning around gave way. They tumbled forward, taking down Percy and Anastacia with them. It was a huge mess of bodies—the biggest comedy of errors Lottie had ever been part of.

"What the—" Anastacia screeched as they clambered to

get up. Jamie moved to assist a very confused Percy, who was looking as though he'd just seen a ghost.

"Okay, that's it." Raphael got to his feet, attempting to sign for Percy's benefit. "I think it's time you all explained what exactly is going on here."

29

It was the day after their midnight adventure, and the fog that had overcome the school was finally dissipating, revealing all that had been hidden in its twisted haze. As agreed, they met before breakfast in the indoor rose garden—they could talk there without anyone overhearing, and most of the students would still be in bed. Water bubbled and gurgled from the cascading steps of the miniature waterfall down into the pond, where the surface reflected the glass dome above their heads. This was the one place in Rosewood Hall where flowers bloomed all year round.

They pieced together everything they knew and explained to Raphael what had been going on, only omitting the truth about Lottie and Ellie. It wasn't fair to leave him out any longer. They told him what Leviathan had done at the summer ball. How Saskia had become a member of a covert evil society that had tried to kidnap the princess of Maradova.

Then it was Percy's turn.

"Percy, can you show everyone the letters?" Jamie signed to him.

Percy pulled out fourteen unmarked letters. He signed and Jamie translated, explaining how each envelope had contained a bar of chocolate and the creepy symbol that they now called the "Leviathan mark." Percy had to be careful not to look at the symbol. They didn't know for sure, but they guessed that during the kidnapping Leviathan had brainwashed him to follow their orders whenever he saw the symbol, so that they could get him to stash poisoned chocolate around the school on their behalf. A cunning, devious plan.

"This is what happened to Saskia, right? They brainwashed her too." It was less a question than a desperate hope Raphael was clinging to.

The royal trio exchanged glances, not sure what to say. Something about Raphael's words felt sticky, like a thick glue you'd use to piece together a broken ornament, but before Lottie could dwell on the feeling, Jamie let out a deep, regretful breath. "No, Raphael. Saskia's motivations were different." He was never one for sugarcoating things.

"But maybe they lured her over; they must have. She wouldn't—"

"*Tais-toi*, Raphael," Anastacia spat.

She'd been sitting on the ledge staring out of the window, not saying a word. Even after their hectic night, her mahogany hair remained immaculate. "She was completely aware of what she was doing," Anastacia continued, turning back to the window.

Raphael spluttered at her words, raising an eyebrow, unconvinced. "This is classic you, Anastacia. You two were always so—"

"You know nothing about us," she barked, that fiery intensity Lottie had seen on the night of the summer ball swirling around her. Anastacia didn't back down at the awkwardness, daring anyone to challenge her. Nobody did. Raphael twitched, eyes flickering as he realized he might not know as much as he thought he did.

Lottie took a deep breath. She had to keep the peace; they would be no use if they were getting upset with each other.

Be unstoppable.

"Listen, everyone," Lottie squeaked. Her voice wasn't coming out as commanding as she'd hoped, but she gritted her teeth and continued. "The good news is that we've found out that Percy was unwittingly distributing the chocolate, and we can stop that from happening now. But we still can't allow Leviathan to get away with this. We can't let them hurt anyone else."

"But what can we do? We have no idea who they are or what their plan is," Lola said.

Jamie shook his head. "We know they're testing what

they have of the Hamelin Formula to try to get the results they want. We know they're trying to control people, and we know that Tompkins Confectionery is involved."

"Our goal is still the same," Binah chimed in. "We have to stop them from perfecting the Hamelin Formula. Lola said that Thumann hid his research, so Leviathan must be looking for it." She turned to the twins expectantly.

"But we don't know where it is either," they replied in unison, their voices syncing together like birds chirping.

"We don't even know where they're looking for it," Lola added.

"Hmm," Binah said, tapping a fingertip against her chin. "What we really need is someone who knows more about the inner workings of Leviathan." Her glance came to rest on Anastacia. "But who would know that?"

"What about Saskia? Isn't she in the palace still?" Raphael offered obliviously. "Can't someone go to speak to her?"

The light reflected off Binah's glasses as she grinned at his reply. "Excellent suggestion, Raphael." It was almost as though she'd led him to make this suggestion. After all, Raphael was one of the few people who could stir Anastacia—and Anastacia was the only person Saskia would talk to.

Man, Binah is good.

Lottie, Jamie, and Ellie all turned to Anastacia.

"What?" she asked indignantly. "This isn't my problem!"

Ellie locked eyes with Anastacia, and something switched in her, a shadow falling over her face. Lottie and Jamie both tensed, preparing themselves to extinguish any fire that might be about to ignite, when Ellie surprised them both and backed down.

"I know that it hurts. I get it now." She spoke so quietly that it was difficult to hear her. "But this is bigger than our feelings."

Silence throbbed between them, and Lottie looked from one to the other, wondering who would snap first.

"Fine." Anastacia sighed. "But it's not like I can do anything right now. She's all the way over in Maradova."

"Well," Binah began, pushing her glasses up her nose, "it's only three days until winter break. It might be time for a little trip . . . ?"

Everyone turned to Anastacia, and her eyes widened.

"No way. *Absolument pas!*" She stamped her foot, hands planted firmly on her hips. "I'm not going anywhere."

And that's how Anastacia Alcroft ended up spending Christmas in Maradova.

❧ 30 ❧

THIS WAS THE FIRST CHRISTMAS Lottie would spend in Maradova. The Maravish kingdom and the festive season were
undeniably made for one another. Trees were daubed in
beautiful bright colors with glittering decorations that
sparkled in the winter sun. Wooden dolls and orbs named
sheniy were painted and adorned with gold and lace trim-
mings and strung up on every tree and on every wall. The
scent of cinnamon and orange hung heavy in the air, steam
rising from the fresh *uyut*, a delicious hot drink whose
name literally translated to "cozy."

Lottie had spent days reading up on the Maravish people's Christmas traditions, and not just because she had to.
The handmade feel, the bright coloring, the glossy wooden
decor—it all reminded her of a Grimm's fairy tale. Sure
enough, as soon as they stepped out of the car onto the
palace grounds, she felt like she'd entered one.

"How does a country so cold and remote manage to be
so wealthy?" To emphasize her point Anastacia shuddered,
grabbing her arms and scowling with such intent it seemed
as if she expected the weather to recoil and apologize.

"Diamonds," Lottie replied.

"Ha!" Ellie cackled, narrowing her eyes. "Is that what they told you?"

"That's what it said in the history book I was given."

"It's a tax haven, Lottie, and it's completely immoral." Ellie kicked some snow up as she spoke, as if she were kicking capitalism. Some of Lottie's happy fairy-tale feelings crumbled at the thought that she might have been reading a rather selective history.

A sarcastic laugh rang out from Jamie. "If you care so much, Ellie, why don't you work on remedying the situation when you become queen?"

"That's not—I'm not . . . *Briktah*, Jamie."

Ellie scowled at him, but he continued to smile at her.

He sighed. "I guess you don't care about it that much, then."

Ellie grabbed a handful of snow to throw at him, but he effortlessly dodged the snowball so that it smacked Anastacia in the face instead.

"Oh my God." Anastacia stood completely frozen. She leaned down and quickly formed her own snowball, arcing it through the air in a perfect hit on Ellie. Within seconds the two of them were pelting each other with snow, clumps of white powder covering their clothes. The assistants carrying their bags gazed on nervously, and Jamie had to give them the all-clear to head inside.

Before Lottie or Jamie could intervene, Anastacia slipped on a patch of ice, landing butt-first onto the frozen pathway with an "oof."

Ellie sauntered over to the very disheveled Anastacia and grinned. "I win."

It was hard to tell if it was the physical exertion or the cold, but it looked like Anastacia was actually blushing as Ellie reached down to help her up. Lottie couldn't help a pout forming, suddenly wishing she was the person Ellie was helping.

"Princess Eleanor Prudence Wolfson." They all froze at the severe tone that came from behind them. "It would be best if we could avoid pummeling our guests with snow in the future, would it not?"

Standing in the doorway was Edwina, the head of the household. She was a dark-haired, remarkably broad woman who looked as if she could throw a whole car. Behind her stood two uniformed members of staff, Midori and Hanna. Lottie could see their shoulders shaking as they tried to hold in their laughter; she couldn't blame them.

There was a prolonged pause as they all waited for Anastacia to take Ellie's hand, but she laughed and batted the hand away. "I can manage on my own, thank you very much."

She clambered back to her feet before dusting herself off calmly and marching to the palace doors. She greeted the household staff with a respectful nod, as if nothing unusual had happened at all. The rest of them swiftly followed behind her, Jamie giving Ellie a curt look that only made her snicker even more.

"Would you like a hot drink, mademoiselle?" Midori asked.

"Or maybe we could run you a bath?" Hanna added.

Anastacia paused, turning to the two maids, who took a nervous step back. She eyed them up and down, clearly bemused at all the attention. Everyone was treading on eggshells around her, desperate to stop her from changing her mind about speaking to Saskia. That made her their very special guest. Her eyes lit up with understanding.

"Hmm, let me see. I'll have an oat-milk matcha latte and a Himalayan salt bath with red rose petals, please. And while I'm bathing, could someone dry these for me?" She gestured to her drenched clothes, her usually perfect hair clinging to her face in wet strands. "And I want a box of Turkish delight to be waiting for me after my bath."

Midori and Hanna nodded and got to work without a fuss, Edwina following behind, looking positively bewildered.

"Wow!" Anastacia watched in fascination as they scurried off to do her bidding. "Remind me again why you don't want to be a princess?"

Ellie groaned, leaning her forehead against Lottie's

shoulder as if it were all too much to deal with.

"It's like having two of my grandmother."

"At least she's fitting in?" Lottie offered.

Everything went wrong on Christmas Day, the day before Anastacia was set to speak to Saskia.

They had eaten the traditional dinner of roast goose and creamed vegetables, serving themselves from a table fit to collapse under all the crystal candle holders, bushels of saffron crocuses, holly wreaths, and gilded wolf ornaments. It was a wonder there was any room for the food. Anastacia had joined them for dinner but then promptly vanished to her room.

The family retired to the lavender study with its purple flocked walls and white piano. Jamie sat at the piano and played for them while Ellie sat by his side, childishly nudging him in an attempt to make him mess up. Lottie, King Alexander, Queen Matilde, and the king's mother, Willemena, all settled down to the family tradition of decorating *sheniyes*. It was odd to see the Wolfsons participating in such a quaint tradition, and yet the king in particular took it very seriously as he sat on the ornamental chair and daintily painted a star on his own *sheniy*. Lottie smiled at the happy family scene as she added finishing touches to her own orbs. Hers were a pair, one with soft peach and gold coloring with suns and clouds and the other with milky midnight blues and stars. She intended to give the peachy one to Ellie and keep the dark one for herself.

Like Christmas friendship ornaments, she thought, smiling.

At the last minute she added one more to the set—a white-and-silver orb with a wolf's face in the center for Jamie.

"You have quite the eye for color." Lottie's skin prickled at Willemena's voice. Ellie's grandmother was small with mounds of spindly silver hair, and absolutely terrifying. Had she just given Lottie a compliment?

"Oh, thank you," Lottie responded quietly. "Actually, I've been painting since I was—"

"You must remedy that mumbling," Willemena scolded. "A princess is first and foremost a communicator of values. You cannot be hesitant if you are to be a great communicator . . ."

Lottie had to swallow her desire to tell this old woman that cutting someone off midsentence was not the hallmark of a great communicator either.

"Okay, we're off." Ellie abruptly stood up from the piano stool, interrupting Willemena's rant. She came over to Lottie and pulled her up off her seat, rescuing her. "Jamie, you too."

Jamie let out one of his long-suffering sighs and looked for permission from the king, who gave a discreet nod. If

Willemena had seen, she'd have blown a fuse.

"I quite think not. This is a family Christmas, and we will be—"

The white double doors clicked shut behind them, cutting off Willemena's words. They'd escaped.

"How'd I do?" Ellie asked when they were safely down the corridor.

Jamie looked down at his watch.

"Four hours and twenty-six minutes. That's a new record."

"What's that?" Lottie asked, leaning on her tiptoes to peer at Jamie's watch.

He smirked. "How long Ellie can stand to be around her grandmother at Christmas."

"If I make it a game, then it's less awful," Ellie said, giving Lottie a wink.

They were heading toward the Vault when they walked past the kitchen and saw something entirely unexpected.

A cascade of mahogany hair as a figure hunched over three bowls of food.

"Too sweet," a familiar voice declared, nibbling at a spoonful of food before moving on to the next bowl. "Ah, too bitter."

A brunette Goldilocks, no less . . .

"Anastacia?"

"*Quoi?*" Her head shot up as she scrambled to hide her

hands behind her back. A telltale smear on her mouth matched the chocolate brown of her hair.

Ellie snorted. "Are you . . . eating chocolate?"

"No!" Then she reluctantly brought her hands back out to show them, fingers covered in melted chocolate. Her expression shifted to a pout. "Yes. So what?"

"No, it's fine," Ellie assured her, still laughing. "Just, why are you doing it so secretly?"

"Because . . ." A furious blush crept onto her face. "When I'm nervous I eat chocolate. Is that really so shocking?"

"I think I'm more shocked by the idea that you ever get nervous," Lottie joked, but a swift scowl from Anastacia told her to quickly shut up. She hastily added, "Sorry."

Be kind, she chastised herself. Of course Anastacia was nervous. Tomorrow, she'd be seeing Saskia. Lottie couldn't even begin to imagine how she must be feeling. She slowly reached out for Ellie's hand, and then Jamie's. They both looked at her, shocked, until their expressions turned soft, a warm understanding blooming. The idea of ever confronting either of them in the same way Anastacia had to face Saskia was too hard to even think about.

"Well," Ellie said to Anastacia, smirking, "if you're craving chocolate, we can help with that."

"Ta-da!" Ellie swept back her arm to reveal their Frankenstein creation. The kitchen looked as though a flour bomb had gone off, a dusting of white powder decorating Ellie's hair like snow.

"It's a Funfetti pancake wrapped around a caramel chocolate bar with a Marshmallow Fluff and popping-candy filling, lightly fried in butter to bring out its gooey goodness." Lottie beamed, admiring their creation. "Although personally I prefer mine with strawberries. It's really up to you what you put in it."

"We call it the chocurrito!" Ellie's teeth sparkled like little fangs as she grinned at Anastacia.

"That is an insult to crepes." Anastacia pointed at the gooey chocolate mess with distaste, her nose crinkling. "Far too much sugar for one person."

"That's what I always tell them," Jamie said.

Lottie still found his dislike of sweet foods downright unholy, but—hey—it meant there was more for her and Ellie.

"Don't knock it until you try it," she said, pinching a mini marshmallow from a bowl on the worktop and holding it up for Ellie, who nipped it from her fingers.

Anastacia's eyebrows shot up with an are-you-kidding-me look, but Lottie was not going to let this slide. Anastacia was going to have a good Christmas whether she liked it or not.

"Come on. It's Christmas, and I promise it'll satiate your chocolate desires." Lottie gave her the very best encouraging smile she could muster.

A swell of delicious warm cocoa scent drifted their way, and even Anastacia couldn't hide how enticed she was, though Jamie continued to shake his head in disgust.

She sighed, rolling her eyes in defeat. "Fine, I'll try it."

Ellie carefully cut the chocurrito into three even chunks and passed them around, the gooey caramel center dripping from the soft pancake wrap.

Anastacia took a dainty bite, the chocolate melting across her dark red lips.

"*C'est magnifique!*" she whispered, as if speaking a tiny prayer.

Lottie couldn't believe it. Anastacia was actually enjoying something.

Ellie grinned at Lottie triumphantly, and for a split second she actually felt that Anastacia might be okay . . . until Ellie said the worst thing possible.

"There is no girl I cannot win over with my chocolate creations," Ellie declared, taking a bite out of her own dessert. "Saskia should be taking lessons from *me*."

Oh dear.

"What did you say?" Anastacia's voice turned cold, but Ellie didn't seem to notice.

"Ellie," Jamie shushed in outraged warning.

The room went very quiet as Anastacia delicately put her dessert down, taking a step toward the door.

"I can't do this." Anastacia sniffed, turning so they couldn't see her. "I'm sorry." She flew out of the kitchen, a single tear escaping into the air like a jewel as she ran away.

"Anastacia!" Lottie called after her, but it was too late.

She turned back to a blinking Ellie, the flour in her hair falling softly down to her shoulders as she shook her head in confusion. "What did I do?" Ellie asked plaintively.

"You really are such an idiot sometimes," Jamie growled.

31

THREE KNOCKS ON THE DOOR with no response.

Lottie tried again. Each time the echo of her knuckles on the wood sounded more lonely.

"Anastacia?" Lottie called her name.

"*Va t'en!*" came the furious voice from behind the door. Lottie had no idea what it meant, but she could make a good guess.

"Anastacia, please. I just wanted to bring you a cup of hot cocoa," she said desperately.

This time there was a rustling on the other side of the door and it inched open. An angry blue eye appeared through the crack in the door and nearly made Lottie jump backward in shock.

"Give it to me," she commanded, her hand lashing out through the tiny gap.

"Anastacia—"

"Give. It. To. Me!" she repeated.

Lottie took a deep breath, knowing she had to be careful in case Anastacia withdrew her offer to talk to Saskia.

"I'll give it to you." Her voice came out shakier than she

would have liked. "But please let me in. Please, I know Ellie can be an idiot. She didn't mean it. Please, Anastacia."

"Urgh." Anastacia rolled her eyes as she opened the door, red nightgown and braided hair coming into full view. "Stop begging." Her arms were crossed firmly over her chest as Lottie timidly entered. "Hurry up!"

"Sorry." Lottie quickly stepped forward, shutting the door behind her and tiptoeing to the other side of the room so that Anastacia couldn't change her mind and force her out. She looked around. To Lottie's surprise, the room was a mess of clothes, different outfits strewn across the bed and over chairs. She realized that Anastacia must have been worrying about what she'd wear when she saw Saskia the next day.

"Okay, I let you in. Now give me the mug and get out." She was still standing by the door, fluffy red slippers perfectly matching her nightgown and robe.

Lottie's hand trembled as she set the mug down on Anastacia's nightstand, knowing it was her only leverage. She just had to hope this wasn't another one of those cases where trying to help would make things worse.

"Anastacia." She didn't know where to start. "I know it's hard, and I know Ellie is an idiot. You can be mad at her. I just want you to know that you can talk about Saskia to me if you want. I will listen. I want to help. I want you to be happy again."

She spewed the words out, squeezing her eyes shut in a desperate attempt not to be intimidated. When she opened her eyes again, Anastacia didn't seem as heated as she had before, the raging fire burning down to a glowing ember. "If you don't want to talk, I get it. I can leave." Anastacia marched over and snatched the mug up, making Lottie flinch. But she didn't order her to leave. Instead a deep sigh escaped her lips.

"I'm not mad at Ellie," she began, surprising Lottie. "I'm fully aware she doesn't think before she speaks. She just . . . *urgh*." Anastacia looked away, clearly mad at herself for whatever she was about to say next. "She reminds me of Saskia."

Lottie quickly bit her lip, but there was no way she could hide her shock.

Anastacia flung herself onto the bed, gazing up at the ceiling. "You and Ellie are so dense, honestly." She took a gulp of her cocoa and leveled a hard look at Lottie. "I just hope it works out better for you two than it did for us." Her voice had turned soft.

Lottie found herself all at once feeling entirely lost, floating adrift in a sea of Anastacia's emotions. If she wanted to understand Anastacia, she needed to go back to the beginning.

"How did Saskia become your Partizan?" She took a hesitant seat on the satin bedspread, next to Anastacia, who had unbraided her hair and let it spill out across the satin in a pool of mahogany.

Without looking at Lottie, Anastacia gracefully sat up, cradling the mug in her palms. It was as though every movement were a dance.

"Did you know that a lot of Partizans end up marrying other Partizans? They know their partners will be the only ones who can understand the importance of their job." She stared off into space. "There were two Partizans working for the Bolivian government who did exactly that. My mother met them when on ambassadorial work, and she also met their child, Saskia." She spoke the name so tenderly Lottie couldn't stop her hand rushing to her chest, her fingers feeling the wolf pendant beneath her dress. "They told my mother of plans to raise Saskia as a Partizan herself. My parents had been considering hiring a bodyguard for me for a while, as there had been so many kidnapping attempts on the children of ambassadors."

"Like Jamie," Lottie whispered. "He was trained as a Partizan very young too."

Anastacia nodded, finally looking Lottie in the eye. "I figured as much." There was a hint of regret in her tone, but she quickly composed herself. "My parents paid a lot of money to have them brought over to Paris so Saskia could be raised alongside me while she continued training. We never saw much of her parents. They were always off doing important work. Saskia was left with us a lot of the time."

"What went wrong?" Lottie leaned forward, enthralled by the story.

"*Mon père*." She hissed the words. "My father is very traditional. I think he always resented how Saskia ended up being a part of the family. He tried to keep his feelings hidden, but kids aren't stupid. She worked so hard to prove to him that she was worth his respect, but the closer we grew the more difficult it became."

"That's awful," Lottie said.

Anastacia nodded, her face twisted with bitterness and something that looked like regret.

"My father has never pretended he was anything other than old-fashioned. We could never let him know how close we'd become. Little did I know someone else had got to Saskia. Leviathan was whispering in her ear, telling her that she and I could be together one day if she followed them."

Suddenly Raphael's idea that Saskia had also been brainwashed didn't seem so far from the truth. The sticky glue of what he'd said back in the rose garden seeped through her brain, stringy tendrils of a theory piecing together inside her head. She thought of Jamie, a boy who carried burdens beyond his years, and her heart ached. Saskia was the same. She might have seemed older, but she was only a year above them. She was still a kid—they all were—and

Leviathan had taken advantage of that.

"It must be hard, to be so young and feel so much responsibility." Lottie couldn't mask the sadness in her voice.

Anastacia laughed bitterly. "That's ironic coming from a Portman."

"I suppose it is. Jamie used to tell me that I shouldn't have been allowed to become a Portman, that I shouldn't have had to become so defensive or careful. But the difference that he could never understand is that I made a choice. He thinks he did too—but it doesn't always feel that way." Lottie thought back to his tortured expression on the field. He'd been so ashamed that she'd glimpsed that part of him, a part he thought he'd killed.

"Saskia made the choice."

"Do you really believe that? I guess we can never know."

Anastacia slowly sat up. "She was my best friend," she said in a pained whisper. "How could she not want to be my Partizan? She said she wanted to be by my side forever." There was a touch of acid in her voice, a wound that she'd been letting fester all this time.

Finally Lottie understood. "Anastacia, just because she might not want to be your Partizan, that doesn't mean she doesn't want to be with you. They're not the same thing."

Blue eyes that burned like fire bore into Lottie's gaze. Then Anastacia stood up, calmly moved to the door, and pulled it open.

"I want to be alone now," she said, all the poison in her voice replaced by a mask of composure.

There was nothing left to say. Lottie climbed off the bed and walked to the door.

Ellie and Jamie were waiting for her.

"Is she still going to speak to Saskia?" Jamie asked, ever committed to his role.

Her conversation with Anastacia had left a hard feeling in her gut.

"Yes," she said, glancing back at the closed door. Lottie hoped her instincts would be proved right. "She'll speak to her."

32

THE KNOCK ON ANASTACIA'S DOOR came at midday the next day. She'd spent the morning in much the same way she had every other day in the palace: lazily indulging in an opulent bath, eating a breakfast of fresh fruit and porridge in her quarters, and trying to ignore the inevitable meeting that loomed ahead. It took longer getting ready that day, and she hesitated, dragging her feet.

But now she was ready.

She was escorted by a tall man with huge muscles and scars that he wore like trophies. There was a dagger tattoo above his wrist, the symbolism of which she didn't care to know. She'd met him before, briefly after the summer ball, and knew he was the king's Partizan. She couldn't remember his name and was relieved when another member of the household called out, "Good afternoon, Sir Olav."

They went down and inward, past the pastel walls and polished marble, which eventually gave way to a cold stone floor and wood paneling. Anastacia wondered with a shudder how many people in the past had been abandoned down here. She braced herself for barred cells and skeletal prisoners, but when they reached the "dungeons" on the floor below she saw no such thing. Instead she found a hallway with a deep-red carpet that led to three containment rooms and a surveillance room. It turned out that the prisoners' living conditions were actually rather pleasant. There was a private bathroom, a place to sit and eat, a double bed, and shelves of books to keep them entertained.

"We've informed her of your visit," Sir Olav said stiffly. "Is there anything you need before we let you in?"

Only my common sense back, please, Anastacia thought as she shook her head.

"Good." He keyed in the code for the first door.

Anastacia could feel her heart rate rising as they approached a second, more simple door. There was no code for this one, only an iron key.

I can't believe these idiots persuaded me to do this.

The door creaked open to reveal a bare, dimly lit room; it was a stark contrast to the rooms that she'd just passed. Anastacia stepped into the room, keeping her chin high. She wouldn't allow an ounce of her composure to slip away. She would not for a second let Saskia think she was nervous. She was Anastacia Alcroft LeBlanc, daughter of Sylvie LeBlanc and Sebastian Alcroft. She could be neither intimidated nor bewitched.

"Ani?" The question came from a figure on the bed.

Anastacia's bravado melted away at the honeyed voice of her ex-Partizan.

Saskia stood up as if welcoming royalty and was given a severe look of warning from Sir Olav.

"I won't speak unless we're allowed to be alone," Saskia said coldly, her voice losing all the sweet notes intended for Anastacia.

Sir Olav held her gaze for a moment before emitting a growl that was so similar to Jamie's that Anastacia found it amusing.

Paritzans, she thought, rolling her eyes.

"We'll be watching," Sir Olav grumbled, before leaving them alone. It was clear he was being quite literal; cameras on the walls moved to focus on the two girls.

As soon as the door shut behind him, Saskia's face flooded with affection and Anastacia smiled in response. This was her best friend. This was the girl who knew everything about her and loved her anyway. The girl who made her realize why she never cared for boy bands or any of the love letters she received from schoolboys. The girl who meant everything to her.

"I've been waiting for you."

"It doesn't look like you've had much choice." Anastacia bit her tongue as soon as the words were out.

Saskia was just as ferocious as she remembered. She

looked exactly the same but for her complexion—her usually bronzed skin had turned pale from lack of sunlight. It was a crime to let a sun lover wilt away in this windowless cell. It took all of Anastacia's willpower not to reach out and hug her.

"Ani, I really was going to come back for you. I had it all planned out perfectly, but *they* got in the way." She spat the word "they" like it was poison.

"Ha." Anastacia couldn't stop a cackle escaping her lips. "Don't kid yourself, Saskia. You did this all on your own."

Saskia's eyebrows furrowed. They'd reached an impasse.

Dropping some of her bravado, Saskia let out a huff of breath from her nose and sat back down again, her arms crossed defensively. "Why did you finally agree to come here? Why has it taken you so long?"

"I'm sure you can imagine that seeing the Partizan who betrayed me wasn't at the top of my list of things to do." She felt a thrill of satisfaction and then guilt as her ex-Partizan looked away with a pained expression.

"Then why are you here?" Saskia said again, more forcefully this time.

Anastacia let out an exasperated breath; there was no way to avoid it. "We need information," she admitted.

Saskia sat up straighter and leaned forward, intrigued. "What do you know?"

"All we know is that your evil little group is working

on some kind of mind control." *Rule number one of getting information: always pretend you know less than you do.* "And we want to know how and we want to know why."

Saskia narrowed her eyes. "If I tell you, you have to do something for me."

Anastacia didn't want to agree to anything before she knew what it was.

"Sit close to me," Saskia continued.

"What?" Anastacia spluttered.

"Just for a moment," Saskia said lightly. "I've missed you so, so much." Her voice was soft, tempting Anastacia to forgive her for everything. She gestured for Anastacia to sit down, patting the mattress beside her, but Anastacia shook her head. "I'll tell you everything you need to know . . ." Saskia trailed off.

There was a long pause, then: "Fine." Anastacia leaned close to Saskia, surprised at how easy it was to give in. Saskia smiled.

"Tompkins is the key," Saskia told her.

"We know that," Anastacia responded.

Saskia raised an eyebrow. It gave Anastacia another thrill to realize that she'd surprised her.

"I wasn't part of the group infiltrating Tompkins, but I heard enough about the plan," Saskia said. "They're after something called the Hamelin Formula, and they've been testing their version on pupils at Rosewood. I even tried to test it on Lottie and Jamie, but it never works how it's supposed to. That's how Jamie ended up falling in the pool." Saskia spoke calmly, as if her words weren't completely and utterly terrifying.

"You were willing to work for a group that's trying to control people's minds? Don't you see how insane that is?"

"You wouldn't understand," Saskia replied, waving a hand dismissively. "Do you want to know the details or not?"

Anastacia's fists curled, but she nodded for her to continue.

"You can't trust the Butter Company," said Saskia. "Richard Butter's been unknowingly under the influence of our master for years."

Anastacia felt a stab in her chest at the word "master." Who was this leader of Leviathan? Who was this shadowy figure who had lured Saskia away from her? Whoever it was, they would severely pay.

"They've taken over the Tompkins Manor. Stay as far away from Julius or Ingrid as possible. They're working undercover as interns at the Butter Company." Her expression turned intense. "Are you listening? Stay away from them."

Anastacia nodded quickly, refusing to let Saskia see how

anxious she was. She recognized the names from Lola, who'd made it clear they made her nervous. Now it was obvious why.

"They know that the formula is hidden somewhere within the Tompkins Manor, but they have no idea where," Saskia continued, though she looked away in a bored way. "If you want to stop them, you have to find the formula and destroy it before they get to it."

The Tompkins Manor. It's in the Tompkins Manor. Stay away from Julius and Ingrid.

Anastacia committed the information to memory. She had been to the Tompkins Manor many times before when staying over with Lola and Micky, and she'd be going back again in only a few months for the Spearion. This was the information they needed. She couldn't stop her heart racing at the realization that they might actually be able to do something to stop Leviathan.

"Now look at me," Saskia commanded, dragging Anastacia out of her thoughts.

Her beautiful ex-Partizan leaned forward, forcing Anastacia to meet her gaze. She found herself reaching out. Gently Saskia clasped her hand and lifted it to her face, moving with such tenderness that it made Anastacia dissolve.

But something was wrong.

She couldn't do this. She couldn't let this happen again.

She'd already had her heart broken once; she wouldn't allow a repeat.

Reluctantly Anastacia snatched her hand away, refusing to let Saskia see the hurt in her eyes. "I have one final question," she said, her voice trembling. She didn't care anymore if she sounded weak. "Saskia, I have to ask you . . ." She clenched her fists hard and spat out the question. "Did you want to be my Partizan?"

Saskia stared back at her in open surprise. "Yes. Of course. I love spending my time with you." This wasn't the right answer.

"I know, but I'm asking—did you *want* to be my *Partizan?*"

Saskia's dark brown eyes darted about. The silence stretched on; it was all the answer Anastacia needed.

"I wanted to protect you," she said at last.

Anastacia held her hand up to her chest, as if hoping to prevent her heart from crumbling. "I just don't understand. Why would you betray my family and then turn around and betray Leviathan and tell me all this information? What do you even want?" she pleaded, unable to prevent the tears from springing to her eyes.

"Isn't it obvious, Ani?" Saskia looked deep into her eyes, begging her to understand. "The only one I'm loyal to is you."

Anastacia barely had time to process Saskia's words

before the door behind her clicked open. Their time was up, and she only had one thing left to say. "Then prove it."

Tears pooled in her eyes, threatening to spill over as she made her way out of the claustrophobic space. Sir Olav stood waiting, but she couldn't even look at him, storming past as fast as she could, making it very clear that she was in no mood to talk right now. Red, everything was red; she was a bull in a rage of swirling furious emotion.

She'd done what she'd come here to do—what she'd promised the others she'd do—and now she couldn't get away quickly enough.

Whatever Saskia did next would decide their future forever.

PART THREE
Enemies

33

THEY ARRIVED BACK AT ROSEWOOD Hall just as the snowdrops were beginning to bloom. They filled the Rose Wood, the delicate white beads spotting the green, reaching right up to the edge of the woodland and the Ivy Wood dorm.

Lottie chanced a smile at Anastacia as they all got comfortable in Liliana's studio, but she didn't return the gesture. This was different from the flippant, haughty attitude they'd become so used to from her. This was a distant lethargy that somehow made Lottie feel far worse.

Ever since talking to Saskia, Anastacia had been distracted. She'd shared with them the information they needed but was adamant that nothing else had happened. Lottie knew better than to bring it up, but it was painfully clear that Anastacia had been upset by her meeting with Saskia, and Lottie couldn't help feeling responsible. After all, hadn't they asked her to do it?

"Okay, listen up, everyone," Jamie commanded, extending a pointer from his hand so fast it made a snapping sound in the air.

They had taken a whiteboard down to their secret base,

propping it up next to the back wall. Binah and Jamie were giving them a cram session on "How to Commit Espionage," going over all the information they'd acquired so far. On the board, in thick bold letters, were five points.

1. Leviathan has infiltrated the Tompkins Manor.
2. Leviathan wants the Hamelin Formula.
3. The Hamelin Formula is hidden somewhere in the Tompkins Manor.
4. We must find and DESTROY the Hamelin Formula before they get it.
5. Do not go anywhere near the Butter Company interns Julius and Ingrid.

"We have less than six weeks until the Spearion. All the teams are staying in the Tompkins Manor, and everyone from Rosewood gets to invite a guest," Jamie reiterated, pointing to a space on the whiteboard that read "*Sixty guests in total.*"

"So we'll have Lola and Micky and Percy there, as their families are hosting, as well as Ellie and Anastacia on the fencing team, and Lottie and Jamie will be their guests." Binah went through the list, jotting down everything as she spoke with unwavering efficiency.

"What? Why don't I get to come?" Raphael moaned, tutting.

"Because, Raphael," Anastacia mocked, "you're not a trained bodyguard, nor are you a princess."

"I could be one of those things," he replied in an equally mocking tone. "Maybe I'm undercover too."

The sharp edge of a retort tingled on Anastacia's lips; Lottie cleared her throat loudly, quickly moving the conversation away from any distraction.

The tournament was taking place only a few days before the Easter break. The only people who were going to stay behind were Binah and Raphael.

"Lola, Micky, Percy—you need to inspect all the rooms and try to find the formula's hiding place before all the guests arrive."

Lola and Micky nodded. They both had lollipops in their mouths, making their serious expressions comical.

"What if we don't find it before the guests arrive?" Percy signed.

"Then we move on to plan B." Jamie spoke while Micky signed everything for Percy. "Lottie, Ellie, Anastacia, and I will help hunt for it before the tour of the factory."

"Might I remind you all that first and foremost I am going to the Spearion to win," Anastacia interrupted. "I'll be spending most of my time scoping out the competition and, if it is called for, 'psyching them out,' as Raphael likes to put it."

"That might actually work," Binah said, making another

note. "We'll need to inspect every room. Psyching out the other contestants could be good cover for getting inside the competitors' areas." She put the pen back behind her ear and pointed to Anastacia. "That can be your job."

Anastacia stared at her in disbelief before reluctantly shoving her sunglasses back on. "Fine."

Lottie could practically hear her eyes rolling from behind her shades.

"So when do we actually destroy the formula?" Ellie asked, not even attempting to hide her delight at the idea of getting to destroy something.

Binah coughed into her fist. "Well, actually, you won't be doing any destroying, Ellie. You're part of the distraction."

"Ha!" Anastacia let out a curt laugh, and Ellie scowled.

"The plan is," Jamie went on, not wanting a fight to break out, "to find the location of the formula before any of the guests arrive and use the commotion of the Spearion to sneak off and destroy it. We can be back in the arena before anyone suspects anything."

"But how much time does that give us?" Lottie asked, suddenly feeling very nervous. "Is the Spearion enough of a distraction?"

"It's not like a usual fencing match." Binah turned the board over to reveal a color-coded diagram. "The whole thing takes place over two hours. There are forty

contestants, and each contestant is entered individually."
She nodded to Anastacia and Ellie, who both returned the
gesture. "They're each paired up randomly for the first
match, where the rounds are quick-fire, leaving twenty
contestants remaining. They're then paired up randomly
again until there's ten, and once more until five contestants
remain. Those last five contestants must have demonstrated
a selection of moves over their previous matches, and the
lowest scorer is removed, leaving four." She pointed to a sad
face in the middle of the board next to four happy faces.
"They are then paired up for three matches each until it's
down to the final two." Ellie and Anastacia glared at each
other, both sure that they would be the last ones in the
arena. "They play three matches until a winner is decided
and awarded the Spearion Trophy."

"That sounds exhausting." Lottie could hardly imagine
completing one intense fencing match, let alone nine in a
row.

"There's a fifteen-minute break in the middle." Anastacia shrugged. "It's more than enough rest time for me."

"Wait," said Lottie, a thought suddenly occurring to her.
"If Lola, Micky, Percy, Jamie, and I are all off destroying
the Hamelin Formula during the Spearion, how will we
watch Ellie and Anastacia fight?"

All eyes in the room turned to her, and she instantly
regretted the question.

"Um," Binah began.

"That's not exactly a priority, Pumpkin," Raphael teased gently.

Lottie felt her cheeks go bright red. Ellie gave her a soft smile to let her know she thought it was sweet, but Lottie couldn't shake how mortified she was. She thought of the king telling her that sometimes she'd need to put Ellie second to put her first. Sure enough, when she looked up at Jamie, his face was dark with disappointment.

"Sorry. Of course! I just, I was looking forward to seeing them . . ." Her voice trailed off.

"Hopefully you'll destroy the formula with enough time to get back to the arena for the last match," Binah offered, ever helpful.

"Sure you will," Anastacia said tonelessly. "Now can someone explain to me what we're supposed to do if we run into those undercover Leviathans—urgh, what were their names?"

"Ingrid and Julius," Lola and Micky said in unison, pulling their lollipops out of their mouths.

"Right." Jamie flipped the board over again and wrote "INGRID AND JULIUS" in big capital letters in the center. "If Saskia, an ex-Partizan, is warning you not to go near these two people, my advice would be that we avoid Ingrid and Julius at all costs. If you run into them, do not engage with them."

Everyone nodded in agreement, and Lottie felt the air go cold, a shiver running up her spine as if the room was trying to warn her about these two people.

"Question," Ellie said, her hand darting up in the air. "How exactly are we supposed to avoid two random people when we don't know what they look like?"

Jamie's gaze fell on the twins, and everyone else's followed.

"Ingrid has long black hair with bangs," Lola began.

"And Julius always wears a cowboy hat," the twins replied together.

"A cowboy hat?" Jamie and Lottie both spluttered.

"Wait . . ." Jamie grabbed his folder of information on Leviathan, pulling out the images Ollie had sent. "Is this them?"

The twins and Percy grabbed the pages from him, their faces lighting up in recognition.

"That's them." The twins' voices lost their usual syrupy sweetness, and they held the papers out for everyone else to look at.

Once again Lottie realized she should have trusted her instincts; these were the strange people Lola had been talking about in the Rose Wood. Ingrid and Julius, the moles in the Butter Company. Those two sets of cunning eyes that had felt like they were watching her through the paper. The idea that they might bump into them at the

Tompkins Manor made her blood turn cold.

"Okay," Binah declared, sensing the shift in atmosphere and clapping her hands together to pull everyone out of their dark thoughts. "Is everyone completely clear on the plan?"

They all nodded again, and Lottie gulped down her worries, not wanting anyone to see how nervous she really was. She was a descendant of Liliana Mayfutt; she should be able to handle anything.

"Excellent," Binah said, wiping the board. "Now, as long as we can find out where the formula is hidden before the Spearion, it'll be a piece of cake."

❦ 34 ❧

WITH ONLY TWO WEEKS LEFT until the Spearion, it was almost impossible to concentrate during classes. While all the other students fretted, preparing for exams, Lottie had bigger things to worry about. She was using every spare moment to figure out where the Hamelin Formula was hidden. Their plan had to work; they couldn't allow Leviathan to perfect something as dangerous as the Hamelin Formula.

It was not going well.

And, to make matters worse, the universe had decided to present her with a new distraction.

"Excuse me, Professor Devine," Lottie began sheepishly, taking a cautious step into the professor's lavish office, "is this royal history trip mandatory?"

She held out the school trip letter for the professor to inspect, trying her best not to be intimidated by the beautiful room. She'd been there only once before, when she and Ellie had been caught up past curfew and the professor had taken it upon herself to teach them a lesson that involved drinking fancy tea in her office.

"Don't worry, Miss Pumpkin." Lottie let out a relieved breath, but the action was premature. "We understand your special arrangement, so I've received permission from Headmaster Croak for your bodyguard Jamie to attend too." She smiled up at Lottie from her desk in a way that let her know there was no chance she was getting out of this. "It should be a splendid day trip."

And so Lottie and Jamie were stuck heading off with the rest of the royal history students to Hampton Court for a very unwelcome distraction.

But it wasn't just losing time that Lottie was worried about. Save for that one time in the library, she and Jamie had not been alone together since the incident on the field all those months ago.

Lottie chanced a glance at Jamie as they walked toward the private cars that were waiting to take the students off to Hampton Court. It was a beautiful spring day, but his expression would make anyone think they were off to a drizzly funeral.

"Jamie, lighten up. What could possibly go wrong?" Ellie said, there to see them off.

"Think of it as a fun trip away before we have to face the big villain," Binah twittered. She'd put her hair in a large bun on top of her head, making a perfect puffy ball that only succeeded in making her look even tinier than usual.

Lottie and Jamie both glanced at each other, neither of

them comfortable with leaving Ellie behind.

Swallowing her worries, Lottie said, "I know the last thing you want to do is be stuck on a school trip with me, Jamie, but we have no choice in the matter, so we might as well make the best of it." She beamed at Ellie, trying to shake off her worry.

Jamie narrowed his eyes at her and she gulped.

She could act as relaxed as she wanted for Ellie's benefit, but she knew Jamie could tell that she was equally troubled by their lack of progress on the Hamelin Formula's hiding place.

"One, two, three, four, five, and Jamie, and seven, and yes, excellent!" Professor Devine and Headmaster Croak went down the line of students, counting each one to make sure they were all present.

"I'll be fine, Jamie." Ellie leaned low so only they could hear her as they got into one of the cars. "Everyone thinks Lottie's the princess, remember? That's kind of the point of a Portman." She tapped his wolf pendant before stepping back. "I'll see you history nerds later."

She gave them a hearty wave and off they went.

After living at Rosewood Hall for nearly two years, it was hard for Lottie to be impressed by any other gardens. She'd become so used to a world of magical lavender and roses with bright petals in every color you could ever imagine.

Rosewood was a dreamworld of flora, a blossoming garden with its own enchanted atmosphere. So to be able to say that the Hampton Court gardens charmed her was a massive compliment.

"King Henry the Eighth was a pompous man. He wanted to astound people with his power and riches, and that was exactly the purpose of Hampton Court." Professor Devine pointed at the lavish decoration, attempting to hide her distaste and failing tremendously. "He had the palace made even more splendid in the mid 1520s after he took it from Cardinal Wolsey."

Headmaster Croak walked alongside the professor, wooden cane in hand, but he made no attempt to hide his disapproval. "Supposedly it was called the pleasure palace, for the level of debauchery that occurred within the walls," he grumbled, almost as if he'd actually witnessed some of these events, and Lottie had to pinch herself to stop from laughing.

"Indeed," Professor Devine replied, "it is not uncommon in royal history to find the occasional sordid story."

Lottie gulped, wondering if the Wolfsons had any "sordid" tales. Suddenly she wanted to run back to Rosewood and dive into Oscar's diary to see if she could spot any.

They continued to walk the grounds, and it became quite obvious to all of them that this was more of a fun sight-seeing trip than one intended for learning. Lottie was trying her best to let go and enjoy herself, but something was causing a deeply uncomfortable itch that she couldn't scratch.

Everyone in the gardens was staring at them.

"Is it just me, or do you feel like we're being watched?" Lottie whispered to Binah.

Binah giggled. "You've never been out in your Rosewood uniform before, have you?"

Lottie shook her head, accidentally catching the eyes of a group of other school students, who all began whispering among each other.

"Doesn't it make you feel a bit funny?" she asked.

The emblems on their school blazers stuck out like a sore thumb, the world-famous Rosewood symbol like a giant red marker. No wonder they were drawing so much attention.

"I'm sure Jamie's used to it," Binah said, laughing. "That's how most of the Rosewood students look at him all the time."

Jamie raised a warning eyebrow at Binah.

"Oooh, so scary," she mocked.

Lottie couldn't help feeling bad that Jamie had been dragged here; he'd barely said a word since they'd left the school.

"I think I need to go to the restroom," Lottie said, suddenly wanting to get away from all the stares.

"I'm coming with you," Jamie replied automatically, before realizing what he'd just said. "I mean, I'll wait outside," he said, correcting himself and leaning against the wall next to the ladies' bathroom.

It took all Lottie's willpower not to burst out laughing at how uncomfortable he'd just made himself, and she felt bad for finding it so funny.

"I'm just going to the restroom, Jamie. I'm not vanishing into the void," she reassured him.

"Well, be quick," he demanded, not moving.

Inside, Lottie went to a sink to splash some cold water on her face, taking a moment to look at her reflection in the mirror. She still found it hard to believe anyone thought she was a princess, and it was even stranger to think that people were impressed by the emblem she wore. Still, despite her doubts, she knew Rosewood was her home. She felt right there; it was her history, her legacy.

So why was she feeling so odd again today?

The water from the tap continued to trickle, disappearing down into the black hole at the center of the gold basin, an endless stream vanishing into the pipes.

She knew the answer to her question, and its name was Jamie Volk.

No matter how comfortable she got, no matter how far she progressed in finding who she was, she felt like she was leaving Jamie behind.

But there was nothing she could do; she'd had to make this journey on her own, and so would he. She just hoped he didn't get lost along the way.

A door on the other side of the restroom opened, making Lottie jump. She turned the tap off, the pipes squeaking as she wrenched the handle. She looked up in the mirror again and a figure appeared behind her so quickly she didn't have time to scream. It reached its hand around her wrist and pulled her backward into one of the stalls. In a moment of sheer feral terror she grabbed the person's hand and bit down hard, making the intruder yell in pain.

Throwing herself out of the cubicle, she let out a manic screech, but Jamie was already there, charging through the door and putting himself between Lottie and the stall.

"Stay behind me," he commanded, slipping into a defensive stance. She readily complied, stepping as close to him as possible, her whole body frozen with fear as the stall door slowly swung open to reveal her attacker.

It wasn't at all who she expected to see. Her whole brain went fuzzy as she took in the confused face before her.

"Ollie?"

❦ 35 ❦

"OH MY GOD, WHAT IN the ever-loving—" Ollie laughed as he tried to come to terms with what had just happened. "You *BIT* me?"

"I thought you were a kidnapper or something!" Lottie shouted, stepping out in front of Jamie and crossing her arms.

"What are you doing here?" Jamie demanded.

"We're on a school trip too—a few days away to see the historic sites around London," Ollie said, still laughing nervously. "I saw you arrive and figured it was my duty to warn you."

"Warn her?" Jamie asked, his eyes narrowing.

"Can she not speak for herself? Jeez," Ollie replied, rolling his eyes as he finally stepped out of the cubicle. "Kate and Charlie are here too. If they see you here, Lottie, your whole princess thing is blown."

Crap, Lottie thought.

For all her worrying, she'd never for a second thought their plan would be brought down by something this ridiculous. One of the reasons that she'd been accepted as Ellie's Portman was that there was little chance of her being recognized by the few people she knew from her hometown, and now here they were!

"Who are Kate and Charlie?" Jamie dropped his defensive posture, relaxing back into his regular only-slightly-prepared-to-kill mode of operation.

"They're friends from when I was a little kid," she explained.

"Bad friends," Ollie interrupted. "Totally ditched her when her mum got ill—"

"Ollie, shhh!" Lottie scowled at him, cheeks going pink. This was not the time to be dwelling on that sort of thing.

"Lottie?" Lottie nearly jumped out of her skin, clutching Jamie's arm as Binah appeared behind them. There were a lot of people in here!

"Binah, you have *got* to stop doing that," Lottie panted, letting go of Jamie's arm, her pink cheeks turning a furious red when she realized she'd been clinging to him like a baby monkey.

"Is this Ollie?" Binah asked, taking a step forward.

"You talk about me?" Ollie held his hand against his chest. "I'm flattered."

But the problem was that Lottie *didn't* talk about Ollie.

"Binah, how on earth do you know who Ollie is?" she asked.

"I overheard you talking about him last year with Ellie

when I was studying in the tunnels. You have a unique way of describing people, Lottie. It was very easy to—"

Lottie groaned. "Binah, no more eavesdropping in the tunnels!"

Binah swished her hand in the air dismissively, not taking Lottie even a little bit seriously. "What's got everyone in such a huff?" she asked, her arms folding over her yellow blazer.

Lottie looked to Jamie nervously. "Some old school friends are here on a trip too, and if they see me then it might blow the whole Portman thing."

"Oh!" Binah said, oblivious to Ollie's enthralled gaze. "Well, that's easy to fix. We'll just have to put you in a disguise."

Without room for protest, Binah immediately got to work. She pulled Lottie's hair up into a knot above her head with strands sticking out in such a way that it made her hair look much shorter than it was, then she used a brown eyebrow pencil to create a wash of fake freckles over her nose and pink cheeks. The delicate concentration on Binah's face as she set about her project put a warm feeling through Lottie's body, like she was a child being dressed up by her mother for the first day of school.

For a final touch Binah took out a pair of spare glasses from her yellow backpack and placed them on Lottie's face.

The whole world became magnified, everything warping as her eyes tried to adjust.

"Perfect!" Binah exclaimed, happily clapping her hands together.

Lottie couldn't stop the gasp that escaped her mouth as she caught sight of her reflection in the mirror. She looked like the spitting image of William Tufty.

"I love it!" Lottie had to stop herself from jumping up and down with the thrill of seeing the family resemblance so clearly etched on her own face. She turned to Jamie with a big grin, forgetting for a moment that he was in a mood, but to her surprise he seemed pleased.

"Very practical," he offered. "Short hair suits you."

Lottie tucked one of the strands behind her ear, looking down at the floor self-consciously. "Thanks," she replied, embarrassed. Compliments from Jamie were like finding water in a desert, especially recently.

Lottie turned to Ollie, but he was too distracted by Binah to pay proper attention.

"Ollie," she called, "do you think this will do?"

He shook his head, like he was shaking off a spell. "Yes, yes, perfect, great," he mumbled.

They made their way back outside, Lottie liberated by her temporary new look.

Ollie, on the other hand, was still entranced with Binah,

watching her skip along the path with the same rapture he usually saved for his mother's cooking or one of Lottie's stories.

Lottie held him back on the path, leaning over so no one else could listen, although it was likely Jamie's inhuman hearing would still pick up their conversation. "You think Binah's cute?"

"Huh?"

"I can tell," Lottie chuckled. "You keep staring at her. But I should probably warn you I don't think she's really interested in romance and stuff like that."

Ollie raised an eyebrow, not quite understanding.

"It's just something I've noticed; she's not really interested in *anyone* like that."

Ollie's eyes narrowed, and she wondered if he still didn't get it, when he said the last thing she expected to hear.

"You're just like your mum."

"Excuse me?" Lottie choked.

"You were both always good at picking up on the small details. It's why you're both so good at telling stories and why you're such a great artist—you capture things other people don't see."

The words struck her hard. The mention of "artist" brought to mind Liliana's paintings and William Tufty's poetry. She looked over at two roses growing next to each other in the soil, pink and red, different coloring but the same structure. Maybe she had more in common with her ancestor Liliana than just their appearance.

The small details . . .

"Thanks, Ollie." Lottie gave him a true smile. "That's about the nicest thing you've ever said to me."

"Well, it's true . . . ," he replied frankly, before a mischievous grin lit up his face. "Oh! And if Binah ever wants to hang out with someone in a strictly platonic way, I'd love to invite her over to try my mum's cooking."

Lottie giggled, giving Ollie a final hug before they parted ways to go back to their own school groups.

Ollie was right: she was good at picking up on the little things—and that's exactly the skill they needed to find the Hamelin Formula. This was her strength, and she knew she could do it.

A surge of determination welled up in her belly like a rising ocean as she looked over the rest of her classmates.

The small details.

This is what Lottie did best, and it was how she would beat Leviathan.

❦ 36 ❧

THE BUS PULLED UP TO the Tompkins Manor as the clock struck twelve noon. They drove through a large white set of gates with two dove silhouettes carved in the wooden panels. Trees lined the driveway, their leaves a halo of pink and yellow, like giant gumdrops. The manor was attached to the factory, where billows of glittering white powder whirled out into the air from tall chimneys.

The second Lottie stepped off the bus onto the white stone path, the aroma hit her senses. It was as if the air itself had been candied; it was so sweet it made her brain feel dizzy.

It's a wonder anyone can think straight in a place like this.

Lola danced off the bus, with Micky following, sucking a lollipop. "Home sweet home," they said in unison.

"It's almost as if they were made in the factory," Jamie said drily. Lottie had to agree.

Jamie tried to help Dame Bolter but was shooed away.

"Not you, Jamie. The Spearion competitors must unpack the equipment. Let's go, competitors!" Dame Bolter ordered, clapping her hands twice.

Ellie rolled her eyes as she stepped off the coach and began to help. Anastacia, on the other hand, seemed less than thrilled about having to carry her own designer bags *and* a tatty duffel bag of fencing gear. She held the equipment bag out at arm's length as though it were a poisonous spider.

"I won't have anyone assisting who's not participating. This team needs to learn that they're responsible for their own success." Dame Bolter threw Jamie a warning look as he loitered around the bags.

Lottie stopped laughing as Dame Bolter appeared before her. Her muscular stature was at odds with the sugary, soft world of the Tompkins Manor.

"If any of the guests on this trip cause a distraction, I will immediately send them back to Rosewood. Is that clear?" Lottie gulped but nodded respectfully, knowing that Dame Bolter did not deal in empty threats. "Good!"

They were greeted at the red doors of the manor by an older woman of South Asian origin wearing a bright pink skirt suit and a broad smile.

"Welcome, contestants. My name is Nadia Kumar," the woman began cheerily. "Please make yourself at home in the manor and rest up before the tournament tomorrow." She gestured for them all to gather in front of the doors. "We will be hosting a tour of the factory before dinner at five p.m. We do hope you enjoy the gift baskets in your rooms and that you will speak fondly of your time at the Tompkins Manor."

Her smile never faltered the whole time she spoke.

"That's the Butter Company's PR lady," Lola and Micky whispered from either side of Lottie. The siblings couldn't seem to pull their gaze away from the woman who was so casually welcoming people into their home.

Lottie took the opportunity to get a good look at the other teams, expecting some fierce faces to emerge from the crowd—but to her surprise they all looked rather tame. She was struck again by that same realization she'd had when talking to Anastacia—that they all really were just kids.

Nadia gestured dramatically with her hands, still smiling pleasantly. "Welcome to the Tompkins Manor."

The glossy red doors chirped as they opened on their golden hinges, flooding the steps with the sweet smell of peppermint, which poured out of the manor all around them. Lottie couldn't help gasping at the magical sight behind the double doors. A rainbow cascaded down in front of them, a split staircase with each step a different brightly colored marble that didn't seem possible. The entire floor was meticulously striped with yellow and pink like the boiled candies from her childhood; it was such a mouthwatering spectacle that she had to stop herself from kneeling down and licking the floor in front of her to check it wasn't really made of sugar. The candy-cane scent that seeped from the walls was overtaken by a thick, mellow odor of licorice as an unfamiliar but instantly recognizable face appeared in front of them: Richard Butter.

He stood in a long black-and-orange robe that trailed over the striped floor of the entryway. Beside him to the left was his son, Percy, eyes down. The similarity was uncanny, but while Percy wore his pale skin and dark presence with a shy, tired manner, his father wore it as if he were a mad scientist. Richard Butter sported a large set of rectangular spectacles that magnified his piercing blue eyes to a comic degree. Percy and Richard together looked like a very strange set of nocturnal humans who should not have been out in the daylight.

"On behalf of Alfred Tompkins, who is currently saving his energy to enjoy the tournament tomorrow, it's my pleasure to welcome you to the Tompkins Manor. We do hope you will make yourself comfortable and enjoy your stay." Richard Butter's voice was nasal and slightly squeaky, as if he might have a cold he couldn't shake.

As soon as the brief welcome was over, the twins skipped off toward Richard, Lola reaching up to give him a warm hug as if they were all part of the same big candy family. Lottie's heart lurched as Percy ruffled Micky's hair, trying to look carefree. They could pretend they were fine, but they all knew how serious their mission was.

Lottie waved goodbye to Percy and the twins, and that was that. The plan was officially in action.

They were given a very brief tour of the manor to show them where they'd be staying, where to meet for the tour, where they'd have meals, and where they could go to practice. The arena was close enough to walk to, but all contestants would be taken via golf cart. Lottie quickly memorized a map of the grounds, knowing they'd need it tomorrow.

The whole manor was a maze of brightly colored corridors and patterned doors, with quirky furniture and still-life paintings almost everywhere you turned. The Tompkins family seemed to have a taste for eccentric and creepy decor; displayed on tables were ornamental dolls with rosy cheeks and murderous grins and little cherubic porcelain animals with bared fangs. And this was the place Lola and Micky called home!

They ended the tour in the reception room closest to the sleeping quarters, a room with large windows looking out over the gumdrop trees, with lime-green furniture and more creepy ornaments throughout.

"Does anyone have any questions before we meet for the factory tour at four?" Nadia asked, a smile still fixed to her face; Lottie had to wonder how her cheeks weren't hurting.

Everyone shook their heads and they were all permitted

to leave. Anastacia gave them a knowing nod as she made her way to the hall, starting her mission to befriend all the contestants and inspect their rooms.

Finally Ellie, Jamie, and Lottie were left alone in the lime-green room.

Jamie glanced around as soon as the door shut, his thick eyebrows furrowed, already plotting his next move. Everything was going to plan. They had a solid four hours to search the manor and even more time after dinner. They could do this.

"I guess we should get started on looking for—"

"Hello," a soft voice purred from the doorway, and they all froze. "You must be our guests."

They turned and saw the two people they were supposed to avoid: Ingrid and Julius.

Jamie tensed, stepping protectively in front of Lottie and Ellie.

"I'm Ingrid Crow, and this is Julius Stub." Julius tipped his black cowboy hat as she said his name, and they both moved to block the door. "We're interns for the Butter Company."

Avoid Ingrid and Julius at all costs. Jamie's words rang through Lottie's mind as she eyed the door, but there was no way out.

Ingrid Crow was a petite young woman with a tiny button nose and a sprinkling of freckles over her round face.

Her hair was so black and silky it looked like oil spilling down her back, but there was something unnerving about her appearance. Hidden deep within her gray eyes was the menacing glint of a professional mischief-maker—a sly, scheming look that could only be attained from years of practice. Everything about her reminded Lottie of a fairy tale her mother had once read, "Master Cat," and much like the trickster cat in the story, she wore thick black boots with a heel that seemed sharp enough to cut skin.

She brought her face close to Jamie's, hands on her hips, as if inspecting a fine diamond. "He's very pretty," she said, looking right through him in a way Lottie knew he'd hate. "Don't you think he's pretty, Julius?"

Julius cocked his head to one side, scrutinizing Jamie.

This is weird, Lottie thought.

"I suppose," Julius drawled indifferently in a thick southern accent.

Julius Stub was the opposite of Ingrid: tall and broad with a thick nose that looked as if it had been broken in the past. He was not an unattractive young man, with strawberry-blond hair and a build one usually associates with football players. But, like Ingrid, there was something about his eyes. They didn't sparkle with the same mischief as Ingrid's; they were empty—the kind of emptiness that allowed a person to do terrible things and feel absolutely nothing.

"I don't know what your parents taught you," Ellie snarled, "but it's very rude to talk about people as though they're not there." She'd already completely disregarded the don't-engage-with-Julius-or-Ingrid rule.

They turned to Ellie and Lottie. Ingrid's leer morphed into a smile and she took a menacing step toward Lottie before lightly brushing a speck of imaginary dust from Lottie's shoulder. "I can't stand dirt."

A low growl escaped Ellie's lips.

"Thank you," Lottie said quickly, rubbing her shoulder. "In fact, we should go and change before the tour. I'm sure we're a mess from traveling."

Ingrid turned her catlike gaze on her.

A lump of fear rose in Lottie's throat, but she swallowed it down, refusing to let her smile falter.

Julius sighed, absent-mindedly inspecting his nails. "Let's go, Ingrid. The guests want to rest, and we have work to do."

At that, Ingrid's expression relaxed and she sauntered over to Julius. "See you for the tour," she said, following Julius out into the corridor.

As they left, Julius leaned to mock-whisper in Ingrid's ear: "We'll have plenty of time to play with our new toys later."

The door clicked shut behind them, and Jamie let out a long breath.

"Did that actually just happen?" Lottie asked.

"They're Partizans," Jamie said, his voice cold.

"What?" Ellie spat, the anger in her not quite dissipated yet.

"They're Partizans somehow. I can tell a trained assassin when I see one."

Ellie stared at Lottie before shaking her head. "Jamie, you mustn't let Lottie out of your sight. That's an order."

Jamie held his breath, knowing he couldn't disobey a direct order.

"I'm going to find Anastacia and warn her," Ellie announced, "then check the other rooms. I'll see you for the tour."

Before she could run to the door, Jamie grabbed her arm, effortlessly pulling her back.

"You need to stay by my side too," he commanded.

Their eyes locked with such intensity that Lottie could almost see the static sparking between them. Ellie tried to whack his arm away, grabbing his wrist with her other hand, but her eyes weren't angry; she looked desperate.

"We can't let them take Lottie again," she pleaded.

Slowly, like a cloud moving over the sun, Jamie released his grip on their princess.

Ellie ran over to Lottie and quickly planted a kiss on her forehead like a protective spell.

"I promise Jamie will keep you safe." Then she dashed

out of the room, leaving the door wide open.

Stunned, it took Lottie a moment to realize what had just happened.

"Go after her!" Lottie cried. "We can't leave her on her own."

The tension was visible throughout Jamie's body, the muscles in his jaw rippling with worry. "I have to keep you safe." He spoke reluctantly, his eyes switching back and forth between the open door and Lottie.

"But—"

"Lottie, I have an order from my princess." He marched her to the door. "So I'm afraid we're stuck until we find this secret formula."

37

LOTTIE COULD BARELY CONCENTRATE AS they inspected the house, in search of any clues. She wanted to find the others and make sure they were all safe. She couldn't get that menacing look from Ingrid and Julius out of her mind.

"We should be sticking together," she said, peering at a bright yellow vase when they returned to the reception room. "That's the number one rule of every horror movie. Never split up."

"We're not in a horror movie, Lottie; this is real life."

Lottie picked up a china doll clutching a giant lollipop from the mantelpiece.

"Are you sure about that?" she said, holding up the doll with its creepy grin.

Jamie gave a tight-lipped smile, clearly not wanting to get distracted.

"You need to concentrate, Lottie. We can't overlook anything." To emphasize his point, he brushed his fingertips along the underside of the mantelpiece, checking for anything hidden.

Although Jamie continued to scour the room for clues,

Lottie saw his eyes flicker to the door, constantly on the lookout for Ingrid and Julius. He never let his guard down.

It was while she was staring at him, watching in fascination as he meticulously checked every item in the room, that a sudden darting light caught her eye from the doorway on the other side of the room. She went over and peered through the glass panel of the door. She gasped as she saw what could only be described as . . . a glowing piano. It was set beneath a circular skylight, and a column of sunshine poured down in a spotlight over the piano. The piano was ivory, with delicate dove motifs etched into the varnish. The instrument beckoned to be played.

Charmed, Lottie pushed the door open and stepped into the magical piano room.

"Lottie?"

"We need to check this room," she called back distractedly. The lure of the instrument was too much to resist, until Jamie came and grabbed her shoulder.

Jamie stared, his hand still on her shoulder as he too became enthralled. "That's a beautiful piano."

"Do you want to play it?" Lottie joked, wandering over to it to get a better look.

Jamie gave her a sideways glance but couldn't stop himself from going over to stroke the varnish.

"I was surprised when you played the piano at Christmas," Lottie admitted, brushing her fingertips along the lid. "Not that anything about you should surprise me anymore!"

"What do you mean?" he asked cautiously, clearly worried she was about to venture into territory he didn't want to go to again.

She shook her head to let him know that wasn't her intention. "I mean, sometimes you do something, like play guitar or recite poetry, and I realize I don't actually know anything about you. Not to mention the sign language."

Jamie chuckled, taking a seat at the piano and running his fingers along the ivories without pushing them down.

Lottie was reminded of what Anastacia had said about Saskia always trying to impress her father, always trying to prove to him that she was worth having in the family. Jamie didn't register the change in her expression, though, preoccupied by the piano in front of him.

"Playing the piano and American Sign Language aren't that different," Jamie began, his voice ever so slightly distant. "Come here." He gestured for her to take a seat beside him on the white stool. She hesitated for only a second before accepting. "When you talk with words, it's a linear process, but with sign language it happens all at once, like the difference between playing one note at a time or hitting a selection of keys together to make a chord."

He demonstrated by gently drawing her hand over to the piano keys and placing his hand over hers. He pressed the tops of her fingers so that they came down, and a few notes echoed through the instrument. Soon they were playing a simple yet haunting melody together.

"In many ways that actually makes it a superior way of communicating." He let her hand go, but a tingle remained, the sensation so pleasant she held her palm to her chest.

Lottie found herself completely entranced as Jamie began working his fingers over the keys. His eyes slowly closed, gripped by the melody, and Lottie couldn't help being drawn in by the delicate music.

"You really love music, don't you?" she said without thinking.

His eyes blinked open, and she regretted breaking his trance.

"I suppose I do," he murmured, looking down at his hands like they were a ghostly vision. His face turned hard again. "We need to get back to work." He stood up abruptly.

Lottie's heart sank, realizing that Jamie was prepared to reject even this—the music that was so important to him—out of fear of losing his composure. She turned away, not wanting him to see the pain etched there. And that's when she saw it.

On the side of the piano, nestled among the carvings of doves, was a beautiful inscription in German.

"Lottie, come on," Jamie ordered. "We've work to do. What's wrong?"

"No, it's just—" Lottie looked closer at the lettering,

gently brushing it with her fingers. "I think Lola's music box has the same words on it."

Um diese erinnerung festzuhalten, musst du sie zuerst zerstören.

It wasn't just the same words; it was exactly the same script, the same writing, the same depth, as if they had both been inscribed at the same time.

The small details, Lottie thought to herself.

Jamie came to take a closer look, but a sound by the door caught them off guard.

"I don't know what you naughty children are up to," a soft voice purred from the doorway, making Lottie jump, "but it's time for the tour."

Ingrid stood, stretching against the doorframe, like a cat stretching on a rug. There was no way of getting past her.

Jamie stepped in front of Lottie, but Ingrid snorted, smiling as if she found them both very funny. They couldn't let on for a second that they'd found anything. Jamie's training kicked in, reminding her of his advice to appear soft. She quickly reached her hand out and grabbed Jamie's, hoping Ingrid would think they'd been caught in a silly romantic moment and not an act of espionage.

Jamie lifted his eyebrow and Lottie squeezed his hand very softly, signaling as subtly as she could to the piano.

To her relief he understood and began rubbing his hair sheepishly as if he were embarrassed. The act was almost too realistic, and Lottie wondered how much of him was pretending.

An eye roll from Ingrid let them know their display had worked, and Lottie felt a thrill at her trickery.

"Would you both stop acting like scared mice? I'm here to take you to the factory." Just in time, three students from the other schools peeked their heads around the door. "Come on," Ingrid said, crooking her finger at them. "We have so much to show you."

The piano would have to wait.

"Distinguished guests, it is our honor to welcome you to the world where all the delicious magic happens"—Lottie held her breath as the giant oak doors swung open and she glanced around, wondering where Lola and Micky were— "the Tompkins Confectionery factory."

For all the color and magic of the Tompkins Manor, the factory was gray and cold—a stainless-steel cave of machinery where you couldn't escape the sounds of grinding and clanking metal or the smell of sugar. It was not the sweet scent Lottie had become used to from the twins, but an overpowering poison of toxic chocolate, like the smell of the faulty Hamelin Formula. Something was definitely rotten in this factory.

Ellie crinkled her nose as they entered the first room, grimacing at the overpowering smell.

"It stinks!" she whispered, forcing Lottie to give her a small kick on the back of her leg to shut her up. This only made Ellie giggle. Even Dame Bolter was struggling not to hold her nose, a scowl contorting her features.

As they made their way past the machinery, Nadia explained the purpose of each piece of equipment. Lottie couldn't stop thinking about the twins. The Butter Company was acting like the Tompkins Manor was theirs. She couldn't understand why Lola and Micky's father was letting them get away with this.

As much as Lottie was trying to pay attention to the tour, she couldn't stop thinking about the glowing piano. The inscription on its side was calling to her. She had to see it again.

"Lottie," Ellie's voice whispered against her ear, "what's up? You seem distracted."

"We can't talk about it here," Lottie replied, shaking her head in warning.

Ellie looked around, narrowing her eyes, not satisfied.

"We can go in there." Ellie jerked her head to a blue door behind them.

Before Lottie could protest, she'd grabbed Lottie's arm, and the two of them slunk behind the door labeled Powder Room.

"Ellie, stop. What about—"

But Ellie's grip was too strong. The door silently swung shut behind them and Lottie watched through the peephole as the rest of the tour, including Jamie, walked off.

"Jamie is going to kill us," Lottie said, hiding her head in her hands.

Ellie didn't respond, jaw hanging open at the sight that lay before them. They were at the top of a set of metal stairs that led down to an endless sea of white fluff. Every surface was highly polished stainless steel, mirroring everything around it in an endless white echo. Fans from the ground floor whirred with a beat like the room's heart, pumping the powder around in clouds that drifted and settled in glittering mounds.

"It's like we're in the Snow Queen's land," Lottie breathed, powder catching on her lips as she spoke.

Ellie reached to take her hand and, together, they walked down the steps into the boundless white world below.

Lottie knew that they shouldn't descend into this sparkling white kingdom, that they should go back. Yet the second their feet touched the stainless-steel floor they both grinned, giggling as they kicked through the clouds of white powder.

All thoughts of Leviathan, of Jamie, of the piano drifted away like they were no more than dust in a breeze.

Sugar particles floated around them, sparkling in the air

and falling in a soft blanket of sweet snow. It felt like they were in a sugar storm, the powder building in a swirling gale. Lottie could feel her skin turn soft and sticky as the sugar powder christened her arms. Every part of them was slowly being covered. Ellie shook her head and clouds of icing sugar flew about her. It felt magical, like they had stumbled into Narnia. Lottie giggled as she shook the powder off. "You've missed some." Ellie leaned forward, running her fingers through Lottie's sticky mass of curls.

"Get it for me," Lottie replied, smiling. As soon as she said the words, something shifted. Ellie leaned in even farther, so close they were almost touching. Her thick eyelashes glistened white from the powder. She looked like a beautiful white demon. Lottie held her breath, her heart thundering as Ellie leaned over her, an intense look on her face. She felt all at once nervous and thrilled, surrounded by their beautiful sugar storm. Slowly Ellie's mouth met Lottie's, and she kissed off the sugar.

An intense jolt of warmth shot through Lottie, leaving an electric tingle on her lips.

Ellie straightened up again. The moment was over so quickly that Lottie wondered if it had happened at all; the only evidence was her heartbeat, hammering away in her chest. Before she could say anything the door opened and Ellie quickly pulled her to hide.

"And this is what we call the Powder Room," Nadia's voice bellowed out, "where we air all the sugar powder to get it as soft and light as possible, before adding it to our mixer."

Ellie was desperately trying not to laugh as they crouched behind one of the fans.

The door clicked shut. Silence fell again, and Ellie risked poking her head out. "That was close," she said, smirking and shaking off the powder. She gestured for Lottie to follow her.

"Yeah . . ."

Lottie felt her fingers go up to her mouth instinctively. That moment had been nothing like her kiss with Edmund last year. It was soft and sweet, and not just from the sugar dust. It made her feel light and giddy and, most of all, it made her feel like she wanted to do it again.

They both jumped as the door swung open. Jamie and Anastacia stood there, looking more than a little irritated at them.

"This is completely irresponsible," Jamie hissed, checking over his shoulder to make sure the rest of the tour weren't watching. Anastacia lowered her sunglasses, and Lottie felt her heart hammer away again, convinced that Anastacia knew what had just happened. "Get back up here now," he demanded.

Ellie gave Lottie one of her side smiles, and they ran up the stairs to rejoin the tour, doing their best to ignore Jamie's tutting.

"What were you two doing in there?" Anastacia whispered as they walked along with the rest of the group. Lottie had to resist the urge to touch her lips again, chancing a glance at Ellie, whose face was inscrutable.

"I don't think I know," Lottie said.

Jamie couldn't get what he'd just seen out of his head.

Before they'd entered the Powder Room he'd glimpsed something through the peephole in the blue door. Two figures leaning in to each other in a kiss. He knew that it was Ellie and Lottie; he'd seen them sneak off and had waited for the right moment to grab them without being spotted.

As he followed the rest of the tour, trying to stay vigilant, the image played over and over in his head. He tried to make sense of how it made him feel.

He glanced at Ellie, his princess, his master, strolling along as if nothing had happened. And Lottie, her Portman, head in the clouds as usual. He had to wonder if he'd imagined it. But why then did that image burn so furiously in his mind? And why, of all the things he'd experienced in his life, did it make him suddenly feel so alone?

38

LOTTIE SAT BOLT UPRIGHT IN bed, a spark running through her as if someone had intentionally shaken her awake. She looked over at the clock on the bedside table—three fifteen.

Something had woken her up.

Everything felt hazy and heavy, her mind still drenched in sleep, but through the mist of slumber she could hear a haunting melody—a melody that was wrong.

She turned to where she expected to see Ellie sleeping in the bed beside her but was confronted with empty space. No calm breathing from her best friend. They were not in the Ivy dorm; she was alone here. For a split second she considered ignoring the music, but the call was too strong; it had trapped her, and she had to find out where it was coming from.

Tiptoeing as softly as she could through the candy-striped corridors of the Tompkins Manor, she followed the call of the song. A part of her brain conjured up images of the Pied Piper of Hamelin and the magical instrument that lured children away against their will.

Before she could come to her senses, she found herself

outside the piano room again, peeping through the glass panel to find the whole room soaked in lavender moon-light.

A figure sat at the instrument, a long white robe spilling over the floor around them. Everything looked silver, a vision so drenched in starlight that it felt more like she was looking at a memory or a dream.

The ghostlike figure repeated the same refrain over and over, each time wrong. Lottie didn't know how she knew it was wrong, but something in her mind told her the melody was missing something.

"Who's there?" The figure turned suddenly, and she recognized the sickly, fearful face.

Pushing the door open, she sleepily mumbled, "Alfred Tompkins?"

It was Lola and Micky's father.

"Who are you?" he demanded.

"I'm so sorry—I'm a friend of Lola and Micky's. I'm here for the tournament tomorrow; I heard the music and I couldn't stop myself from following it." She took a deep breath, finally waking up. "I'm so sorry," she repeated.

He narrowed his eyes at her and she got a proper look at him. His hair was almost entirely gray and patchy on his gaunt skull, as if it had been falling out. Lines etched his face, making him seem far too old to be the father of the twins. He looked like he was about to say something when his hand shot up to his mouth and he began coughing violently.

Lottie instantly rushed to his side, rubbing his back. Memories of her mother in a similar state infected her mind, and she knew she'd have wanted someone to be there with her too.

"Let me help you," she said, offering him an arm to guide him back into his wheelchair. He took it reluctantly, and they hobbled across the glowing moonlit floor.

The coughing didn't stop as he sat in his chair, and Lottie started to worry.

"I'll go and get help," she said, but he held up his hand.

"No, no, I'll be fine in a minute; you stay right there," he ordered.

So she stood by him as he wheezed and spluttered, until finally he settled back down.

"Are you really okay?" Lottie asked nervously.

He looked up at her, a scrutinizing gaze, as if he didn't trust her. "You're the princess, aren't you?" he said at last.

Lottie hesitated. She knew it was her job to be a Portman, but somehow, alone in that room with this sickly old man, she felt like she was lying. Something about this situation made her feel like she had to tell the truth.

"Yes, I suppose I am," she replied.

"Why did you follow the melody?" he asked suspiciously. "Tell me honestly."

"Well." Lottie gulped. "If I'm being honest, it sounded wrong."

"What?" he spluttered, coughing again.

"That is to say, the tune was wrong. I don't know how I know; I could just tell, as if I'd heard the song before."

He stopped coughing and gave her another once-over. Lottie felt embarrassed in her pink Disney dressing gown, like a silly little girl.

"That's quite a keen ear you have," he said unexpectedly. "The song I'm trying to play, you see, it doesn't exist." He gazed over at the piano, his voice going distant like he was talking to himself. "There's no record of it."

"You mean you made it up?" Lottie asked curiously.

"No, no, no, as in, it's a secret. A puzzle I've never been able to solve." He shook his head, not looking at Lottie. "I suppose I lack the attention to detail." He laughed at this, which led to more coughing, and Lottie couldn't understand what was so funny. She remembered what Lola had said all that time ago in the woods, about her father losing his mind.

The woods.

Lottie knew where she'd heard the correct melody: it was in Lola's music box. Again, the two items, the piano and music box, were intertwining. But why?

These were the small details; she just had to figure out what they meant.

"Where is this piano from?" Lottie asked, her curiosity winning again.

Alfred eyed her once more, deciding whether to answer her.

"This piano," he began slowly, almost as if he still wasn't sure he was going to finish the sentence, "was one of only two things that my wife inherited from her father, and she left them both to our children."

"It's magnificent," she replied honestly, not hiding any of her wonder.

"It is, it is, but sadly I am no use to it." He frowned, and Lottie wished she could help him. To grow old and lose the ability to do what you loved seemed so awful. "Now, young princess, would you kindly wheel me back to my room? I am very tired."

Lottie nodded, relieved that he was letting her take him to somewhere he could rest.

She wandered back afterward in silence, back down the candy-striped corridor to her lonely bedroom. As she drifted off to sleep, the mad words of Alfred Tompkins repeated in her head like a round.

Secret

Puzzle

Detail

Before she could put her finger on it, sleep consumed her.

꧁ 39 ꧂

ELLIE AND LOTTIE DIDN'T SPEAK of the kiss; in fact, Lottie had very nearly convinced herself that the whole magical sugar-powder memory was just a ridiculous fantasy she'd made up. She'd considered asking Ellie what it had been about, what it meant, but there was no good time. That, and she didn't want to be a distraction, not when Ellie should be focusing on the tournament . . . which was less than half an hour away.

"Did you enjoy the tour?" Lola and Micky asked.

"Yes, it was great. Loved the, erm, chocolate part. Very cool." Lottie stumbled over her words, realizing to her embarrassment that she'd been in a complete daze. It certainly didn't help that she'd had such interrupted sleep, although she thought better than to upset the twins with the story of their sickly father worrying himself into a coughing fit.

"Lottie," Jamie cautioned, "stop getting distracted."

She nodded, hating that he could pick up on her state of mind so easily. Today was crucial; they needed to use this time during the Spearion to destroy the Hamelin Formula, but there was one huge problem.

None of them had found where it was hidden yet, and the contest was only moments away from starting.

They were outside the arena, surrounded by crowds of people milling about before the tournament began. They'd been trying to think of the most likely hiding spot for the formula, but they'd drawn a complete blank. It was starting to feel as though their plan was destined to fail.

"Excuse me." A group of people around their age squeezed past them, all wearing T-shirts in support of someone called Alistair.

"Sorry," Lottie apologized, moving out of the way so they could get through the door. "I hope Ellie and Anastacia are okay," she mused, watching with envy as other people got to go and support their friends.

"Oh, Anastacia's fine," Lola chirped happily.

"She came to our room this morning to ask for some chocolate," Micky added.

A very unladylike snort escaped from Lottie's throat, and she quickly had to cover her mouth to feign a cough. She remembered how Anastacia ate chocolate when she was nervous.

"I need you all to pay attention," Jamie pleaded, the stress of their looming failure etched on his face. "We need to try to think where the formula could be."

"What if we can't?" Percy signed, chewing his lip.

They all knew as well as Jamie that if they hadn't found the formula by now, they probably never would, and they just had to hope that meant Leviathan would never find it either, or they were all very much screwed.

"Could all guests please take their seats for the start of the Spearion?" a voice called out from hidden speakers.

Lottie tried to give Jamie a reassuring smile, but it was clear nothing was going to get him to relax.

"Worst comes to worst, we'll have to find some time after the tournament," Lottie offered.

Lola and Micky nodded at her, but Jamie looked inconsolable. She reached out to him, but he shook his head, marching off and leaving the rest of them to follow behind.

The arena was an odd building converted from an old warehouse, with tiered seating that didn't quite match the dark wood that surrounded it. It was not the grand building Lottie had been expecting, but it was completely packed with enthusiastic spectators, giving it the sense of a vast stadium. Lottie even recognized a few other Rosewood students sitting in the stands. There was an infectious energy in the air. They took their seats near the back in case any of them needed to sneak off. The whole time Jamie's jaw twitched.

They could see Dame Bolter below, roaring strategy to the rest of the Rosewood team as if they were in an end-of-the-world scenario. Lottie felt her hands clasp in her lap, desperately trying to figure out which was Ellie and which was Anastacia, until they all pulled off their helmets at once, following an instruction. And there she was. Her hair fell in dark inky clumps around her sharp face. Her lean frame stood skinny but strong in her blazing white uniform. This was the version of Ellie that Lottie could never quite get out of her head. The fierce, princely sword fighter who would storm through the snow in bare feet to save her.

Lottie realized she'd never get used to it; she would always be in awe of Ellie. The way she held herself, how smart she was, how loyal she was, and, most of all, the way she made Lottie feel about herself. Ellie balanced her; she was the bitter to her sweet, the night to her day. Together, they were two halves of one whole.

Her hand instinctively went to her lips, remembering the moment in the Powder Room.

What did it mean?

A nudge at her side had her plummeting back down to earth hard. She turned to see Jamie's eyes boring into her, a look she knew all too well; it meant "stop getting distracted."

"Sorry," she said, although she wasn't quite sure what she was apologizing for.

"This is getting serious, Lottie," Jamie said sternly. "We have to think of every small detail we may have missed."

Detail, detail, detail.

This was supposed to be Lottie's strength; this was how she'd told herself she'd find the Hamelin Formula's hiding place.

She rubbed her forehead, a million images and words erupting inside her skull.

The song from the music box, her strange encounter with Alfred Tompkins, the words on the piano that she couldn't even read . . . It all came rushing back. She'd been so caught up in Alfred's health that she'd forgotten what she'd learned about the piano.

"Lola!" Lottie exclaimed, before she even knew what she was doing. Lola turned to her curiously, head tilted to the side. "I never asked you. What does that German inscription in your music box mean?"

Lola shrugged, shaking her head in apology.

"It's gibberish, really," she said regretfully. "They think it was a bad translation."

"It means"—Micky cleared his throat—"'To keep the memory safe, you must first destroy it.'"

"See?" they said in unison. "Gibberish."

But Lottie was hardly paying attention. Alfred Tompkins's words swam in her head, the words she'd thought were the ramblings of a sick old man. He couldn't solve the puzzle because he couldn't play the melody.

Her lungs burned with the temptation to squeal with

excitement. She grabbed Jamie's arm, pulling him out of his seat toward the exit.

"Lottie, what is it?" he asked, his face still awash with worry.

Just as he spoke, the horn blared for the start of the match.

She glanced back toward the arena, where Ellie was about to start the biggest fencing tournament of her life. A stab of guilt shot through her at not being able to be there for her friend.

"Lottie," Jamie repeated, irritation building in his eyes.

She'd realized what her main distraction was—it was Ellie. She finally understood King Alexander's words when he had told her and Jamie to stay vigilant. She couldn't let her feelings for Ellie stop her from doing the right thing for the crown.

She closed her eyes, remembering what the king had told her. *"There may come a time when you will have to put Ellie second in order to put her first. I trust you'll understand should that moment arise."*

"Jamie." She took a deep breath. "We have to leave. I know where the formula's hidden."

❧ 40 ❧

Lola placed the music box on top of the piano and slowly lifted the lid to reveal the elegant white dove inside. The bird danced merry little circles, completely unaware of his importance.

Jamie closed his eyes, listening to the melody. "Hmm. Explain it again to me."

"Well, Lola and Micky's mother gifted them this music box," Lottie began, smiling at the twins as she recited their story. "She said to always keep it safe. They've never been able to find the song anywhere else, and no one has ever found out its name or where it comes from."

The sun outside was setting. The bright white light that had lit up the piano was now a deep burnt orange, the whole room ablaze.

Percy was standing by the door on lookout, but he peeked in a few times to check that they were okay.

"She gave it to us when she started to get sick," Lola added, affectionately stroking the china dove as though it were a real bird. "We've never really understood the inscription." She reached her other hand out to Micky and squeezed it.

"I think this song isn't really a song," Lottie mused, tapping the music box. "It's actually a key. I think she entrusted it to you because she wanted you to find the Hamelin Formula and she wanted you to destroy it. I think she left this to you and your father as a clue."

"But . . . ," Micky said somberly.

"We can't play the piano," the twins said together, shrugging in perfect time with each other, "and we don't know the music."

Lottie turned to Jamie, and he let out a long breath, knowing exactly what she was thinking.

"I can try to play it by listening to it, but—" Jamie paused for a moment, closing his eyes to take in the melody again before opening them, defeat washing over his features. "It's a complicated piece. It could take a while."

"I'm sure you can do it, Jamie." Lottie beamed at him. This was their only shot; she couldn't let him doubt himself. She handed him Lola and Micky's white dove music box, its trill still singing around the room.

And then Lottie did the worst possible thing she could have done.

As she passed the box to Jamie, their fingers brushed with a touch as light as a feather, but it was enough to make her jolt; the shock in his eyes let her know he felt it too. It was just enough for them both to falter. Lola and Micky gasped as they watched the music box slide out of their hands. For once Jamie's lightning reflexes did not kick in, caught as he was in a momentary daze at his own stupidity, and they all witnessed the treasured item crash to the marble floor, sending out discordant notes as it smashed.

"No!" Lottie cried, throwing herself down to try to salvage their mistake. "Lola, Micky, I'm so sorry." Tears were welling in her eyes, making the world at her knees a blurry mess, but she could make out the little white dove cold and cracked on the hard ground. She imagined her tiara in its place, imagined it broken into pieces by one careless act.

How could I do this? How could I be so awful?

Lottie slowly turned to glance at the twins, terrified to see the look on their faces, so sure they would hate her forever, and she wouldn't blame them if they did.

"What's that?" Micky asked as he stared at the remains of the box.

"Lottie, look." Jamie got down beside her and very gently handed her a silk handkerchief. The twins and Percy came to stand over them, everyone staring.

Lottie quickly wiped her eyes and looked down. Perched within the mess, under the dove, was a piece of folded paper. Without hesitation Micky bent down to retrieve it.

"Is that—" Jamie leaned over to get a better look, his eyes going wide. "It is!"

"It's sheet music!" Lola cried as she squeezed Micky's arm.

Even Percy was smiling, relief washing over him as he affectionately ruffled Micky's hair.

"And it even has the name of the piece." Lola was practically dancing around the room now. "The secret song has a name." She clutched the paper to her chest, holding it against her heart in a way Lottie had done many times with her tiara.

"'*Süß aber Bitter,*'" Jamie announced. "Sweet but bitter, bittersweet."

"*Can you play it?*" Percy signed, his eyes turning serious again as they locked with Jamie's.

"*I'll try.*"

Lola placed the sheet music on the piano and they all gathered around Jamie. Lottie could hardly contain herself. *A secret magical song that opens up the piano.*

It was as though she were truly in a fairy tale.

Percy went back to the door to keep watch while Jamie sat at the stool. His lips moved silently as he practiced in his head a few times, his fingers flitting over the keys without pushing down.

"Okay," he said, his chest expanding as he took a calming breath. His fingers pressed down on the first notes, and in an instant he wasn't Jamie the Partizan anymore. His poise, his sensible black shirt and trousers, his ever-scruffy dark hair and brooding mood morphed into the face of an artist, someone with a deep well of emotion just waiting to be tapped. This was Jamie without the burdens he gave himself. This was the secret Jamie, who he locked away beneath his responsibilities.

The melody came to an end as quickly as it had started, but Lottie knew the sound would linger in her chest, resonating through her like a sweet warm drink. Everything was falling into place. Two more bars and the piano would open.

The distrustful face of Alfred Tompkins materialized in Lottie's mind. He'd been so worried, so nervous for her to find him there. What was he so afraid of?

A dark feeling crept through her as a terrible thought dawned on her. Just like the music, someone else had been playing them.

The next second felt like the longest moment of Lottie's life. Her throat began to swell up, and she tried to speak, but it was too late. Jamie had finished the piece, the perfect melody closing flawlessly as his hands lifted from the keys and a loud click echoed through the room. There was the whirring of age-old cogs kicking into gear from somewhere inside the piano. The side of the instrument popped open, a tiny hatch revealing itself in the intricate carvings. A small black box lay nestled inside the beautiful piano.

"Jamie, I think—" But as Lottie spoke, the door swung open. Percy cried out in shock and was promptly yanked backward out of the room. Before either Partizan or

Portman could react, a hand roughly covered Lottie's mouth from behind, choking her.

"Hello, you naughty children," purred Ingrid's voice, her inky-black hair wrapping around Lottie as she held her tight. "Thanks for finding the formula for us." She gave a mocking laugh.

Julius sauntered in behind her and Jamie jumped to his feet, blazing forward with ice-cold resolve, but Ingrid lifted her hand to circle Lottie's throat. "Ah-ah-ah, I wouldn't do that if I were you."

Julius stepped aside to reveal the last person Lottie expected to see.

Saskia San Martin.

She casually strolled into the room, a bag over her shoulder that looked much too heavy for one person to carry. She narrowed her eyes at Jamie before lifting her finger to her lips. The whole room seemed to grow small and claustrophobic.

Julius walked menacingly up to Jamie, reaching over him to take the small black box from the piano. Jamie was poised, ready for any opening he saw, but it was clear there was nothing they could do.

"Hello, old friends." Saskia grinned as she pulled lengths of rope out of the bag. "Don't take this personally."

41

ELLIE WOULD BE LYING IF she said she wasn't feeling a little underwhelmed. There was something missing, something that she couldn't put her finger on.

"Everything feels rather anticlimactic, doesn't it?" Anastacia sighed, pulling her helmet off as they headed to the changing room where the rest of their team and Dame Bolter were waiting.

"Congratulations, Ellie! How does it feel to come in third?" Dame Bolter was wearing one of her rare smiles as she patted both girls on the back, and Ellie couldn't help leaning into it. She respected Mercy Bolter, and to know she'd pleased her was high praise.

"Oh! Did I win something?" Ellie smirked, feigning modesty and earning an eye roll from Anastacia.

Neither of them had won first, as they had both been knocked out in the penultimate match, but Ellie had scored a little higher, earning her the third-place trophy. Much to their irritation, the two girls hadn't had a chance to duel each other.

Tom and the rest of the team playfully nudged Ellie in

praise, and she joked along, but her heart wasn't quite in it. It felt empty, just as Anastacia had said.

Ellie squeezed past the rest of the contestants to follow Anastacia out of the back to find the others. They'd agreed to meet after the tournament was over.

"Let's hope they found the formula," Ellie said, looking down at her watch. "They're late."

"Are they?" Anastacia said, casually checking her fingernails. "I didn't realize we had a specific meeting—"

Thundering footsteps caught their attention. They both looked over to see Percy hurtling down the corridor toward them. He was moving so fast they feared he might charge right into them. He came to an abrupt halt, bending over as his chest heaved.

Anastacia began rubbing his back to help him calm down.

"Percy, what's—" Ellie froze, realizing that speaking was totally useless, but he didn't need to say anything. There was panic in his eyes when he finally looked up at her. Something had gone wrong.

She grabbed his shoulders and looked him straight in the eye, trying to understand what had happened. He shook his head and grabbed her arm, tugging on her white fencing gear. Whatever had happened, they needed to go now.

"Anastacia," Ellie growled. "Get our swords."

✳

They stormed through the manor, sliding along the floor. Percy had to stop them just before they approached the piano room. He led them very slowly to the door so they could peer in through the glass.

Anastacia took a step back, her hand going to her mouth, and Percy wondered what she'd seen. Ellie leaned over to her, whispering something, and a furious resolve took over both their features. Percy leaned forward, trying to see Micky.

He knew Lottie and Jamie would be fine—they were both so strong—but Lola and Micky were delicate. Micky in particular was a soft, fragile creature. It's why Percy liked him so much. They might have looked like opposites, but they both found the world a strange and unsettling place, and each other's company was one of their only comforts. He let out a relieved breath when he saw that Micky and Lola were unscathed. He was about to take a step back when his eyes passed over something that made him freeze. The red Leviathan mark on Ingrid's arm.

Red. Red. Red.

He couldn't get the color out of his head. The image consumed him, but he couldn't look away. He tried to squeeze his eyes shut, but all he could see were hands and faces signing at him, smiling at him.

Open the door. Bring them to us.

The words weren't his own, but all of a sudden he couldn't think for himself.

Percy's eyes glazed over, all the light behind his gaze blinking out in an instant, leaving only a shell. The Leviathan mark had taken over.

An arm grabbed at his side, but it was useless, nothing could get through to him—and, before the two blurry girls on the periphery could stop it, invisible marionette strings pulled him forward, reaching his hand out and pushing open the door.

⚜ 42 ⚜

"Brilliant," Ingrid said, grinning, without even turning around. "Our pet has arrived."

Lottie tried to shout out a warning to Ellie and Anastacia, but her mouth was covered with tape, and all she could manage was a strained squeal that made her sound as pathetic as she felt.

There was nothing they could do. Ingrid had held on to Lottie, making it very clear she would hurt her if Jamie and the others didn't comply. So here they were, gagged and tied up on the floor, forced to watch Ellie and Anastacia go through the same thing.

Ellie and Anastacia had no time to react, the shock of Percy's actions leaving them entirely unprepared against three Partizans.

"Don't touch me, you dollar-store cowboy." Anastacia finally found her voice and screeched as Julius pulled her sword away from her. Ellie growled, sprinting around the other side of him, but Ingrid was there in moments, effortlessly tripping her and slamming her down to the floor with all the grace of a cat pouncing on a mouse.

Lottie squealed again, flinching, and desperately turned to Jamie, who had been placed as far away from them as possible. His hands and feet were bound, restricting his only means of defense, but his face remained cold and blank.

Panic burned within Lottie's skin, leaving her in a state of paralysis. She felt like she was in a nightmare, continuously willing herself to wake up, but she was stuck, tied up again and defenseless on the hard floor with Lola and Micky behind her. She could feel them shivering with fear, Lola's back shaking as she tried to hold back sobs.

Lottie's worst fear had come true. Lola, Micky, Jamie, Percy, Anastacia . . . Ellie. They were all in danger—danger that Lottie had promised herself she'd never let anyone else experience.

All the while Percy stood staring vacantly. It was like he'd turned into a wooden puppet, standing limp, waiting to be told what to do.

"Saskia, you coward." Anastacia kicked violently as Julius picked her up like she weighed no more than a kitten.

Saskia refused to look up at Anastacia. She took Ingrid's place, leaning close to Ellie's ear and whispering what Lottie assumed was a threat. Whatever she said, it scared Ellie enough that she stopped fighting back.

"Can you shut that one up, please, Julius?" Ingrid pointed to Anastacia without turning her gaze from Jamie. They were not giving him even the tiniest opportunity for escape.

Satisfied that Ellie and Anastacia were not going to be a problem, Ingrid leisurely strolled over to Percy like a cat toying with its prey. He didn't respond, still caught in whatever trance they'd put him in.

"This has been far too easy," Ingrid purred, sliding her long black fingernails under Percy's chin. "When we sent Percy to Rosewood to plant test specimens for us, we never expected it would be *this* easy."

"What did you do to him?" Ellie growled.

Ingrid seemed thrilled by the question. "I'm so glad you asked," she murmured happily. "Percy was our first great success. He demonstrates great potential." She patted his head. "You see, the problem is the sense of hearing. When we're not there to control the environment, the subjects become distracted by sounds; makes them go all loopy." She giggled, and Lottie remembered the horrified screams of everyone they'd poisoned. "With his father's permission we took Percy in as our little lab rat and planted him in your school to test our version of the Hamelin Formula. We needed to prove to our master that the formula was viable. We also hoped it would lead you to us."

Lottie felt sick. Percy's father hadn't been an unwitting accomplice; he'd agreed to all this. He'd had his own son kidnapped.

"What do you mean lead us to you?" Ellie asked, incredulous but calm.

Lottie was bewildered by Ellie's behavior; it was so unlike her to remain calm, especially in a situation like this.

Julius let out a low laugh, his mocking tone making Lottie incredibly angry.

"What we mean is," Julius drawled, "why would we go to any effort when we could just get you to do all the dirty work for us?"

A thick dread built in Lottie's stomach as the reality slowly dawned on her. All at once the restraints felt too tight, like they were squeezing all the air out of her.

"You think it was just some fairy-tale coincidence that this year's Spearion was hosted in the Tompkins Manor? That we only tested the formula at your school?" Ingrid was practically cackling. "You think we just let you wander around the manor looking for the formula without interference because we were busy painting our nails?" She let out a short bark of a laugh before wandering over to Jamie again, casually sauntering around him. "It wasn't easy getting little Percival to room with you, but now he's going to tell us everything about you." She grinned again, supremely satisfied with herself.

"Don't forget about sending them on that field trip so we could look through their stuff," Julius added, flicking his hat up to wink at Lottie.

She felt her heart sink, unable to believe how stupid they'd been. They'd *wanted* them to find out about Percy; they'd *wanted* them to find the formula. All this time they'd been playing directly into their hands.

Julius laughed, leaning his face close to Lottie's. "We've been patiently waiting like snakes in the grass," he said, and his rich drawl made her shiver. "And now we have two more perfectly ripe little mice to take with us."

Lottie desperately looked to Jamie again, and his eyes widened as Ingrid stroked a hand through his hair.

"They'll be very pleased we got the princess *and* her pretty Partizan." Ingrid traced her fingernails along the skin on his arm.

Why are they so obsessed with Jamie? She couldn't stop a muffled scream as Ingrid touched him. The scream worked. Ingrid straightened up, coming to her senses and checking her watch. "We'd best be on our way, then."

Ingrid moved Percy to the side of the room and gestured for Julius to grab Lottie. As Ingrid walked back toward Jamie, Anastacia began screeching and kicked her half-tied leg out, catching her on the shin.

"Oh, would you shut up?" Ingrid hissed at Anastacia, whose eyes were furiously focused on Saskia.

But she wouldn't. Anastacia kept screaming, the sound completely feral, even with the tape over her mouth.

"I said *shut. Up.*" In an act of bratty exasperation, Ingrid kicked Anastacia in the stomach. Total shock and pain overtook Anastacia as her whining turned to gagging. "There, now you won't be making any more—"

Ingrid didn't have time to finish her sentence. A roar escaped from Saskia, her whole expression twisting into a fiery rage as she leapt into the air and pounced. Saskia's fist met with Ingrid's face so hard and fast it sent sparks through Lottie's vision in a moment of empathy.

Julius grabbed Saskia and pulled her backward by the scruff of her shirt, but this gave Ellie enough time to force herself up off the ground where Saskia had been holding her, grab her sword, and dive forward to free Anastacia.

A horrible crashing sound echoed through the room as Julius effortlessly threw Saskia down in a rage. She writhed on the floor, the wind knocked out of her.

Anastacia pulled the tape off her mouth. "Don't you dare touch her," she snapped as she grabbed her own sword.

Ellie reached out and helped Anastacia up so that the two of them blocked the two rogue Partizans. But then, to Lottie's horror, Ingrid pulled two elaborate knives from her shirt pocket, flexing them outward ceremoniously as a twisted smile cracked her bleeding face. Despite the chaos, Lottie could make out the handle of each blade: a black spider curled around a rigid green-and-silver grip. A horrible thought occurred to her—were the blades dipped in venom?

"You two little girls want to fight?" Ingrid purred, spinning one of the knives as if she were performing a circus act.

Julius let out a low mocking laugh, but just as it seemed they were about to close in on Anastacia and Ellie, Saskia sprang to her feet again and dove on Julius, pulling him back.

That's when the fight really began.

43

SASKIA AND JULIUS SMASHED INTO each other with all the force of opposing hurricanes, their powerful bodies locked in a perfectly matched battle. Lottie was reminded that Partizans fight to win, whatever the cost. They both moved so quickly it was impossible to tell who had the upper hand, neither of them letting the other get a single critical hit in. But Lottie's attention was soon drawn elsewhere—because Ellie and Anastacia were determined to fight too.

Lottie had regretted not seeing them in the fencing tournament, but she'd never imagined she'd end up witnessing a *real* sword fight.

Anastacia glided across the room with the grace of a ballet dancer, pivoting out of Ingrid's reach, while Ellie ferociously swung her blade with lightning precision.

"Ha!" Ingrid cackled, deflecting Ellie's blade with her own, and the sound of steel on steel reverberated through the room. "For two soft little rich girls you sure put up a good fight." She spun to avoid a strike from Anastacia. "Shame you're on the wrong side." Ingrid spat blood onto the white marble floor. "Oops!" she said, laughing and swinging her blade around to stop Ellie's over-the-shoulder strike.

"Don't touch my princess, you poisonous snake," Ellie snarled, her eyes blazing with thunderous fury. The demonic wildness that had been triggered by Lottie's kidnapping last year now raged within her once more.

Ingrid laughed again before swiping her blade up through the air, taking advantage of Ellie's blind fury. Ellie leapt backward as fast as she could, but a thin red line bubbled on her pale cheek, the blood pooling and then trickling down her skin.

Lottie desperately wanted to shout encouragement, but the tape on her mouth was too tight. She felt utterly useless trussed up on the floor. She hated this more than anything. All her fears of having to watch Ellie at the mercy of a Partizan were coming true, and she couldn't do anything. There was nothing unstoppable about her right now.

She squeezed her eyes shut, trying desperately to conjure up the image of Liliana, that furious force whose blood was in her own body. She had to do something.

"You're too soft." Jamie's words echoed through her mind. *"Lull your enemy into a false sense of security."*

And then she realized that was her weapon. They didn't consider her a threat; they weren't paying attention to her.

She turned as far as she could to Lola, who was tied up behind her, and reached out her fingers as best she could to brush her hand. Lola jumped at the touch, her eyes wide. Softly Lottie curled her fingers around Lola's exposed thumb and squeezed, letting her know it would be okay. . Then she began working away at the rope binding Lola's wrists.

It was harder than she expected, and the whole time she was terrified that Ingrid or Julius would notice, but they were so caught up in the fight that they paid no attention to Lottie, Lola, or Micky. She managed to loosen the rope and quickly squeezed Lola's thumb again to warn her against wriggling free. *Not yet.* Lola nodded and slowly tucked her feet beneath her thighs. Then they both began working on the ropes around Lola's ankles. Lottie kept her gaze trained on Jamie as he struggled against his own bindings. Their eyes met for a moment, but he quickly looked away again, not wanting to draw their enemies' attention to her. Did he have any idea what she was doing? Lottie grabbed the last section of rope and felt it loosen in her hand.

Just a little more.

Lottie tugged the rope sideways—and there! She felt the rope slither to the floor; Lola was free. She leapt to her feet and charged toward the door.

Julius and Ingrid were stunned for only a moment before kicking into action.

"Don't you dare—" Ingrid lunged for Lola, but, still tied up, Lottie rolled across the floor, throwing out her bound legs to trip her. Ingrid stumbled, giving Lola enough time to make it out of the door.

If Lola could get help, they might be okay. That was, if Ingrid didn't get to Lottie first.

Ingrid turned her attention to Lottie, her face twisting with rage as she swung her knife out in a menacing circle. "You're going to regret that," she spat.

Lottie had never felt fear at this level. It consumed her, freezing her in place like she was made of stone. She snapped out of it and desperately rolled to the side again.

Just as Ingrid raised her arm to strike at Lottie, two swords appeared above her, forming a protective cross over her head. The weapons whistled through the air and clanged against each other.

Lottie peered up to see two fierce female warriors standing over her.

"Julius," Ingrid screeched from behind them, swiping her other knife upward and forcing Ellie and Anastacia to the side. "We have to go NOW!" she roared.

Julius tried to move away from Saskia as Ingrid violently swiped at Anastacia. But Saskia wasn't done with him. She grabbed his arm and pulled him back into the fight. He let out a furious bellow as he turned to land a punch on Saskia. She ducked just in time, reaching up to grab his arm midswing, the two of them locked in a battle of strength.

"You'd betray the whole cause for that spoiled brat?" he spat.

"Yes," Saskia growled before dropping his arm. "Because she's *my* spoiled brat."

She pulled her fist back, roaring as she planted a hit directly on his face. Julius let out a horrified shriek, recoiling as he grabbed his bleeding head, reeling from the pain in his eye. Saskia drove one final kick into his stomach, knocking him over.

"JULIUS!" Ingrid screeched. She flipped the knife over in her hands, running to Julius's side. Grabbing him under the armpits, she pulled him up and charged to the door, knife held out in front of her, ready to throw it if anyone took a step toward them.

They disappeared through the door. Saskia lunged to go after them, but Anastacia reached out and grabbed her.

"We have to stop them," Saskia howled.

"No, we have to help Percy," Anastacia replied.

Seconds later, Dame Bolter and Nadia Kumar came rushing into the room with Lola following behind. She'd found help, just as Lottie had hoped she would.

"What on earth is going on here?" Dame Bolter cried, her glance taking in the swords in Anastacia's and Ellie's hands and the three tied-up students. "*Saskia?*" She nearly choked as she took in her old student in all her ripped clothes and bruised skin.

There was a groan of pain from the side of the room. Percy Butter's trance had finally become too much for him. His eyes rolled back in his head and he fell into Saskia's arms.

᥌᥈ 44 ᥊᥏

PERCY WAS RUSHED TO THE hospital, where he lay in a private room, propped up on a mountain of pillows, surrounded by machines that beeped as they monitored him. There was a pungent scent of flowers and a boy by his side who refused to let go of his hand.

He was going to be fine. The doctors had informed them that there was no permanent damage but that they couldn't let him go until they were sure they'd broken the association that had led him to this dangerously hypnotic state.

So here they all were in the hospital, nervously waiting for Lola and Micky to emerge from Percy's room and give them more details. With them was Dame Bolter, who'd followed the ambulance in her car. She kept saying over and over how sorry she was, how she should have known . . . But there was nothing anyone could have done differently. Lottie was learning that when Leviathan was your enemy it was hard to protect the people you cared for.

Lottie and her friends—and Saskia—were in the hospital waiting room, refusing to leave. They all felt responsible for what had happened. They should have looked after

Percy; he'd been a pawn in this whole game. They'd been too caught up with finding and destroying the Hamelin Formula. Lottie smiled bitterly. They hadn't even managed to do that. Ingrid and Julius had used them to lead them to the formula's hiding place, and then they'd arrived to pluck it from their hands. They'd failed on so many levels . . .

The clock ticked anxiously on the wall while other sad faces dipped in and out of the waiting room. Lottie didn't know any of these people; she didn't know their stories or who they were here for, but her heart ached for all of them. She knew exactly what it was like to sit in lonesome fear in the purgatory of a green-lit, sterile hospital waiting room.

"Hey, Lottie!" Ellie's voice softly whispered to her, and she turned around in the uncomfortable green seat.

Ellie had been given a dressing for the wound on her cheek, but it would probably leave a light scar—which she was utterly thrilled about. But Lottie felt the opposite. She would remember this day whenever she saw the scar. It was a permanent reminder that would follow them forever.

"Shhh, look!" Anastacia pointed up at the muted TV in the corner of the room. The news was playing, with subtitles scrolling beneath the headline story.

In a shocking turn of events tonight, Richard Butter, head of the renowned confectionery business the Butter Company, which recently merged with Tompkins Confectionery, has been arrested under charges of collusion and child endangerment for his work with an unknown extremist group named Leviathan.

Very little is known about Leviathan or their intentions, but it has come to light that they may have been responsible for a number of kidnappings and attempted kidnappings made on children of world leaders over the last few years.

It was official. Leviathan was no longer an undercover threat. They were real enough to make headline news. Whatever their plans were, they were surely in motion already.

The government urges anyone who might have any related information to come forward immediately.

They all turned to Saskia, who was sitting with her legs casually thrown over the side of her chair.

"No," she said bluntly without looking up from her magazine.

"Listen, Saskia," Jamie said. "You might have come through for us today, but let's not pretend you didn't join them in the first place and that you didn't go right back to them the moment you were freed. You're lucky we don't hand you in right now."

"Urgh, whatever." Saskia rolled her eyes. "I wasn't on their side this time. I had a long time to think when I was locked up. I heard that the princess was attending the Spearion at the Tompkins Manor, and I guessed what might be happening over here, so I told the king's goons that I could stop Leviathan's plans: I was going to wait until we had the formula, then destroy it. I knew I just needed to get Ingrid rambling. That snake just cannot help herself. I swear—"

Anastacia coughed loudly, interrupting Saskia's monologue. "Saskia will have a meeting with the Partizan council, and they will decide on an appropriate punishment for her based on the circumstances. We're pleading brainwashing," she said calmly before giving Saskia a severe look.

"But there's something you guys should know." Saskia picked casually at one of her nails, still not looking up. "Remember last year when I, erm, attempted to kidnap Lottie?"

They all gave Saskia a cold look and she quickly continued. "Well, remember how I said she was the highest on their kidnapping list?" Lottie remembered what Saskia had said to her in the van, the first time she'd heard the word "Leviathan." "Well, she isn't highest anymore."

Their curiosity spiked.

"Isn't that a good thing?" Ellie asked. "For us anyway."

Saskia shook her head. "It definitely isn't a good thing for you, because the person at the top of their list now . . . Well . . ."

She pointed to Jamie, standing against the wall, trapped in his thoughts. He caught her eye and looked away, striding off down the corridor.

He hadn't spoken a word since they'd been freed from the Tompkins Manor, and Lottie couldn't even begin to imagine what was going through his head right now. He prided himself so intensely on his role as Eleanor Wolfson's Partizan.

"Jamie?" Ellie practically choked. "What? Why?"

Saskia shrugged. "Your guess is as good as mine." She flipped the page of her magazine.

"Can't you take this a little more seriously?" Lottie cried, surprising herself and everyone else. Jamie was in such a dangerous place right now; he was vulnerable, and to know that Leviathan was after him at such a crucial moment in his life made her want to scream. She looked at their shocked faces and shook her head, marching off to find him.

Ellie called after her, but she had to speak to him. This might be her only opportunity.

She found him sitting on the floor, staring out of the window into the electric light of the streetlamps outside.

"Jamie," she began, but she wasn't really sure what to say. He'd made it very clear to her before that he didn't want any help, but part of her knew that if he still didn't open up now, she might lose him forever.

"Everyone's safe," she said at last. It was the truth: they were all safe, even if they didn't feel like it. None of them were hurt, and that was the most important thing.

"They have the formula now," Jamie said, his voice entirely emotionless.

"Yes, but—"

"I didn't do anything," he murmured, the hesitant way he spoke making Lottie flinch.

"What? Jamie, get up, come back and—"

"Lottie, I didn't do anything. That's my job, Lottie, and I couldn't do it. I did nothing."

"Jamie . . ." There was something so intensely wrong about seeing Jamie this unsure of himself, so utterly frozen by doubt. "There was nothing you could have done." As soon as she said the words, she knew they were wrong.

Jamie doesn't want any help, the voice in her head reminded her.

She stood up slowly and held her hand out to him, a stabbing feeling striking through her heart as he looked up at her, his disheveled dark hair casting shadows over his brown skin. But there was something more; another, different shadow loomed over him. That inner torment and the demons he refused to face were rising, gnawing at his heart where the wolf pendant hung on its chain like a noose.

Without saying another word he stood up, rising into the shadows.

He didn't take her hand. And she knew, deep down, that he never would.

❧ 45 ❧

THE GREAT WHITE-AND-GOLD HALL WITH its cherubic paintings towered around Lottie, but it didn't intimidate her in
the way it used to. Now she entered the room with purpose, Ellie and Jamie at her side. Her last conversation with
Jamie before they had come to Maradova had made her
realize something crucial—now was the time to act.

The king sat on his golden throne, his mother, Willemena, on the left, and his queen, Matilde, on the right.
Simien Smirnov stood behind him beside Nikolay. They
were arranged like a perfect arrowhead, and Lottie was the
compass determining all their futures.

"Our future queen has sustained an injury the likes of
which will inevitably leave a scar." Willemena scowled at
them, a unique look of distaste for Lottie, Jamie, and the
future queen herself. It did not sting Lottie the way she'd
expected, but instead left a cold feeling of fear—not for
herself, but for Jamie. "Let the mark be a warning, to all
three of you." Her voice was rasping but powerful. "Every
action has a consequence."

Lottie could only think about Jamie behind her, torturing

himself over the events that had unfolded. Her hands balled into fists at her side. The truth was, she agreed with Willemena. They had to learn and they had to grow; it was all they could do. They had made a terrible mistake this time, venturing completely out of their depth, and they were lucky things hadn't turned out far worse.

The king let out a deep, pained sigh. "They're still after the Maravish princess for reasons we don't know," he said, "and now Jamie too?" King Alexander and his wife shared a brief look that Lottie couldn't quite understand. "Maybe it's all to claim a ransom."

"Actually, I don't think that's right, Your Majesty," Lottie interjected, gripping her hands behind her back. "I don't think Leviathan is kidnapping for ransom."

The king gestured for her to go on.

The thought had been growing in Lottie's mind ever since Raphael had made that desperate comment about Saskia being brainwashed. It had been seeping through her mind like glue, all the pieces sticking together, the idea cementing into a theory.

"I think they're trying to control the next generation of powerful people."

Lottie noticed Willemena's hand squeeze tighter on the golden wolf on her cane, the veins blue beneath her skin.

"It's why they're going after Partizans too, and why they wanted the Hamelin Formula," she continued, refusing to falter, even though she could feel Jamie's eyes burning into the back of her head. "They want to manipulate the most powerful, strongest people of tomorrow."

King Alexander's eyes flashed. He indicated for Nikolay to join him, and the two of them drew their heads close together to deliberate under their breath, leaving Lottie to stand anxiously, hands shaking behind her back. Finally he leaned back in his throne. "This is indeed troubling information. But it is advantageous that we have it."

"Lottie Pumpkin."

She looked up as Queen Matilde spoke her name like it was a magic spell. "Something has changed in you."

Changed?

The word somehow felt good; it felt right. Remembering how she'd stood in this very hall at the end of last summer, lost and unsure, haunted by her own self-doubt.

"You have uncovered a remarkable amount of information so far this year," the king added, though his face remained stern. "And all the while Eleanor has remained safe and secure enough to thrive at Rosewood."

Lottie couldn't stop herself quickly glancing at Ellie, who seemed equally shocked by the praise, her eyes glowing.

"It is as though a true Portman, the likes of which they write fairy tales about, has been born in front of us," the queen finished, and to Lottie's utter astonishment Willemena banged her cane on the floor in agreement.

An intense light seemed to grow around her until she was sure she was floating. Lottie stood tall, releasing her hands from where she'd been gripping them behind her back. All the time, though, she was acutely aware of Jamie behind her.

"You may leave." The king waved a hand through the air.

"Thank you, Your Majesty." Lottie bowed respectfully before walking to the door, Ellie and Jamie following.

The second they had left, Ellie relaxed. "They praised you!" she said. "And me. Kind of. They said I was thriving." She shook her head, as if expecting herself to wake up.

But Lottie couldn't revel in the approval yet because a shadow still remained cast over them, the shadow she'd tried so hard to shed some light on.

She turned to Jamie, who stood motionless in front of the great oak doors. "What are you going to do?" Lottie asked him.

Ellie finally seemed to feel it too, that darkness seeping out from him, curling around her.

"Jamie, what's wrong?" she asked, but he didn't respond. "Tell me, what's wrong?" she insisted. Her gaze traveled over him and her voice suddenly cracked. "You're not wearing your wolf."

Lottie nearly gasped. Sure enough, when she looked at Jamie, the wolf they had shared was gone. She gave him a pleading look, but the instant their eyes met she knew exactly what was going through his mind.

He shook his head, turning away from Ellie again. "I don't deserve to wear it now." His voice was an icy wall between them. "I failed you and your family."

"How dare you!" Ellie yelled unexpectedly, pushing him with little effect. "How dare you think of yourself that way?"

"Ellie." He said her name so coldly it made Lottie shiver, the anger in her growing at his determination to hate himself so much. "You will never understand."

"No." Ellie was furious now, tears streaming down her face. "*You* don't understand. Every time we fight, I pray that this time you'll get sick of it. I pray that this time you'll have had enough and you'll leave forever to live your own life, away from the stupid spoiled princess and the stupid Maravish royal family. But you never do. You're so loyal! How can you say you've ever failed us?"

Jamie looked at her blankly. Her words didn't seem to hit him at all.

"I failed. That's all there is to it." He moved to leave.

"No!" Ellie cried, grabbing his arm. "We failed you. You shouldn't have to do anything. You shouldn't have anything to feel bad about. Both of us, you and me, we should be able to live how we want, Jamie."

Something in her words made him freeze. He twisted

back to face them, a cynical gloom in his eyes. "And what about Lottie?"

There it was again, the one thing Jamie could never understand. Lottie had found her home this year, in Ellie, and in her own royal connections. But Jamie refused to find himself, clinging to the path that had been laid out for him. He was all alone and he was determined to stay that way.

"I found my place," Lottie replied, not letting Jamie look away. "I know where I belong. But you . . . Don't you see? You're lost."

He held her gaze, and something briefly stirred behind his eyes, but then it was gone and he turned from them again.

"Jamie!" Ellie called, but Lottie knew there was no point. She gently reached her hand out to calm Ellie.

Jamie disappeared into the gloom of the corridor. In that moment Lottie understood completely what being a Partizan meant to Jamie. It was his greatest excuse—his excuse to never explore who he really was. He clung to the illusion that being a Partizan was in his blood, so that he never had to confront his demons.

But if he didn't confront them soon, they were going to eat him alive.

❧ 46 ❧

"No, Ellie, we can't help him." It was a relief to finally say this out loud. "Jamie has to come around on his own. All we can do is ride this phase out with him."

"But I can't stand it," Ellie said, pacing her room. "It's this stupid family."

"He'll come around," Lottie repeated, but it was more of a prayer than an assurance.

She lay back on Ellie's bed and pondered what the queen had said to her. It was hard for Lottie to put into words, but knowing that the change in her was tangible, knowing that Ellie's family could see it, made it far more real. Although Jamie was lost right now, she was sure if she could find herself, he could too. "It's not something we can force on him, trust me."

"When did you get so wise?" Ellie asked, hurling herself onto the ebony silk bed throw. She sniffed back another furious set of tears.

"Didn't you hear?" Lottie teased. "I *changed*."

Ellie snorted, unable to stop herself from laughing as she curled up on the bed beside her. "You're such an idiot," she said, playfully ruffling Lottie's hair.

Lottie was so relieved to see her smile again that it took her a second to notice how close they were. The memory of their sugar-dusted kiss crept up on her.

The room turned quiet, silver moonlight filtering through the curtains and filling the room with a milky blue glow. Lottie imagined Ellie and herself as a moon and sun, opposite but the same.

Lottie knew she had to ask; they couldn't let it remain unspoken. She'd seen what suppressing painful things had done to Jamie, and she wouldn't let that happen to them.

"Why did you kiss me?" Her question split the air like a crack of thunder.

Ellie's dark gaze pierced her own. "Lottie . . ." Her name was drenched in anticipation. Ellie closed her eyes, and a short breath left her lips. The moonlight dipped. But when she opened her eyes again the storm had passed and she was smiling. "I was just playing. Don't think anything of it."

Everything dissolved as the magic light of possibility blinked out.

Lottie felt herself shiver. The words hurt, a bruise forming deep inside her, spreading through her chest. "If that's what you want," she said, tearing her gaze away from Ellie's.

"It's for the best," Ellie said slowly, resting her palm over Lottie's hand.

Ellie's words reminded Lottie of what the king had said, and part of her feared that she was right. Ellie meant too much to her; she could never think clearly if she allowed this feeling to grow. She had to squash it; she had to tell herself it meant nothing.

Fighting back the sting of tears, Lottie put on her best smile, the one she had perfected for times just like these.

"Of course!" She beamed happily. "We're fine." At least now she knew.

Ellie gave a brittle smile back.

They sat together in silence, a million words left unspoken.

Lottie wasn't entirely sure yet what she was feeling and what it meant, but if it didn't mean anything, then why did it hurt so much?

Before she could think about it further, Henry Pitkin and Liliana burst into her head, trying to tell her something. It was a part of herself that she'd only just discovered, a part of herself that made her realize that she and Ellie had so much more to learn about themselves, if they were to be strong enough to face their enemy.

She ventured one more glance into Ellie's ebony eyes. She had to do right by Ellie, and if that meant locking this memory of the kiss away for when they were both ready, then she would. A new determination rose within her, crushing the pain and the doubt. She would defeat

Leviathan, protect Ellie and Rosewood. Most importantly, they would be there for Jamie when he found himself, however long that took. They were a team, and she would keep them together no matter what.

"I'm going to head to bed," Lottie said, yawning. She headed back to her room, leaving her princess to rest.

As she strode down the grand hallways toward her bedroom, she knew there was one thing she had to do before she could sleep.

Returning to her quarters, she stood in front of her gilded mirror, preparing to do something she hadn't done in a very long time.

She reached into her bedside table and extracted her velvet box. Inside lay Liliana's tiara, her mother's tiara.

My tiara.

She placed the sparkling object upon her head, the crescent moon glittering in the beams of moonlight that pierced her room. She slid the wolf pendant around so that it came to rest over her heart where it belonged.

Then she stood and gazed at her reflection. There she found the truth she'd been searching for. The girl before her was larger and stronger than she remembered, both in body and in presence, her petal-soft skin glowing pink, messy straw curls framing her face. Yet the tiara still fit perfectly, and the pendant no longer felt heavy.

The girl in front of her knew her place. She knew the

worst was still in front of them, their biggest challenges yet to emerge, but she was ready. Wearing these precious pieces like armor, she repeated to herself, *"I will be kind, I will be brave, I will be unstoppable."*

This was Lottie's story. This was where she was meant to be.

Her heritage on her crown, and the wolf at her heart.

❧ EPILOGUE ❧

GREEN LIGHTS WHIRRED OVER THE hospital bed where Julius lay, his body surrounded by a steady beeping of machines, in time with his breathing. He was asleep, bandages covering his face completely. The surgeons had had to remove his left eye where Saskia had punched him; the damage was too much to fix.

"An eye for an eye . . ." Ingrid repeated the words to herself over and over, as if she were singing a lullaby to a crying baby.

It was late and the compound was dark, but footsteps still echoed up and down the corridor outside the infirmary. Leviathan never slept; there was always movement, always someone training or plotting, always awake and ready.

"Crow."

Ingrid turned furiously in the direction of her name. She did not want to be disturbed right now.

"What?" she hissed, looking over at the young recruit who didn't even flinch at the venom in her voice.

"The Master wants to see you," he replied steadily.

Ingrid's face instantly softened, and she carefully pulled her hair back neatly from her face as she prowled toward the boy. He held still as she stroked a long-nailed hand over his hair and patted his head softly.

"You keep watch over Julius for me," she purred, leaning down to look the boy in the eye.

He nodded without saying a word, moving to take the seat she'd just vacated.

Everyone was like that here; nothing could intimidate you when you had nothing to lose.

Ingrid stood poised outside the heavy door where their master worked and slept. People came and left the compound regularly for missions, but Ingrid and Julius had spent the most time there. In many ways the strange, twisted complex had become their home ever since they'd met as children.

She knocked but only as a formality, letting herself in without a response. The door creaked shut behind her, clicking into place.

"It appears that the media are making quite the fuss over our little assemblage," their master mused from where he sat on the floor, his back to her as he trawled through pages of various newspapers scattered around him. "Come closer," he commanded, gesturing for her to move forward before standing up in one swift motion, revealing his true, grand stature. He kept his back to her, gliding across the concrete floor to gaze out at the valley through the large window on the back wall.

"Why are you so disappointed, Ingrid?" he asked softly, looking over his shoulder only slightly so that the light of the moon reflected in his sage eyes. "You should be celebrating a great success in bringing me the Hamelin Formula."

Ingrid was struggling to keep focused on his face, a furious pout forming on her lips as she remembered the events that had unfolded. "But I failed," she grumbled in response. "I was supposed to bring you the Partizan and the princess as well." She sniffed as she spoke, feeling like a child who'd lost her favorite toy.

"Ahh, the princess . . ." He laughed, turning away again. "She is proving to be quite slippery." He looked up at the sky, his shadow stretching over the room, creeping toward Ingrid's toes. "It's a shame about Saskia."

Ingrid bristled at the name, the fury rising inside her again.

An eye for an eye. An eye for an eye.

"None of you could have guessed she'd cut a deal with the king of Maradova."

"I'll make it up to you," Ingrid added hastily.

"You will," he agreed, without looking back, "but that is not why I have called you in here." She watched with curious fascination as her master tapped his chin in thought, wishing she could see inside his glorious mind. "The formula works, Ingrid."

A tickly anticipation fluttered in her stomach, a jittery thrill she got whenever they inched closer to their goal.

"What shall you have me do with it, sir?" she asked instantly, failing to hide the purring delight in her voice.

Her master turned his head ever so slightly again, emerald light casting thick shadows over his pale face where a rapacious grin emerged. That dazzling smile, enticing and full of promise, was the same smile that had welcomed her into Leviathan all those years ago. She wanted to always be the cause of that expression, to make him proud.

"We're going to turn the world against them," he uttered matter-of-factly. "And when we're done, we won't need to force them to come to us." His voice took on a melodic trill, excited by his own plotting. The feeling was infectious in the air around the room. "When we're done, the Partizan and his princess will be begging to join us."